WHILE THE GETTING IS GOOD

ALSO BY MATT RIORDAN

The North Line

MATT RIORDAN

A NOVEL

WHILE THE GETTING IS GOOD

HYPERION AVENUE
LOS ANGELES . NEW YORK

Copyright © 2025 by Matt Riordan

All rights reserved. Published by Hyperion Avenue, an imprint of Buena Vista Books, Inc. No part of this book may be reproduced or transmitted in any form or by any means, electronic or mechanical, including photocopying, recording, or by any information storage and retrieval system, without written permission from the publisher. For information address Hyperion Avenue, 7 Hudson Square, New York, New York 10013.

First Edition, August 2025
10 9 8 7 6 5 4 3 2 1
FAC-004510-25163
Printed in the United States of America

This book is set in Baskerville MT Pro, Broadletter JNL
Designed by Amy C. King

Library of Congress Control Number: 2025931991
ISBN 978-1-368-10145-5
Reinforced binding

www.HyperionAvenueBooks.com

Logo Applies to Text Stock Only

PART I

ONE

Eld watched his son raise the binoculars to his eyes. The boy didn't put the strap around his neck, and Eld almost said something in the way of a warning about the binoculars finding their way overboard. He opened his mouth but thought better of it and said nothing. The boy had arrived at the age where telling him things wasn't so much teaching as nagging, and a flash of annoyance was getting to be a familiar look on the boy's face. Besides, Eld had picked up those binoculars in France.

Eld never said "war." He always said "in France." Even to himself. They were good binoculars, too expensive to replace, but they weren't French. Eld had plucked them from the mud near the body of an almost dead English horse. If those binoculars went to the bottom of Lake Huron it would be one less thing Eld had from France, which was fine by him.

"Yup," Doc said, "that's Charlie McCallister's boat." The boy held the binoculars one-handed and rolled at the hips with the swell. "He's painted the old scow, blue of all things, but that's his, all right."

Doc turned and moved toward Eld, each step across the yawing deck light and certain. Eld watched him and knew how the world seemed an easy place to a young man, more so for a young man like Doc. There was no point in telling him otherwise. Doc would just stare at him, and anyway that information would reveal itself soon enough. Eld smiled at his son and took back the binoculars. He put the strap around his neck before sweeping the rolling blue for Charlie's boat. It hadn't been half an hour since the rain quit, but the sun was sparkling down the slope of the bigger rollers, forcing Eld to squint. It was indeed Charlie's boat, and Doc was right. He'd repainted it. Blue. If some dark November night Charlie didn't come back on time and his wife sounded the alarm, Eld and the rest of the fishermen in town would be out here looking for the upturned blue hull of his boat, in all that blue water. Charlie knew that.

"I don't see any gear out," said Doc.

Eld focused on the stern. Doc was right again. No nets were visible and no cork lines trailed from the stern. Charlie was nowhere in evidence either.

"He's just drifting," said Doc. "We in Canada? Close?" The boy looked at his father and cocked an eyebrow. "'Course, little thing like an international border, that wouldn't stop Charlie from fishing."

Doc had been out on deck when Eld dead reckoned their course on the chart table in the wheelhouse. Eld figured them at a couple miles over the Ontario line. He didn't have the papers to fish here any more than Charlie did, but there was less competition than on the Michigan side. Fishing over the line was illegal, but Eld didn't feel wrong about it. The fish didn't know they were Canadians.

Eld put the binoculars down. "Let's go take a look. Might be he needs help."

Doc followed his father into the wheelhouse.

"That fool Charlie needs a tow, he's gonna have to wait till we're full up. We don't have the fuel or the time to run him back twenty miles."

"There's been days I needed help," said Eld, but he didn't counter his son.

Lately Doc was given to expressing some unchristian sentiments, and when he did, Eld could hear those same words coming from Doc's mother. He saw that thought for the poison it was and chose instead to think of Doc's sentiments as a symptom of youthful impatience. Anyway, they could sort out what to do when they talked to Charlie. Eld bumped the throttle arm twice with the palm of his hand and the engine clatter made further conversation impossible.

If Charlie needed help, he should be out on deck looking for it, but he wasn't there. Eld weighed the possibility that Charlie was working alone, and that he had gone over. He'd be floating somewhere, on his back probably, in the twenty miles of open water between here and land, and there'd be almost no point in looking for him. Eld knew he would look anyway, until he had to run back for fuel. A whole tank of fuel burned and no fish to show for it would put his month in the red. That would make two out of the last three, and that would mean a conversation with Maggie. Like her son, Maggie would say Charlie was a damned fool and Eld didn't need to make his family go hungry for every fool who got it in his head to be a fisherman. All of that was true, and reasonable, and just the same, Eld, if need be, would go looking for Charlie.

At a hundred feet out, Charlie's head appeared over the rail, but only his head. He was sitting on the deck. Another head popped up. The second head had a fedora on top of it and a face on the front that Eld didn't recognize. Charlie and the other man stood.

You don't need a rifle to catch herring. That's a plain fact. All the same, the second man held a rifle.

"Aw hell," said Eld, and he backed off the throttle. As the distance between the two boats closed Charlie turned to the second man and spoke a few words. The second man peered at Eld and Doc for a moment before disappearing into the wheelhouse.

"What's that about, you think?" asked Doc. "Maybe he's worried about the Canadians?"

"Maybe," said Eld, but he doubted the rifle was for the Canadians. In Eld's experience the Canadians were not a particularly warlike race. Certainly, the Canadians he had met were not the kind of people who might initiate gunplay over a few herring.

When they were twenty feet away the man with the fedora reappeared without the rifle and put a foot up on the rail. He was wearing leather street shoes. Charlie waved and smiled but said nothing. Eld knocked the engine into neutral and they drifted closer. Inside of ten feet Eld saw that Charlie didn't have any nets aboard. If Eld asked him about fishing, Charlie would have to say something, something like maybe he forgot to bring a net, so Eld was out of things to say before he opened his mouth. He nodded at the man in the fedora, but that man looked like he had never been so bored as he was just then, encountering Eld and Doc.

"Everything okay, Charlie?" Eld knew it was Doc's voice, but it sounded deeper, older. There was nothing of fear in that voice, so Eld was afraid for both of them. Doc was standing at the rail. Eld wanted right then to get his son as far from this situation as possible.

"Yeah," said Charlie. Grinning. He started to say something else and then stopped. His face was frozen for a second, his lips forming the half word he had uttered. "You?" he asked, although the word came out without the *Y* sound at the front of it, so that it sounded like *oo*.

For a second or two there was silence. The blue lake water made gentle lapping noises on the sides of the hulls. Then Charlie spoke again. "How 'bout you?"

"Good," said Eld. He was watching the man in street clothes. "Scouting. You know."

"Sure," Charlie said. "See you in town."

"Guess so," said Eld. He knocked the throttle into reverse and backed twenty yards without taking his eyes from the man in street clothes. He didn't speak to Doc until they were out of rifle range, and then he asked if there was any coffee left.

Doc went below and reappeared shaking the thermos. "There's a swallow in there yet, maybe two," he said as he handed it to his father. "So you figure the guy with Charlie, the guy with the rifle, he was a Canadian. Maybe he had an Ontario permit so they could fish that side of the border?"

"Maybe," said Eld, "but he didn't look Canadian."

"How does a Canadian look?"

Eld swallowed cold coffee and looked at his son. The boy should get some other kind of a job. This job, it was an honest living, but you were at the mercy of everything. Weather, accidents, some bank, they all had you, and you never got very far ahead of them. Then maybe some depression or a war popped up and you couldn't get out of the way. Eld was old enough to know he couldn't change those things, that they came down the pike at you no matter what, but he believed that with a little luck, and a lot of moxie, you might put yourself in a position to get the hell out of the way. Making it so Doc could get out of the way, Eld figured that for his job.

"No," said Eld. "I don't think it was Canadians that got Charlie to paint his boat blue, or send him out here drifting over the border with no fishing gear. Somebody down in Detroit put Charlie up to this. Somebody in Detroit or maybe even Chicago, and that somebody, or somebodies, they sent along the guy with the street shoes and the rifle to watch over their investment."

Eld didn't say the word "whiskey." He knew he didn't have to. Doc was fourteen, old enough to know that the shiny new trucks popping up around town came from running whiskey over from the Canadians. They were still making it to beat the band over there, for export to the States, Prohibition be damned. Old Man Seagram didn't give a fiddler's fuck who they were exporting it to, and it had to get to Detroit somehow. What Doc understood without being told, that worried Eld.

It was break-even fishing that day, with just enough herring to keep Doc occupied while Eld thought on the cost of fuel and what they had seen. That operation they had stumbled on, it was the kind of plan Charlie would come up with. A half-assed plan. Meeting out in the middle of the damn lake with no nets on board. Anything other than a clear day—hardly a reliable occurrence even in summer—and the boats wouldn't be able to find each other. More, moving cargo from one boat to another in open water was a questionable proposition even in the best of weather. Eld knew it to be difficult with fish, and fish didn't come in bottles that shattered when dropped. Charlie hadn't done anything to hide his tracks either. Without a net on board, the purpose of the trip was obvious. Even the laziest police would know at a glance what they were up to, and the load was right there for anybody to see. Charlie was an indifferent fisherman, and it seemed that his work ethic for smuggling was the same. If Charlie lost a load, or got himself pinched, the whiskey would find another route and any opportunity would be gone.

The smart play would be to take on extra fuel and run all the way over to Grand Bend on the Ontario side. Then you could pick up a load and ferry it back in the dark with the running lights off. If you fished a little on the way home you might catch enough to cover the load with fish. There were better ways to run whiskey, and men more reliable than Charlie McCallister.

Eld heard a shout and looked up to see Doc jumping from the rail and cannonballing into the water. His clothes and boots were in a pile on the deck. Walking to the rail, he saw Doc floating on his back, his toes breaking the surface.

"How's the water?" asked Eld.

"Wet," said Doc.

Eld hung a thick hawser line over the side before stripping off his clothes.

"How were you going to get back up?" said Eld. He climbed up on the rail.

"You mean, if I hadn't brought you along?"

"What if I wasn't able to help?"

"Like maybe you had a stroke in the ten minutes I was swimming and couldn't throw me a line?"

Eld didn't answer. He stood on the rail for a minute and looked down into the water. He didn't know how deep it was. Hundreds of feet, anyway. He didn't know what was down there, but he had a fisherman's sense that it wasn't a friendly place. Nothing in the lake died of old age. Doc had his eyes closed, as if he were about to nap, drifting with his back turned on all that darkness. Eld didn't know if he admired that about the boy, but he did know that it didn't come from him. The boy was brave. Eld knew what happened to the brave. He had seen it. At that thought he dove, and before he touched the water he decided to look up Charlie when they got back to town.

There was no sound, knifing down into the dark. He kicked and swam deeper.

Money. Money would protect his brave son. Enough money might even protect Doc from himself. Eld stopped swimming and opened his eyes. Below him the blue turned black, and above him he could see Doc and the white hull of the boat. He was between the dark and Doc floating up on the surface, but he could stay there only so long as he could hold his breath. He paused as long as he could and then started for the surface.

The sun on his face and his lungs full of new air, he thought he had a plan by the ankle. He would get more money. Enough so that his little family could get the hell out of the way. He climbed the hawser and swung a leg over the rail. The nets on the deck, the boat, the fuel in the tanks: the bank had put up the money and the bank held the note. There was a mortgage on the house too. They weren't hungry, and there were lots of folks worse off, but fishing lake herring was a working man's life, start to finish.

Running whiskey wasn't safe, and it wasn't legal, but it wasn't really work either.

Eld smiled and dove again.

TWO

Charlie was smiling, sitting with his new friend, who was not. A week had passed since Eld had first seen him on Charlie's boat, and he was still here in town. The man had introduced himself as Leon, but he hadn't said anything more. His fedora was on the kitchen table. Charlie was talking again and you could see he thought himself clever. Eld knew he was not.

"There's more money in whiskey than there is in herring," Charlie said, grinning at his observation.

The three men were in Charlie's kitchen, sitting at the table drinking beers. When Charlie fetched the bottles from the icebox Eld saw dozens more in rows. Charlie's wife, Marie, was nowhere to be seen, which was a feat considering the woman's size, but the kids were making kid noises from the room adjacent to the kitchen. A screen door banged and the kid noises moved from the room out into the yard.

"Right," Eld said. "That's right, and more boats means more money, and my boat is even bigger than yours, Charlie." Eld used the words "even bigger," instead of just "bigger," so as not to offend. Just the same, Charlie's smile faded. The penny had dropped.

"Why you?" Charlie said.

Eld explained his ideas—running all the way to Grand Bend, making the return trip in the dark, covering the load with tarps and fish.

"And, Charlie," Eld said slowly, lifting his beer bottle, "much as this goes down nice on a hot day like today, a man in your line of work shouldn't keep beer in the house. Probably I'm not the only one who's figured out what you are up to."

When Leon looked over his shoulder at the icebox, Eld figured he was going to get his shot.

"I'd need to make a few changes to my boat," Eld said, "put in an extra fuel tank, but I could be heading over by September."

Charlie looked annoyed and started to say something, but Leon interrupted.

"More would be better," Leon said, "and I like the idea of running all the way across, but you'd need a crew."

Charlie spoke up. "Eld's got crew." His voice was eager, happy to show Leon he knew things. "Doc—that's his son—that's the only crew I ever saw on the *Nancy*."

Eld wished that Charlie hadn't just then been trying to be so helpful, saying Doc's name out loud. "He'll be back in school come September. I can handle the runs myself."

Leon shook his head. "That's not the way we work. You don't go anywhere with our load where there isn't one of us on hand. Especially if we don't know you—and we don't know you."

This was where Eld wanted to go, and he jumped right in. "What if it wasn't your load? What if it was my load? We treat whiskey just like herring. I pay for it. Pay the Canadians. You buy it from me only when it gets here. I lose a load, something breaks, that's on me. Just like herring. I take all the risk."

"I don't know about that," said Leon. "Seems like we'd be setting you up in business. The whole point is we need the supply. What's to stop you from selling to the highest bidder?"

"You," Eld said. "We work out the price before I go across, and then the load is yours. I'm not looking to get sideways with Detroit, and you guys, well, you're not really much use on a boat anyway. No offense."

"None taken," Leon said. "I don't like the life, living and working in fish stink." He shot a glance in the direction of the kid noises. "Don't like the women up here either."

"He gets seasick," Charlie said, a trace of smirk at the corners of his mouth. Eld was reminded that Charlie didn't go to France. Eld came home from France convinced that it was better to let things slide when possible. Taking offense, getting excited about a dead duke, fighting over some notion of honor or a dozen yards of desolate swamp in the Argonne, that was for the soon-to-be dead. Charlie took offense, and now he was taking liberties with Leon. Eld wasn't afraid of them, but neither would he take any liberties with Leon, or the men Leon worked for, whoever they were.

Leon looked at Charlie. "How come you didn't think of this? Seems we're in business with the dumbest fisherman up here." Leon got up from his chair and walked toward Charlie's bathroom. "Your wife, being connected, that's the luckiest break you ever got."

When Leon left the room, Eld leaned toward Charlie and lowered his voice. "Charlie, we go in on this together. There's a couple more boats in town we could get to help. Reliable men. We keep on fishing, business as usual, but from time to time run some whiskey, or whatever they want. We throw in together, share the risk. If somebody loses a load, gets arrested, whatever, the rest of us take the hit too. Nobody gets wiped out."

"And I suppose you're the one's gonna run this outfit, means we all work for you."

"We work together," Eld said.

"I heard they made you a sergeant over there. On the spot. Put you in charge of guys."

"Was a long time ago, and it's not like I got a taste for it. I didn't want the job. I got it 'cause the Germans missed me. All I wanted was for them to keep missing me."

"I'd be working for you."

"You wouldn't," Eld said. "You'd be working for yourself."

Charlie. Eld was going to have to watch Charlie.

"Anyway, you rather work for me, or for them?"

Eld stopped at the butcher on the walk home from Charlie's house. He bought two pounds of peameal bacon with money that he owed to the bank. He liked peameal bacon just fine, but Maggie had a particular love of the stuff, and Doc ate everything with wolfish indifference. Two pounds would be enough, depending on Bea's appetite. You could never tell with Bea. A year younger than Doc, she seemed to be maturing on a faster but inverted course. Her thoughts grew daily more impenetrable, where her older brother's temperament flashed in obvious ways. Bea might smile and say the bacon was the best thing she ever ate, or she might spit it out. She might do both things with the same food within a few days' time. Eld smiled at the thought and walked in the middle of the road, shiny where the town had laid some oil to keep the dust down.

Maggie was in the doorway when he came up the walk. It was late in the afternoon, too late for lunch, but he thought he might cook it up to get her in a cooperative frame of mind. He wanted the part of her that was resourceful, and clever, but first he had to get past her temper. She would be angry that he got this far down the road without asking her first. She might say he was disrespectful. If he could get her past that, get her thinking about running this, he would sleep easy. He didn't know when he married her that she had a mania for commerce, but she had something in her blood that told her how to run things. It was an unlooked-for bonus. He needed every card in his hand to make this work, and she was a big one. The army made him a sergeant, but it was Maggie who knew how to tell people what to do.

"That grin," Maggie said. "Eldridge Mackey, I seen it before."

"I have a proposition for you."

"It's too hot." Now she was grinning. "And anyway, two kids not enough for you?"

The woman's appetites, whether for bacon or marital congress, were another unexpected bonus. She continued to stand in the doorway, her arms crossed, as he put the bacon in a pan. He told her about seeing Charlie drifting in the middle of the lake as he poked the meat around the bottom of the skillet. The smell of it frying blossomed in the room and made his mouth water. He noticed Maggie watch the bacon. When it was crispy on the edges but still had chew in the middle, he put three pieces between thick slices of bread and put the sandwich on a plate. He took the chair across from the plate and finished telling her his plan. She walked around slowly before sitting. She was looking at the table when she picked up the sandwich with one hand. He watched the maneuver with concern that one of the slices might fall out on the floor, but he didn't mention that. She was listening.

He told her it was just an idea, that they didn't have to do it. He wasn't sure he could back out, now that Leon had taken the train down to Detroit to talk it over with his bosses, but he knew it would be easier to get Maggie on board if she thought she had a choice. Once she got moving in the right direction, Maggie was hell-bent and hard to stop. He leaned on her, and they made decisions together, but sometimes Eld gave her information in pieces, and in a certain order. Sometimes he had to steer her a little bit. He wasn't proud of it.

"Thought I noticed you were quiet last couple days," Maggie said. "Always a cause for concern. Been thinking on this?"

"Could be," Eld said, and when Maggie didn't respond, he confessed what she already knew. "Guess that's right."

"Thinking how you were going to get me to go along? With you, us, throwing in with gangsters, starting a life of crime?"

"Been thinking about that too," Eld said. "You been reading the paper? They're gonna repeal the law, maybe as soon as next year, and this chance, it'll be all over. The cops are making it hard on them getting over the river down in Detroit, not like it was five years ago, and they can't get enough across. That's why they are up here now looking for anything that floats, in business with a jackass like Charlie. We got a year, maybe less, before the law swings back the way it was, and then they're hauling it on rail cars in broad daylight. After that, we got nothing they want. They got no use for a fisherman, so they go back to whatever it was they did before. We'd be done with them."

"And you go back to herring?"

"That's just it. I was thinking we get enough to get out of the fish business altogether. Year before last was our best year ever. Made around fourteen hundred for the year, counting money Doc and I made hauling ice. I did some math. I'd want you to check it, but I think I could make that every month."

Eld could see on his wife's face that the numbers had a persuasive power he did not.

"But you like fishing," said Maggie. "So does Doc."

"I do at that," Eld said, "but not so much that I'd keep doing it if there was a shot at something better. We could pay off the mortgage, get set up in a business, send Doc down to Ann Arbor for more school."

He thought himself cheap for saying that, for dangling that life for Doc before her.

First Maggie made him show her the newspaper stories that said Prohibition was likely going to end. He had saved two of them, folded them and put them in a high cupboard she couldn't reach without asking him. Then she got out a pencil and did the math over and over, figuring it with different prices for fuel, and even counting on losing a load. It was dark and Bea was asleep when she stopped figuring.

Maggie took the pack from his shirt pocket and lit one of his cigarettes. "We'd maybe do better than you said."

She was smiling. It was her plan now. But then she pointed her pencil eraser at him.

"So where's the money come from to get started?"

Eld said nothing. It was her plan. She would know what to do. They were getting older together, but the years made him softer. She was getting harder.

"The fuel," she said, "*that* we could get on credit, but how are you going to pay the Canadians for the first load? That's called working capital, and we don't have it."

"I was thinking," Eld said, "we would ask for an advance. Just to get started. It's peanuts to those guys."

This was a lie. Eld had no intention of getting in hock to Leon. This was a hard steer of his loyal wife, but it had to be done.

"Oh no. I don't think so." Maggie got up and took the coffee pot off the stove. She poured two cups and sat back down. "I've seen that guy, the guy who's following Charlie around town. Don't like the look of him. We don't want to owe him money. People in town say he's Purple Gang."

"His name's Leon. I don't know who he works for. Might be Purple Gang, might be somebody else. Thing is, they have money that we don't."

"Mom does."

Eld felt a pang of regret when Maggie said this, as he'd suspected this was where Maggie would end up. If Maggie hadn't suggested it, he would not have mentioned his mother-in-law.

"I'll go see her tomorrow," Maggie said.

They sat up smoking and talking it over until there was a loud belch out in the yard, reminding Eld that the evening was quiet and the windows were all open. Doc came in smiling, a Coke bottle in his hand and the pink dome of a mosquito bite visible on his collarbone. The mineral smell of lake water rose from him and filled the kitchen.

Eld heard Maggie's breathing settle and he knew she was asleep. He lit a cigarette and blew smoke at the ceiling. If he told her tomorrow that the deal was off, that the Purple Gang decided they didn't need him, she would push him to find a new buyer. She would find one herself. One way or another, good, bad, or indifferent, he would run Canadian whiskey over the border until Prohibition was repealed.

It was her plan now, and that was his doing.

THREE

The first trip to see the Canadians took an extra day. When he got to Grand Bend there wasn't any whiskey, and the man he was supposed to meet wasn't there either. Eld got a haircut he didn't need, for which he paid in American dollars, in the hope that the conversation would come around to where he might find a warehouse full of whiskey. When the discussion took no such turn, focusing instead on farming and the sorry state of local road maintenance, Eld sat silent and listened to the Canadians stretch out their vowels. He did not know how to ask directly. He rented a room near the harbor and spent a fitful night considering many risks that had not previously occurred to him.

In the morning there was a man waiting on the dock, standing near the *Nancy*. Eld had his mother-in-law's money in his pocket and he wished he didn't.

"Soary," the man said, and it took Eld a second to translate.

"Sorry for what?"

"We missed you yesterday. Got held up in Sarnia. Got word you arrived yesterday. Been on the road since four this morning so we could catch you before you went back across."

The man said his name was John, but didn't say how he got word that Eld had arrived yesterday. Eld didn't ask. This man, he wore his pants tucked into his boots like a fisherman, but his clothes were clean. He might be the police. Might be a highwayman. Might be fucking anybody at all. John apologized several more times, and then he offered to treat Eld to breakfast. Eld wasn't hungry, but he agreed anyway.

Instead of the café Eld had seen in town, they walked a few blocks to a house. It was a big house, recently painted, with a wide white porch, but that didn't stop Eld from thinking it was a good place to shoot somebody and take their money. There were four teenage boys sitting down to breakfast when they got inside. They stood up when Eld came in, shook his hand, and introduced themselves. Eld drank their coffee and ate a bear claw as they asked him how he wanted his boat loaded. The taste of the bear claw didn't register but he chewed anyway. He didn't want to admit that he had never done this before, so he guessed at a load plan, and he said he wanted nets and gear stacked on top.

After breakfast the Canadians walked him into the garage. He was close to certain they were going to shoot him then, and his mouth went dry, but instead they showed him a brand-new truck, loaded high with cases of whiskey. They were proud of the truck and explained that its purchase was what held them up in Sarnia. The smell of paint rose from the frame, and flecks of mud stood out from the glossy black.

"Which one?" asked John, gesturing at the cases.

When Eld shrugged, John drew circles in the air with his finger and then picked a case in the middle of a stack. The boys retrieved the case and plucked out a bottle. John removed the stopper and handed the bottle to Eld. He took a pull. The liquor was clean and it warmed as he swallowed. Something fantastic rose in his chest, something he couldn't afford. The Canadians were all smiles.

"Nobody made that in their fucking bathtub," said John.

He replaced the stopper and handed the bottle to Eld.

"That one's for you," he said, "and you'll find this load is a dozen cases over what was asked for. We can throw in some free once in a while. Our way of apologizing for leaving you high and dry here. That won't happen again."

The whiskey was loaded aboard the *Nancy* in bright sunshine, right in front of god and anybody else who might have cared to look. Apparently, nobody did. The loading took an hour, during which Eld spoke only once, to ask one of the boys to stop whistling. He had started speaking without thinking, a fisherman's learned response to the sound of a whistle, but then he had to follow through.

"It's bad luck to whistle on a boat. You might whistle up a storm."

Eld thought that was an idiotic superstition, but he enforced it just the same. The boy looked up at the clear sky but said he was "soary."

Eld had started the engine when John ambled up, smiling. He bent down to the wheelhouse window. "You forget something?"

Eld said nothing. The boat was still tied up.

"The deal was FOB." When Eld remained quiet, John continued, "Free on board. We deliver and load the goods."

"That seems right," Eld said.

"Right," John said. "Then you pay us."

Pay. Eld hadn't paid them. He went below and got the envelope. John asked permission before he stepped down to the deck of the *Nancy*, and he counted the cash quickly.

"Happy to help our friends down below," John said, "and American dollars are always accepted."

Tobacco from Eld's cigarette stuck to his lip. His hands were rubbery and the first two matches went out. It was past noon, Grand Bend a smudge on the horizon, when he succeeded with the third match.

"Jesus," he said, exhaling the smoke.

He'd meant to pick up a lunch, but then he'd spent the morning waiting to be shot by the Canadians. There was no coffee aboard either. He took a long swallow from the bottle of whiskey. The water ahead rolled at the bow in small humps, and a slight headwind gave the illusion that the *Nancy* was moving faster than she was capable. After a second pull he started to smile. His stomach unknotted and he realized he was starving. It was two hours to the border, an imaginary line out in the middle of the lake. There he would drift and wait for darkness to cover his return.

Four hours after Eld had smoked the last of his cigarettes, the *Nancy* bobbed in the dark, running lights off, three hundred yards from where he thought he was supposed to bring her ashore. For the dozenth time Eld scanned the dark lumps of the shoreline and wondered if he was within a mile of the spot. Easy to make a mistake in the dark. Flashlight beams blinked, short and long, signaling the all clear.

He motored the *Nancy* up slow into the shallows, bracing for a boulder to buckle the hull. Someone put a flashlight beam in his eyes as he approached the rickety finger pier. For the second time in two days he prepared to be shot, but he was better at it now. He managed to curse and call out for them to shine the lights at the water. At the pier he saw Leon and two men he didn't recognize. Charlie was there too. When he was satisfied that the *Nancy* was moored properly, he asked if they had any food.

"What, like a picnic?" asked Leon. "No. We don't got any food."

They walked the cases one at a time down the narrow pier and then used a wheelbarrow to take them on a path that led up the embankment. Where the path got steep a cave had been dug into the face of the bank. Tucked behind a thick grove of sumac, the cave had no door, but it was lined with red brick, and stout timbers held planks across the ceiling. When all the whiskey was in the cave, Eld remembered the extra cases.

"There's a dozen extra here," he said. "I had the room, so I took on more. If you don't want 'em now, leave 'em here and I'll put them toward the next load."

Leon nodded. "No. We'll take those too. Every trip, you take all you can carry." He looked at Charlie. "See that? That's initiative." Then he barked a little laugh, like a puff of smoke into the cool air of the cave. "Almost as good as being married into the outfit."

Leon paid in crisp fifties. It was the most money Eld had ever seen in one place. That record had previously been held by the money he had given the Canadians that morning. Leon's men waited for Eld to return to the *Nancy*, but before he had cast off they were removing the planking from the narrow pier, leaving only steel supports that were barely visible above the water. Eld watched the men remove the last plank. It was a calm night, but they would not all be calm, and Leon's temporary pier was on unprotected open coast. In big chop, the pier would be useless. This worried Eld, but then he remembered the envelope of fifties in his jacket. He would worry more, but later.

He walked home from the harbor after midnight, carrying only the bottle and the envelope. There was a pack of cigarettes on the kitchen table when he came in. Maggie called his name and was coming down the stairs before he could answer. He smiled at her and took two water glasses from the cupboard. He poured them each an inch and lit a cigarette. When he sat down she gathered her robe about her and sat in his lap. He held onto her as she put her chin on the top of his head.

"You're late," she said. "A whole day. Wasn't my best day. I thought plenty about the money, but I hadn't thought about that, about you not coming—"

"The Canadians," said Eld. "They were late. Gave me extra to make up for it. There's more in the envelope than we counted on."

"Extra?"

"Yeah. They were sorry about being late. *Soary*. Real polite, those people. They tried to feed me breakfast, but I didn't eat much because I thought they might be fixing to shoot me. In a polite way."

He felt Maggie's body freeze. They sat together like that for a long moment before Maggie spoke.

"Were you afraid?"

He knew he was meant to shield her from this part of his plan, that he should have said no, but he was tired and had been drinking good whiskey on an empty stomach. He managed to say nothing.

"Well," she said, "if you thought they were gonna shoot you, why didn't you eat hearty?"

"That line of thinking, the 'being shot' line, has a way of preoccupying you so that you aren't hungry."

"I see." She poured more whiskey into her glass. "You hungry now?"

"Good god, yes. Haven't eaten since. This gangsterin', it works up an appetite, worse than fishing."

With a little laugh, she got up from his lap and took butter from the icebox. She spread it on a heel of bread and handed it to him.

"Any jam?" he asked.

Maggie shook her head. She picked the envelope up from the kitchen table and counted the cash.

"Lord."

"That's what I was thinking too." He drained his glass and stood up. The envelope was delivered, and that seemed like a good place to end this day.

"When Doc came home tonight," Maggie said, "he smelled like beer. I didn't say anything, but I think he was drunk. He fell asleep and snored."

FOUR

The second run was supposed to be two weeks later, but Leon moved it up. Soon Eld was across every Tuesday morning, back in the dark of Wednesday night, giving Leon time to get the whiskey down to Detroit for the weekend. Eld's mother-in-law was paid off without his ever having a single conversation with her. Since he never saw a police boat, Eld gave up the idea of covering the load with fish so he could fit more cases in the hold. Still, Leon wanted more.

Eld drove his boat and counted his money, but never without a nagging fear and an eye on the calendar. Until he started running whiskey, he had worked for every dollar that passed through his hand. The easy money made him nervous and left him wondering who still had the dollars to buy good whiskey. Banks were closing and Ford's detectives were shooting unemployed hunger marchers down in Dearborn. Eld didn't know what was coming down the pike, but he was certain it wasn't going to be good. In France Eld had seen panic, seen idiots in charge, seen every man for himself. He was uneasy, but determined to get his family out ahead of that, one load of whiskey at a time.

One morning in October while she was counting money at the kitchen table, Maggie announced she would vote for Roosevelt come November. Maggie's grandfather had fought for General Grant at Vicksburg, and her family had voted Republican every election since the Civil War. If Maggie was voting for a Democrat, whatever was coming was almost here.

Eld approached three other captains in town. Two jumped at the chance, but the third, the best of the lot, turned Eld down flat. Eld had spoken to him on the village dock while the man was icing a load of herring so small that it wouldn't cover the cost of a tank of fuel. Eld was confident. The first two captains had been grateful for his offer. He got a dozen words out of his mouth.

"I know all about it. And the answer is no, Eld. No. Hell no," the man said, shaking his head.

Eld started to explain it was only temporary, but the man stopped him.

"I'm not judging. Hell, I'd be happy to buy a bottle from you," he said, "but I'm not doing business with those people." He turned and walked away, but then stopped to say over his shoulder, "You shouldn't either. You lie down with dogs, you get up with fleas."

Eld met with his two new recruits, Eugene and Andy, at Charlie's house. Eugene was older than Eld, and a foot shorter. More than once Eugene had asked Eld for help carrying bulky gear down the pier to his boat. He was a smart man, with a reputation for hard work, but after a life of fishing he seemed always to be in dire financial straits. Eld sometimes thought he might be Eugene in twenty years, or something close, and he'd offered the man this shot at smuggling whiskey because he felt the world had not been fair to him. Now, looking at Eugene, his hopeful round face under a Tigers cap, Eld saw that perhaps Eugene was simply unlucky. Eld was not tasked with redistributing luck in the world, and saddling yourself with the unlucky, especially in an endeavor as risky as smuggling, was sentimental and foolish.

Eugene sat next to Andy, a gangly man Eld liked chiefly for his imaginative use of profanity. Andy was the least successful of four brothers, the only one who had chosen to make fishing his life's work. Andy's older brother owned the hardware store in Minden. Eld owed the man money. Andy stroked his beard and nodded vigorously at everything anyone said.

They sat at the kitchen table while Marie cooked two big steaks. She was apparently angry about something, as she dropped the steaks on the table without speaking and followed her kids out into the backyard. They were thick steaks, cut off the bone. Eld's mouth watered. Marie had put a rough-cut chunk of butter on each but didn't leave any plates or cutlery. Without offering an explanation Charlie retrieved a knife from a drawer and cut off an end piece before handing the knife to Andy. He pinched the meat between his thumb and forefinger and popped it into his mouth.

Eld watched the other men eat the steaks in the same fashion as he explained the proposition.

"We buy from the Canadians and sell to Leon. Keep the difference. The profit. We work for ourselves, not some Detroit outfit." That way of putting it made Eld feel better about Leon. Selling to Leon was different than working for Leon. He hoped that way of putting it would make the new men feel better too. "If you don't have the cash to finance your first trip, I'll lend it to you, but since I'm taking the risk, I get a third of that take."

That last part was Maggie's idea. She had said that if he wanted to get his family on the road to something better, he needed to start thinking like he wasn't a fisherman. She could be a hard woman. He looked down at what was left of the steaks, and at Charlie licking his fingers, and he was thankful once again that Maggie had said yes to his marriage proposal, written with a shaking hand in a trench in France, while he spat out flakes of tobacco that had stuck to his lip from cheap French cigarettes.

"It's already October," Eld said. "We keep running across, one load each, once a week, until the ice sets up, on our side or over there. The rest of the week we keep fishing, just like always."

"Christ." Charlie spoke through a mouthful of steak. "I quit fishing. I'm doing this so I don't have to fish. That's the whole idea."

"We keep fishing, Charlie. We keep fishing so nobody in town notices anything out of the ordinary. Be careful with your money."

Eld forced himself to stop looking at Charlie. Every day the man proved he was a fool, but maybe even a fool could do this work for three months. "Don't buy cars. Spend some of your money at Christmas if you want, but nothing flashy. We're all done by the first of the year, maybe sooner, depends on the ice. Next year, the whole country is going back wet, and this will all be over. We go back to what we were doing, or whatever the hell you want. It's a free country."

Andy stroked his beard and nodded vigorously. The man appeared happy to be included, finally judged worthy of some sort of selection, even if it was to commit a crime. "All fine by me," he said.

Eld turned to Eugene. Maggie had seen Eugene's wife leaving the back of the Methodist church hall with a bag of groceries. He had to say yes.

"This ain't my life's calling," said Eugene. "I'm no gangster, don't want anybody thinking I am. To tell the truth, if it wasn't Eld that asked me, I would have said no."

Eld was thinking about that, about him leading men into this, like the sergeant he never wanted to be, when the screen door opened. Before Charlie could get up from his chair Leon stepped over the threshold, followed by a man Eld had not seen before. The conversation evaporated and everyone stared. Eld didn't know how to look except like he'd been caught.

The second man was smiling as he took in all the faces in the room. Eld followed his stare, saw undisguised fear, and tried to screw up the courage necessary to meet the man's eyes. Leon gestured at Eld.

"This right here is Eldridge, our Northwoods tycoon."

The second man nodded. "Mickey wants to meet you," he said, without introducing himself. "Says that if he's going to make you rich he wants to see your face. Shake your hand. Take your measure."

"Sure," Eld said. His mouth was dry. "Where and when?"

"That's the great part," said Leon. "You're invited to a *party*."

FIVE

Every man on the *Nancy* was wearing a dark suit. Most were pinstriped, but a couple were windowpane. Eld's was more subdued, a charcoal gray, with a little shine on the front of his thighs where he had rested sweaty palms every time he had worn it. The four women on board were younger than the men, and they wore skirts that ended just past their knees. Most of the men were musicians holding instruments in cases. They stood because there was no place for them to sit.

Eld counted again. Nine. Until they had pulled up in two big Buicks at sunset, he had never seen any of them before. Before that day the most the *Nancy* had ever had aboard was four, when Eld had taken his family out for a summer evening picnic. His passengers had brought a basket with liquor and glasses, and most of them now held a drink. One of the musicians came over to where Eld stood by the wheel and offered him a glass. Eld had seen plenty of Black men in the army, but they were a rarity in Minden.

"Not just now," said Eld, "but I might take you up on that when we tie up."

The musician smiled. "That's when you quit, but I start working. You like music? Maybe some dancing?"

"My wife's at home."

"Everybody's wife is at home. You never been to one of these before?"

"I can't dance."

"I believe that," the man said, raising his glass at Eld. "Since you're driving, I'm guessing you know where I'm going."

"You don't know?"

"People we work for, they pay cash, but they don't volunteer information, and they don't like questions."

"We're going to Sanilac Island. Not sure why. Eight miles offshore. Used to be a big fish camp there, but it closed last year. Not a place I would have a party."

"Mickey's outfit doesn't do anything half-assed. The place, the food, the music, all of it's going to be first-rate. You can count on that."

Eld recalled the bunk cabins, the mess hall, and the icehouse. The last time he was on the island, stacks of dead sturgeon lay dried out in crisp fall air. Monstrous fish, with bony plates on their backs and mouths blooming meaty white whiskers, some of the carcasses were longer than Eld was tall. The dried fish were sawed into oily chunks and used for stove fuel. Eld's memory, of greasy smoke and the accompanying smell, was hard to reconcile with dancing and musicians.

"Do you know Mickey?" Eld asked.

"Seen him. Know of him. Spoken to him on a couple occasions. Can't say I know him."

"I'm supposed to meet him," Eld said. "Why I'm here."

"He's a talker. He's good at it. Anyway, I like hearing him talk. I suppose you know he's the boss. One of 'em, anyway. You want to make damn sure he likes you. If you are going to do more for him than just drive his band out to an island, hell, even if that is all you do for him, do just exactly as he asks. Don't get any ideas."

"Too late. I had an idea. Now I got a boat full of strangers headed to a three-day party."

The musician nodded. "If he wants to meet you, you're in it now."

Even in the twilight Eld could see that the Sanilac Island he had known was reborn. Twenty-five yards out and he saw a garden lit by hanging lanterns. He backed off the throttle and smelled grilling meat through the exhaust fumes. He had to nose the *Nancy* slow through a group of big Chris-Crafts and sailboats bobbing at anchor. Some of the boats had crew aboard who waved as he passed.

The *Nancy* eased up to the pier in full view of twenty staring people, but no one moved to take the tie-up lines. When his passengers didn't move either, Eld scrambled from behind the wheel. The lines fast, he held out a hand to the ladies as they stepped up to the pier. Sweating a little in his suit, he was glad for the movement. Whatever was going to happen was now happening. The waiting part was over.

He followed a line of lanterns up to the building that had been the salt barn. The mounds of salt were gone, and the fish barrels were repurposed as tabletops. He looked into the crowded room for a long moment and saw how things could change. Somebody, not him, had seen what could be, had seen that the salt barn could be a nightclub with a buffet arranged along one wall. The floor planks were painted blue and old nets were hung on the wall. His musician passengers were setting up, joined by men who must have come on other boats. Smiling couples milled around with plates in their hands. Eld realized he was standing at the end of the buffet line when two women stepped up behind him. He excused himself and one of the women laughed.

"We don't bite," she said, her voice full of money.

Eld walked to a bar in the corner and fished in his pocket for a cigarette. The bartender came over and lifted a red glass table lighter.

"I don't want anything to drink," Eld said. "I'm supposed to meet Mickey."

"Fair enough," said the bartender, "but I just pour the drinks."

"You don't know Mickey?"

"Didn't say that."

Eld heard his name called and turned to see Leon. He heard a clarinet, and then a cacophony. Leon's lips were moving but Eld couldn't make out words. The musicians were tuning up.

Leon leaned in. "Have a plate," he said, nodding at the buffet. "Mickey's busy just now, but you're on the list."

The gangster waved over a woman standing in the buffet line. Eld tried to say something, but somebody in the brass section was running through a scale. The woman had shiny black hair, cut short. She smiled in a practiced way as she approached.

"This is Georgia," said Leon. "Georgia, this is Eld. He's new. Doesn't know anybody. Can you keep him out of trouble for a while?"

"Sure." She put her arm through Eld's and smiled. "I'm hungry, and I don't like to eat alone. I read how it's bad for the digestion. Come on with me and we'll get in line." She tugged his arm and Eld saw silver filigree woven into the black fabric of her dress. He looked up and Leon was gone. In a minute he was answering questions.

"Fisherman. I'm a fisherman."

"That sounds about right. Your hands are a mess." She had his arm held out with one hand, rubbing his upturned palm with her free hand. "Feels like the bottom of a foot."

"It's honest work."

"I hope you're not here because you're honest. Are you?"

They had arrived at the front of the line. A man in a white tunic cut Eld a thick slab from a standing rib roast. Georgia told the man how she wanted him to carve her off the breast of a duck. There were oranges cut in halves arranged around the ducks. Eld thought briefly of pocketing some and bringing them home. He didn't recognize most of the other food, so he took a pile of mashed potatoes and let Georgia lead him to a table. She did a lot of leading, this woman.

"What's your name?" he asked her.

She made a face. "It's Georgia. Leon just told you that. Of course, that's not really my name."

"What is really your name?"

She shook her head, but she was smiling. "Nice that you asked. Georgia is good enough for most men."

Something must have crossed his face, because she stopped smiling.

"It's not like that," she said. "Don't make me take back what I said about you being nice."

"I don't know what you mean," he said.

"I'm a nurse, just like you are a fisherman. There doesn't seem to be much need for nurses or fishermen at this party, yet here we are. We could just leave it at that."

A nurse. He looked into his plate and cut a piece of beef.

"Bon appétit," Georgia said.

"You were in France," he said. It was a hunch.

She laughed. "Yes. Like I said. I'm a nurse."

"I was too."

"You were a nurse? No. You were in France. But I don't remember seeing any fisherman."

"They wouldn't let me bring my boat," he said.

He was chewing the meat. It was probably delicious, but he was having a hard time concentrating on it. The woman filled the dress she had on. He was drinking with a woman not his wife. It had been ten years, more, since that had happened. He remembered not to talk until he had swallowed. Charlie spoke with his mouth full. Charlie. That fool was just this second sitting in his house not ten miles from this spot. He might as well have been sitting on the moon. Georgia was working on a piece of duck. She looked up at him as she put the fork in her mouth. She did something with her eyes.

"I have a wife, family," he said.

She shrugged. "That suit"—she was gesturing at him with her knife—"the last time you wore it, were you burying somebody?"

"Yes," he said, looking down at his suit and remembering the hole in the ground and the white of spade-cut roots poking through black Michigan dirt.

"What do they want with a man like you?"

"It's supposed to be a secret."

"Then you better keep it."

The band started up and it was hard to be heard. There was a clarinet solo and then the tempo picked up. Georgia put down her knife and came around to his side of the table. Her hands were at her waist but she leaned toward him and touched his neck with her cheek. Her fingers were snapping. The arm she pulled on had his fork in the fist, so that he was walking and chewing and waving a fork in the air.

"C'mon," she said.

"I can't dance."

"I believe you."

The floor in front of the band was already crowded. Georgia backed away from him a step and swung her arms. She turned and said something he couldn't hear to another woman who joined them. They both looked at Eld and laughed. He put the fork in his jacket pocket and tried to copy their movements. He felt a hand on his shoulder and snapped around, ready to send off the wiseass who might be cutting in. It was Leon.

"I'll bring him back," Leon said.

Eld wanted to stay, but he followed the other man across the floor and up a flight of stairs to a door that hadn't been there a year ago. Leon knocked twice and opened the door. The loft above the salting floor had been finished and turned into an office with a peaked ceiling. Two men were headed out. They both looked him over.

"Hick," said one of them, low enough so that only Eld could hear. The word came out fast, and when Eld stopped, surprised, the man grinned and stopped too.

"I'm right here," the man said.

Eld didn't lack for courage, and it hadn't left him, but he wondered then about the world to which he had invited himself. A world populated by men who hurled insults at strangers, inviting violence as a matter of habit.

"This is Eld, our guy up here," Leon said, interrupting the standoff. Eld's antagonist shrugged and headed for the door.

"Did you get something to eat?" The man speaking was up and around the desk with his hand out before Eld said anything. He had the quick step of a man who enjoyed sports, but he was gray at the temples. Eld put him at about forty. His suit was double-breasted and he wore a bow tie.

"I did," Eld said. "Thank you." He noticed then that one of the walls was covered in a mural. A shirtless man rose from the sea with a trident in one hand. At the height of his waist the foam of waves became a team of white horses.

"Neptune," the man said, following Eld's gaze. He still hadn't introduced himself. "He watches over our business."

"Are you Mickey?"

"You didn't know that?" The man was smiling and was shaking Eld's hand.

"Last time I was here, this building was full of salt and herring, and there wasn't a band either. You've done a lot with the place. With the whole island."

Mickey held up his arms. "Look on my works, ye mighty, and despair," he said. When Eld didn't respond, he continued. "When I bought the place, the chief quality was the evil, evil stink."

"Yeah, if you're a fisherman that's the smell of money. This island smelled like money. Strong enough that you could smell it a couple miles offshore."

"Funny you say that." Mickey motioned at a chair and went back behind his desk. "You ever lain down on a pile of money? Reeks. Reeks of a thousand sweaty palms, deep dirty pockets in the urine-soaked trousers of desperate old men, fingernails with shit under them."

"No," Eld said.

There was quiet for a moment. Mickey lit a cigar and puffed.

"I have never had a pile of money to lie down on," Eld said.

"It sounds like a fine idea," Mickey said. "Like a fine way to spend an evening, maybe with a lady friend or two, but I can tell you from experience it's not what it's cracked up to be. You get to rolling around, you can't tell if the smell is from you, or your friends, or the money—but then, it's all those things. A sickly sweet odor. There's even a strong fecal note. That's money. It smells like pussy."

Eld thought about that, and about the women Mickey might know. "So, what was it you wanted to see me about?"

"They tell me you were in the war."

"No secret about that."

"I'm told the army made you a sergeant. Gave you some medals too."

"The other guys kept getting shot."

"Are you one of those guys who went over there, saw horrible shit, came back a nihilist?"

"A nihilist?"

"Do you think life is meaningless? Do you desire the abolition of the existing moral and social order of things?"

"I don't think so. There's things I'd change, but mostly no."

"Myself, I'm on the fence about those questions. Better for me that I don't dwell on them. It's the unexamined life for me. It helps that I have other things to do. You see, commerce, it pollutes the life of the mind. For me that's a mercy. You stay busy selling widgets or what have you, whiskey in my case, you don't have time to contemplate how you are wasting your days. I take on new projects like this one, I don't think about why I'm here."

Eld wasn't sure what this man wanted him to say, or if he wanted him to say anything at all. "Seems you got it sorted out."

"Maybe. In the meantime, happens I'm in need of a sergeant." Mickey spun his desk chair around and plucked a bottle and two glasses from the top of a credenza. "Did Charlie tell you why we are using boats way up here?"

"No, but I guessed it was because of the police. Read that in the paper."

Mickey snorted. "No. The police are not a problem. Neither are the newspapers. They are an expense. A service. A line item on my budget. The competition, on the other hand, now they are a problem. They hired away some of our friends in law enforcement. Which is fair enough. That's capitalism, and I'm no red. Are you? Are you a red?"

"No." Eld could sense Leon moving around behind him, but he resisted the urge to look. If they were going to shoot him, they'd have done so by now.

"I'm pleased to hear that. I understand the romantic appeal, but I want sound business managers working for me, not revolutionaries with some wild-ass ideas about a paradise for the workers. For the time being I can't use the river down in Detroit, so we moved up here in the woods. Turns out moving up here was good business. I don't need so many people on the payroll." Mickey drew a circle in the air with his cigar. "All the judges, cops, lawyers, drivers, even my guys who make everything go smoothly, guys like our friend Leon, I don't need them. Minden is a very small town. I had more people on my payroll in Detroit than live in Minden. You know what—I haven't paid anyone up here. No one has even asked. But if they did, I could put the whole town on the payroll and still come out ahead."

Mickey poured whiskey in the glasses and held one across the desk to Eld. The band had started another number, a slower song. Eld looked at the whiskey and thought about who might be downstairs dancing with Georgia. He took the glass even though Maggie had asked him not to drink and he had said he wouldn't. He told himself he knew what he was doing, that this part of the endeavor was for him to handle how he thought best. He didn't tell Maggie how to raise the money or handle the books. That's what he told himself, but the truth was he took the glass because he thought he might do things that would later require an excuse.

"See, I'm not any different from Mr. Ford," said Mickey. "I run an organization that has a lot of moving pieces. I make decisions to optimize profits. Running Canadian whiskey has been a good business for a long time. We all made money, but the competition caught up with me, and anyway the days of Prohibition are numbered. There's no point in spending more money to chase that business into the ground, and I sure as hell don't intend to get shot over it."

Eld swallowed some whiskey. "So what do you want with me?"

"Like I said, I need a sergeant. The money I made, I used a lot of it to buy this island. I'm going to call it the Sanilac Lodge. A business almost entirely within the law, but part of the appeal will be the scandalous origin. That draws your bourgeoisie types. This party, it's a dry run. My guests are getting a preview, and they are just the right people to spread the word, but we got to strike now, while the iron is hot, get while the getting is good, you understand?"

"I think so," said Eld, though he wasn't sure. There being a depression on, the iron didn't seem too hot.

"Prohibition ends and everyone is going to want to get a snootful. The fucking Presbyterians who've been teetotaling are going to come out of the woodwork. Fortune favors the bold, so I'm going to seize this chance, open a resort with gangster style. Sell an ocean of legal booze. We open next season for real. First of June to Thanksgiving. This building is the main restaurant and nightclub. I'm clearing timber to put in a golf course and tennis courts. Using the logs to build the cabins going up."

Mickey gestured in the direction of the band. "The people out there tossing back my liquor have the money to spend a couple expensive weeks in the summer up here. Swimming, sailing, golf, tennis, horseback riding, whatever they want. But you know, it's an island. I need somebody who can run a fleet to ferry the guests out, eventually to help me run the place."

"I'm a fisherman."

"Exactly. You can drive a boat. You're honest. At least until proven otherwise. My current associates, they have other qualities, but they aren't . . . well, they aren't the men you ride into retirement with."

"Can I think about it?" Eld was imagining the conversation with Maggie, right up until he thought about Georgia the nurse slinking around downstairs.

"Sure. I think you're the guy for this, but don't get the idea you can't say no. It's not that kind of offer. Worst that happens if you say no, I might have to ask Charlie."

"Would it pay?"

"More than chasing herring, anyway, and you'd get a long off-season."

Eld finished the whiskey in his glass. "Don't ask Charlie. Give me a couple days and I'll get back to you."

"Good. Now, for the rest of the evening, and tomorrow too, enjoy yourself. I am—we are—in the recreation business. If we aren't having a good time, why would anybody else pay for our products? This island, these parties, even me, it's all marketing. Now you are too. Go have a drink."

Halfway down the stairs Eld felt the smile on his face and knew there was a little evil in it. He stopped to sort his thinking and fumbled in his jacket pocket for a cigarette. There was an angle here, to be more than just another honest piker available to get evicted or otherwise screwed in whatever fashion was convenient for the people who did the screwing. Just that wanting, Eld knew it was sin. He was covetous, maybe. Alone in the stairway he lit his cigarette and listened to the band. He would drink soon. To excess. The time to be honest with himself was now, while he was still capable of it. His honesty was why Mickey made him the offer, but his honesty was what kept him a working man waiting on a bad letter from a bank. His honesty, and his other ideas about what was right, maybe that's what he needed to change. He needed a new deal, just like Roosevelt said.

Georgia was at the bar. He took up the spot beside her and motioned at the bartender. The music was loud, and under that was the happy noise of voices and silverware on plates.

Georgia leaned close to be heard. "Don't you have a big smile," she said. "Must've gone well."

"Do you still want to dance?"

Eld had always been lucky with women. They seemed to like him.

In an hour his shirt was damp with sweat and he had loosened his tie. The only light on the dance floor came from sconces on the walls, and moving bodies blocked even that. Georgia was close. He wondered if he had asked for this, or if it had just happened. The wanting, that was sinful, he was sure of that, but he wasn't sure he had come out here wanting this, specifically.

In the dark he put his hands on Georgia in a way that made his intent unmistakable. She stopped dancing and looked at him, but he couldn't read her expression in the shadows cast by other dancers. He waited to be slapped. She leaned into him and put a hand on the back of his neck. Her other hand reached down and cupped everything between his legs. In the dark in the middle of the dance floor he kissed a woman who was not his wife.

"Same again," he said to the bartender on their way out into the night. His voice was hoarse from shouting over the music. He was drunk, as he had set out to become, on an island stacked high with steaks and dancing gangsters. The good whiskey and the life Mickey was dangling, and, if he was honest, the looks Georgia was giving him and the smell of her neck swept him up and carried him along. They left the hall when Georgia said she wanted to get cigarettes from her cabin. A few steps outside and she said she wanted to go to the boat.

"My boat? Why?"

"Does it have a bed?"

Eld hesitated. The daybed below deck was just then under a pile of nets he had moved there to make room for passengers. There were no sheets on the thin mattress, and the Pendleton blanket was smudged in places with marine-grade grease.

"I've never done it on a boat," Georgia said.

"There's a bed."

He took hold of Georgia's hand. Eld knew what he was doing, but his real life, the one where he chased herring and was chased by mortgages, seemed far away. The things he might do here, they could be meaningless. He could be a nihilist, in opposition to the moral order of things, if only for a few days on this island.

SIX

He had nodded off on a sofa in the living room when Doc shook him awake.

"It's the police," said Doc. His voice was a hoarse whisper. "C'mon and get up. The police are here. They want to talk to you."

Eld swung his feet down to the rug and looked around the room. The newspaper had slid off his chest to the floor. Open windows let in a lake breeze.

"Where's your mother? Bea?"

"They're in town. Why do the police want to talk to you?"

Eld stood. "I don't know," he said. He was in his stocking feet but couldn't remember where he had left his shoes. "Wait here."

He walked through the kitchen to the front door. Two policemen he didn't recognize were in the yard talking to each other. They weren't local. Fifty yards past them, coming down the street, he could see Maggie and Bea. Maggie was carrying a box.

"What can I do for you?" Eld called through the screen. He held open the door and stood on the porch. Doc followed until Eld put a hand on his chest at the threshold. Doc's chest was warm under his hand. Eld pushed him back into the house.

One of the policemen turned. His cap had a visor. "Oh no. It's what we are going to do for you." Eld saw their gloves first, and then the motorcycles parked in the street. They were Michigan State Police.

"You work for Mickey Solomon," said the second policeman. It wasn't a question.

"I work for myself," Eld said. He let the screen door shut and stepped down from the porch. The yard was cool and he felt it through his socks. He put three strides between himself and Doc.

"I'm a fisherman," he said, lowering his voice.

The trooper stepped closer. He was a tall man with a pencil mustache.

"Mickey is supposed to be retired. Working on his country club out there. You and the other fishermen running for Mickey, you get this warning because you don't know any better. You stop running whiskey and go back to fish. You are in charge of the fishermen, so we came to you. If it doesn't stop, it's you who will get another visit. This is the only warning you get."

Bea had reached their motorcycles.

"Warning from who?" Eld asked. "From the state police?"

"You wouldn't know, but Mickey, he doesn't have friends anymore like he used to."

Eld wanted to ask more questions, but Maggie and Bea were now within earshot.

"Well," said the trooper who had issued the warning, "you let us know if you see anything out there."

Tall boots, shined to a gloss, crossed the lawn and swung over motorcycle saddles. Eld saw service revolvers holstered with the butt forward. He saw his wife with a box of groceries. One of the troopers nodded at her and touched the brim of his cap. Maggie was smiling because she was a smart woman who kept her nerve, but Eld saw her eyes.

The troopers made a show of kick-starting their machines. Eld's family, everything in his world, was looking, but only Eld knew what was happening. Gasoline was passing through the carburetors of the machines, mixing with air, to be fed into cylinders, compressed, and ignited with a spark. Also, the Michigan State Police had come to his home and threatened his life.

The noise was less a roar than a series of individual yet overlapping explosions. Sound slapped against houses on the street and brought Doc out through the screen door and onto the porch. One of the policemen, astride his rumbling motorcycle, pointed his index finger at each of them in turn, as if he were counting. He ended on Eld. Then they were off down the street.

Eld stood with his family until the last echo had faded. Maggie and the children were all looking at him.

"Well?" Maggie said.

"They asked if I knew anything about boats hauling Canadian liquor."

Eld didn't like lying, but he had a good reason. He loved Maggie and didn't want her to suffer. Worrying her wouldn't help matters any. That was the same reason he would lie about Georgia. He wasn't lying about Georgia yet, but only because nobody had asked. Before running Canadian whiskey was Maggie's idea, it was his, and he had told her that the little family they were raising wouldn't be involved in the business of gangsters. He had been wrong, apparently. He had steered his family straight into gangster business, and himself straight into bed with a woman not his wife, and now he was a liar to boot.

Maggie was watching him. She had a funny look on her face. He shrugged. What she didn't know wouldn't hurt her. They would all be dead in a hundred years and what he did, whether he lied, none of that would matter anyway. He tried to smile, pretending for a moment to find comfort in that notion. This nihilism shit didn't come naturally for him. It was going to take practice.

"Christ." Maggie put down the box she was carrying.

Bakery bread and butter. Items she wouldn't have bought a month ago, before the whiskey money. There was a cabbage in the box too, because Maggie hadn't lost her head. Maggie always boiled the cabbage, so boiled cabbage, the exact taste of disappointment, was in his immediate future.

Eld nodded. "Yeah. Christ."

———

The Pontiac Hotel was on the northwest corner of the two main roads that crossed in the center of Minden, a ten-minute walk from Eld's front door. The café had been a bar before Prohibition and there were half a dozen rooms above. Eld knew that Leon had two of them. A third room was taken by the bachelor druggist who ran the town pharmacy, and the other two rooms were vacant. Eld hadn't asked anyone for that information, but he knew it just the same, as did probably all of Minden's six hundred and thirty-eight permanent residents. Eld also knew that Leon liked to spend his mornings in the café drinking coffee and reading the papers.

When Eld came through the door there was only one customer. A man with his hat pulled down was using toast to mop egg yolk. His shirt sleeve was stained and bandages covered his wrist. When Eld took the seat across from him, Leon looked up with a start. One of his eyes was blackened.

Leon looked back down into his plate. "Want something? The breakfast here is the best eats in town." His voice sounded like he had a cold.

"I ate. But I'd have coffee."

Leon flagged down the barman and asked for more coffee.

"Seems you got the same message I did," Eld said. "Except yours was maybe more emphatic."

Leon pushed his plate away. "I've had worse."

"Two state policemen came to my house on their motorcycles and told me to stop running whiskey for Mickey."

"Did they hit you?"

"No."

"Could have been worse then."

"What does Mickey say?"

"He's headed back. On his boat. Won't be back to Dee-troit till tomorrow." Leon said *Detroit* like he was from out of state. For the first time, Eld wondered where Leon was from.

"Okay. In the meantime, I'm not going across."

When Leon reached into his jacket pocket Eld stood up fast and his chair fell backward onto the floor. Leon's hand came out with a pack of cigarettes. He lit one and returned the pack to his pocket.

"Seems their warning did the trick. You're a little jumpy. Thought you were some kind of war hero."

Eld remained standing. He spoke loud enough for anyone to hear, if there had been anyone in the café, which there wasn't.

"I'm a fisherman, not a gangster. I'm not going to see the Canadians until Mickey gets this sorted out."

Leon leaned back in his chair and looked up at Eld. "I'm sure I could convince you to go. That's what Mickey pays me for, to convince people. I'm a professional convincer. But I'll tell you what, right now I got my hands full. Don't want the distraction. So maybe you don't go. *You* don't go, but everybody else, they keep on as usual. Your visit from the staties, you can just keep that to yourself. You do that, I don't see a need to convince you."

"The other guys, how are you going to protect them?"

"What they don't know won't hurt them. Besides, how is anyone going to know whether the shipments have stopped?"

"Same way they knew about us in the first place. Maybe somebody in this outfit is talking, maybe somebody is watching."

"Maybe. You sit tight and let me worry about the competition. I'll let you know when this situation gets sorted."

"The cops, they said they would come looking for me if we didn't stop."

"It's not the cops that would come looking."

SEVEN

Maggie bought cabbages straight into November. She said the grocer had a big pile of them and they were cheap. Since Eld wasn't fishing, he didn't have much to do, and he watched the cabbages come in the door a couple at a time. He stayed close to home, shaved every day, and from time to time he thought about gangsters, the other captains, or Georgia. He did not complain about the cabbage. Each time the aroma filled the house, and again when the pile of translucent leaves appeared heaped on a platter at dinner, he was reminded that he was a family man, that he had chosen this life, and that it required sacrifice.

Eld had met enough women, chiefly the hectoring wives of other men, to consider himself lucky to have Maggie. When he'd come home from France and seen Doc, he'd marched to the altar without a particle of hesitation. He'd waited in the mud for the Armistice, reading a lot of talk in week-old papers about a peace with honor. Eld knew by then that honor was a notion for old men far from the smell of cordite smoke and dead horses. He didn't give a shit for their honor, considered the idea obscene, but he was damn sure ready for peace. His own peace turned out to be the clean smell of a chubby toddler and a wife who didn't make a show of disappointment. Better than what a lot of guys got. Better than he deserved.

Eld still believed those things, but Georgia had a way of encouraging flexibility, and maybe getting him thinking about the virtues of nihilism. With every watery bite of cabbage, tinged with bitterness, he took in the faces of his family gathered around the table and wondered if he couldn't ask for just a little more out of life. When the grocer ran out of cabbages and Maggie switched to boiling potatoes, he took it as a sign and went fishing.

The earthy kind of rot that thickened the air on an honest herring boat had dissipated in the weeks since Eld had fished the *Nancy*. He took deep breaths through his nose and could detect only the faint scent of old rope and lake water. He had the engine started when Doc appeared on the wharf, five feet above the deck. Eld watched him move and tried not to smile. Doc stepped off the pier casually, dropping through the air with a look on his face like he was thinking about something else. Then his feet touched the deck, he sank into a crouch, absorbing the force, and stood. It was one fluid movement.

Eld looked at him closely. He would permit the boy certain freedoms, as he was no longer a child, but he would finish school.

"Why aren't you in school?"

"It's Saturday, Dad. They don't have school on Saturdays."

Eld laughed then, but he didn't want Doc around if he got a visit from anyone in the whiskey business. Not Leon, not the competition, not the Michigan State Police. He told Doc he could handle it himself.

"We haven't been out together since school started. I want to go, and the boys at school have been saying the fish are thick." He held up a canvas bag. "Mom sent me with lunch."

"Cabbage?" Eld had seen a forlorn head in the pantry. He was hoping that Maggie had missed one and that the grocer had not secured another supply.

"I believe it is, yes."

Eld hadn't heard anything about whiskey from anyone for two weeks. Probably Mickey had sorted out whatever the issue was. Anyway, they were going out fishing, not running whiskey. Eld dug in his pocket and handed Doc a dollar bill.

"Go up town, get us a couple sandwiches. I'll wait."

The first fish came aboard at eleven in the morning. There was a cold wind, but the work kept them warm. Doc talked about the Tigers and his friends in school while the net went in and out. By two they were halfway to a full load. They broke for lunch and ate the sandwiches on deck while herring flopped at their feet. The fish were nearly a foot long, as fat and healthy as Eld had ever seen. If the fishing was always like this, he wouldn't have gone over to Canada.

Doc took a thermos from the bag, and a bowl with wax paper tied over the top. "That'd be the cabbage. But there's ham in there too."

"I'm good, but you help yourself." They both looked at the bowl, but neither of them moved.

"We can't have it with us when we go back," Eld said. "Your mom, she's a practical woman, but she has feelings. We will bring back an empty bowl, and if asked, it was good." He jerked his thumb over his shoulder and reached for the thermos. Doc turned and dumped the contents of the bowl over the side. A greasy sheen spread where the ham entered the water.

Doc held the bowl in one hand but didn't turn back to his father. "Who's that?"

Eld stepped to the rail. The boat headed toward them was three hundred yards away but moving fast and close to full throttle. Eld scrambled to the forward day bunk and retrieved the shotgun he had stashed under the mattress. When he returned to the deck, he took Doc's shoulder in his hand and pulled him away from the rail.

Doc was looking at the shotgun. "Where did that come from?"

"Get on the wheel. Be ready to gun her."

Eld kept the shotgun just out of sight inside the cabin door as the other boat approached. Too fast to be a fishing boat, it passed fifty yards off the stern of the *Nancy* without altering course, revealing the profile of a sleek forty-foot cabin cruiser. When the cruiser throttled down to a stop, Eld stepped into the cabin and snatched the French binoculars from a shelf, barking at Doc to stay inside. The *Nancy* was still rocking in the wake of the other boat when Eld tried to fix the cruiser in the narrowed view of the binoculars. His eyes slid over windblown blue chop for a few moments until he found it. There was a man on the other boat, also with binoculars, looking back at him.

"That's a Remington, isn't it?" Doc asked.

Eld didn't answer.

"It looks new. Those are expensive."

"Boost the throttle a little," Eld said. "Keep the course we're on."

"Who are those guys?"

"I don't know. City people. Out for a cruise."

"In November? That'd be a first."

The cabin cruiser didn't follow them, and after a few minutes it too continued on its course. Eld had to squeeze past Doc to put the shotgun away.

"So some of the guys in school, they work at the fish company. They say they haven't seen much of you the past couple months, that you haven't delivered a lot of fish. Maybe not a single one. You been doing those overnight trips, but no fish, and now we got a new Remington twelve-gauge."

"We're doing fine. You don't need to worry."

"I'm not worried." Doc throttled the *Nancy* down. "I'm not worried, and I'm not stupid. There's lots of talk in school about those caves north of town, about whiskey coming across from Grand Bend, how it's getting here. People say you are running the whole thing."

"That's not true."

"What's not true?"

"I'm not running anything."

"So are we smuggling whiskey?" Doc was smiling, on an adventure. Probably the honest truth wouldn't help, but it was worth a try.

"Look," said Eld, "not everything I do is the right call. I think I made a mistake. I got this idea I could carry a few loads and get a little ahead, but to tell you the truth I'm beginning to regret it. The people in this business got their own way of doing things. It's not like selling herring."

Explaining things to his son, in as few words as possible, Eld saw his own foolishness.

"Are we going to be rich?" Doc asked.

"No. Maybe we make enough to pay off the house, but even that, I'm not sure. Right now I'd like to be done with this."

"Why?"

"There's a disagreement—I guess is the way to put it—and some of the guys at the top want us to stop. Your mom, she doesn't know that. I don't want her to worry. So that's another thing you don't tell her. Like the cabbage."

"Who do they think they are, telling us what to do?"

"They think they are Detroit gangsters, because that is what they are. Probably killers. Not anybody we should fool around with. Maybe the guys in that cruiser were working for them, and we are not going to get involved in their fight."

They set the net again and drifted for an hour to let it fish. Eld drank coffee and watched his son most of that hour. Doc sat on the deck with his back against the bulkhead. He had his hands palms up in his lap and his lips were moving like he was talking, but Eld couldn't hear anything.

"I told you what's going on because I want you to be careful," Eld said. Doc looked up as his father spoke. "When you hear things at school, around town, you don't say anything."

"I could help you," Doc said. "I could go with you on a run. You go across to Grand Bend, right?"

"No. I want you to stay out of this. I don't want you to be worried, but the guys in this business aren't like you and me. They do things every day that people like us can't even imagine."

"But over in France, you saw things like that, did things like that."

"That's not really the same thing. Pay attention to me now: if anything happens to me because of this stupid idea I had, you will be the man of the house. You understand that?"

Eld silently composed a longer lecture, where he would say the job of a man was to be useful, to provide, and if need be to suffer, so other people didn't have to. He might say gangsters with their flashy cars and their gin-swilling whores were frivolous children, no good to anyone but themselves, the opposite of useful. He feared he could not deliver this wisdom with the solemnity it deserved, now that he was running gangster whiskey and might even have his own mistress. He looked at the unease on his son's face and resolved to try. He was already a coveter and adulterer. If he added hypocrite to the list at least it would be in service of making Doc a better man than his father.

Doc was watching him. "Nothing is going to happen to you, right?"

The boy was rattled. There would be time for longer lectures later.

"That's the plan," Eld said. "That's why we are out here fishing instead of heading over to Canada, but I need you to stay clear of this. If anything happens to me, it's up to you to look after your mother and sister."

"Okay," Doc said, smiling. "But I don't think Mom needs taking care of."

"Well then, you just eat her cabbage and do as she asks."

"Do we get to keep the money? The money you already made?"

"Well, I ain't giving it back."

"Good. And the Remington?"

"What do you want with that?"

"Rabbits, pheasants, whitetails. The way I hear it, if you can't kill it with a Remington twelve-gauge, you best just leave it alone."

EIGHT

On their return to the harbor, the ice man watched them tie up from his seat on an overturned bucket. Eld greeted him and the man lifted one arm but said nothing in reply. Eld saw other fishermen, and the fuel truck man, and none of them said anything either. They looked at Eld, and at Doc too, and they made a show of being busy with one thing or another.

Doc was a step ahead all the way to the fish shed at the base of the dock, and he took a cart from the half dozen leaned on their ends up against the wall. Eld helped him load up their fish and wheeled the cart back to the shed. The ice man appeared, and together with the Huron Fish Company superintendent, they weighed and iced the herring. They didn't look at Eld and neither of them cursed while doing their work. Not even once. The ice man left as soon as the fish were iced and went back to his bucket down the dock.

"Nice catch," the superintendent said when the last of the herring was packed and in the company chests. "Do you want to get paid cash now, or settle at the end of the month?"

The Huron Fish Company had not once in ten years ever offered cash on the spot.

"End of the month is fine. Like always," Eld said.

Doc was quiet on the short walk up the hill from the harbor into town. Eld wanted to go into a store, the butcher or the hardware, just to see how the clerk would react, but he didn't want Doc to see. Eld wondered what Doc was thinking, what he had noticed.

"Remember," Eld said, "you don't say anything to your mom."

"Dad, the Fish Company, they know. The ice guy, everybody at school. Everybody knows. They all think you're a gangster now. They're afraid of you. Mom is going to know too, sooner or later."

So he had seen. He'd seen the downcast gaze of intimidated men, just the kind of responses that would appeal to a teenage boy looking for a way to live in the world.

"I'm not a gangster," Eld said. "I'm a fisherman. It's honest work and I'm proud of it. This little sideline, it was supposed to stay quiet. I should have known better. I've lived in this town my whole life, except for when I was in the army, and everybody knows everybody else's business. I don't know why I thought I could be different."

"They're afraid of us. So what?" Doc was smiling. "Nobody was afraid of us when we were just fishermen."

"Not us. *Me*. They're afraid of me. More important, you know who's not afraid of me? The actual gangsters."

Doc walked a half step ahead of his father through town and cut across yards when they turned corners. Eld had to hurry to keep up, walking just fast enough to make it a little difficult to speak. When they made the last turn and the house came into view, he reminded Doc about the cabbage, then told him he was going to run an errand before going home.

Doc stopped walking. "I'll come," he said.

"I want you to get home, look after your mom and your sister."

"What if you need help?"

"I do need help. That's why I asked you to go home, because I can't be there."

"I'm not scared."

"I know you're not."

"Are you scared?"

Eld thought for a moment about what he might say, what was true, and how he wasn't sure about either.

"There's different kinds of scared. I'm not the kind of scared where you throw up or piss yourself."

That much was true. Eld had been that kind of scared and done both those things, and he didn't feel that way now. Doc's eyebrows moved a little.

"I'd say I'm *worried*," Eld said. "How's that? I'm worried and I need you to look out for your mom and sister while I try to sort this out."

Doc stuck his hand out, and for a moment Eld didn't understand that he wanted to shake hands. Before he could smile a lump was in his throat, and then he wanted to live up to the moment and be worthy of the young man his son had become. When they were done Doc turned without speaking and made his way home. No longer slowed by his father, Doc jogged. There was a lot of good in the boy, especially courage. Eld hadn't taught him that. The pudgy toddler he had met when he came home from France, now a brave young man, had come to him like that. Doc was full of things to be admired and feared, a mysterious gift. Eld was still watching when Doc reached the house where all Eld's other gifts were.

He walked to the long bar at the Pontiac and wished he could buy a drink. Instead he lit a cigarette and asked for a cup of coffee. When it came he asked the barman if he had seen Leon. Eld knew the barman in the way everyone in Minden knew everyone else. Eld knew, for example, that the man's name was Mike, that he had been a good baseball player, good enough to try out for the Tigers just after the war. Mike played center field, Ty Cobb's position. Ty Cobb kept his job, and Mike poured coffee at the Pontiac. It was a story that Eld thought he might envy just then.

"He left this morning."

Eld stabbed out his cigarette and reached for another. "He say when he was coming back?"

"No."

"He say where he was going?"

"He paid his bill and left. I didn't ask him any questions. Man didn't invite a lot of conversation."

"He checked out? Took his bags?"

Mike found a spot on the bar that didn't need wiping, then rubbed it with a white bar towel. The towel had a blue stripe.

"Look," Mike said, "I don't want to get involved."

"Involved? Involved in what? I'm just asking you if Leon checked out."

"You fellas, your business, I'm not speaking against it, but it's not for me."

"What the hell business are you talking about?"

Mike flipped his cloth over his shoulder. "The man paid his bill and left this morning. More than that, I just couldn't tell you."

Eld walked home past houses so familiar he noticed the one where the color of the curtains had recently changed from tan to red. Who hung red curtains? It was almost dark by the time he got home to a kitchen full of the smell of roasting chicken. It was warm and steamy under the low ceiling. The pot Maggie used to boil potatoes was on the stove. Bea was at the table with a stack of old newspapers and Maggie was behind her with a pair of scissors. They had a dish of flour paste on the table in front of them and were laughing at something.

When the potatoes had boiled sufficiently, Maggie asked Eld to mash them. Mashing the potatoes was not physically demanding, but somehow that job had been permanently assigned to him. In his house it was a man's job to mash the potatoes, so much so that Doc sometimes tried to take over. Eld did not permit this, though he did allow Doc to melt butter in a saucepan of warm milk. The two of them stood over the pot, mashing and adding hot liquid, mashing again, adding a handful of salt and then tasting. When the potatoes were perfect for Eld, though not yet salty enough for Doc, he pronounced that portion of the dinner ready. By then the table was set and the remaining dishes were ready. Maggie handed him his good carving knife and he stood at the end of the table carving up the chicken. He handed out drumsticks and breast meat and twice asked the children to save him some gravy as they ladled lakes of it over mountains of potatoes.

Eld smiled as hard as he could, trying to overcome the ache, the ache at how he had marched all this, all this vulnerability, the only things he ever had that were worth anything, right out into the no-man's-land of whiskey and gangsters. How had he done that? He looked back to his decisions, his motives. Greed didn't get him in this spot. He wanted no more than the next guy and had no interest in lording it over anyone. No. He had been hopeful. He knew better than to be hopeful. God had sent a whole war, a war in which Eld had participated, to teach men about hope, but somehow Eld had forgotten.

After dinner he drank two cups of coffee with his pie, which on this night made it hard for him to get to sleep. His eyes were closed when the knock came. He sat up but didn't get out of bed, unsure that he really had heard a knock. It came again. Maggie was awake. He heard Doc move downstairs and that got him running. He was on the steps, moving and thinking. Moving his bare feet fast on the cool wood so that it was only the balls of his feet striking the floor. Thinking he must get to the door before Doc, then thinking that if they had come to hurt him, to make an example, to do whatever, they probably wouldn't have knocked.

He met Doc at the bottom of the stairs. In the dim moonlight coming in from the windows he put his hand on Doc's chest and motioned that he should return to his room. Doc didn't move. The knock came again. Eld went out the back door with Doc on his heels. They crept along the wall until Eld could see around the corner to the front porch. There were two men there, both staring at the door. Eld eased around the corner. One of them held a bucket. It was Eugene. The other man was not a man at all but a teenage boy.

"Eugene. What is it?"

Eugene turned and faced Eld. "My boat. Somebody went down to the harbor and burned up my boat."

There was a note in his voice that Eld recognized. Fear, but something else too, a note of complaint, a note of shock at the injustice. They stood there a moment in front of Eld's house, the four of them in the night, two fathers and two sons.

"The fire department?" Eld asked.

"There already."

"How do you know it was somebody that did it, not just an accident?"

"You can smell the kerosene clear up the hill. See the slick in the water. They doused it good first, then dropped a match. They weren't trying to hide anything."

"You got any enemies, any idea who would want to do that?"

"What do you mean, like my wife? Damn it, Eld, I don't have enemies. What I got is this business, with you and the Canadians, and somebody isn't happy. I know the Canadians got paid. Paid 'em myself. So who is it? Your friends from Detroit, up here burning my boat?"

"I don't know, Eugene." Eld had been lying to Maggie. Now he was lying to Eugene too. "But keep your voice down. My neighbors don't need to know our business."

Eld put on his boots and the four of them walked together down to the harbor. Eld smelled smoke, and then kerosene, before he could see the lights of the wharf. The Minden volunteer fire department was packing up their truck, and Eld greeted several of the volunteers by name. They nodded to him, or waved, but they didn't speak. There was no obvious reason Eugene would have fetched him to the scene, and the firemen would know that. The *Nancy* was there, apparently in no worse shape than when Eld had left her that afternoon.

"Well, look at that, Eld, your boat is here," Eugene said. "Tied up in plain view, and it's just fine. Looks ready to go."

They walked another twenty yards, to Eugene's boat. Taut tie-up lines dove from the wharf to the cleats of a boat visible mostly through a few feet of water. Dock lights reflected on the oily surface, obscuring the view of the submerged deck. The part of the superstructure above water was charred and smoking. The thick scent of kerosene unearthed memories of Eld's youth filling lanterns. His mind wandered into trying to sort how he got here from there.

"What am I going to do now?" Eugene said. He was pleading now, but it was unclear with who. "I got a loan on my boat, and I went into business with you so I could pay off the loan. Now I got all of that loan to pay, and none of the boat."

NINE

Eld spent the first hour considering in turn each of the other men in his train car. He wanted his life, his family, but he had reason to envy the other men too, in their suits and ties, a few without the good manners to remove their hats. Those other men were not foolish. At least, they didn't look that way. Eld was sure he was wearing all of that on his face.

He didn't have a phone number for Leon, or an address other than the Pontiac Hotel. He didn't know how to find Mickey either. What he had was a number for Georgia, written in grease pencil on a torn scrap of butcher paper. She had slipped him the paper on Sanilac Island, without a name on it, or an explanation. When Eld called the number a man answered and told him it was a shared phone in the hall. He gave Eld the building address but said he didn't know anyone named Georgia.

At the Michigan Central Station Eld got off and bought a *Free Press* and a fresh pack of cigarettes. He hadn't been down to Detroit in more than a year, and it seemed to have grown even busier since the last time he was there. Thousands of people churned through the station while Eld drank coffee and ate a sandwich in the station diner. He'd thumbed a lift from Minden down to Port Huron and caught the morning train without having breakfast. To show up at Georgia's door both unannounced and hungry would be rude. He would surprise her, that couldn't be helped, but at least he wouldn't put a dent in her groceries.

After asking directions from a porter, Eld caught a streetcar to Georgia's neighborhood and found the building. The redbrick structure came out almost to the street, but the entrance was recessed so that the shape was a right-angled horseshoe. He hadn't sorted out how he was going to handle this part, so he stood out front and smoked a cigarette. People walked around him in ones and twos, nodding but uninterested, the way city people do.

The five-story building was pretty. Prettier than his house. Prettier than anyplace he had ever lived. He had glimpsed the Ambassador Bridge from the streetcar on his way there, and he was sure you could see it from the upper floors of the building. You could get in a car and drive to Canada, have breakfast over there with the Canadians, and be back for lunch in Detroit. The people in Minden, they spat the word "city," trying to make it sound dirty, but Eld always heard the jealousy and resentment in their words, and maybe a little fear. A woman entered Georgia's building. Eld noticed her shoes. She was followed by a man in a navy wool overcoat. These city people, their lives, he could see the attraction.

A glass pane on the lobby wall covered a list of names and corresponding apartment numbers. There were only three women's names. None of the names were Georgia, but she had said that wasn't her real name. The idea just then occurred to him that she might be married, or living with a man, and her name wasn't on the list at all. He dismissed that idea and looked the names over again. Two looked Italian. Eld had met Italians in the army, from Chicago, and they all told him right away that they were Italian. Georgia hadn't said anything about being Italian. He took the stairs up to the top floor and found the apartment of the third name. He stood in the hall and looked at the door. He was there to find Leon and Mickey, to get him and his family and his friends out of this jam. He knocked.

A voice from inside said, "Yeah." It was almost a man's voice, but not quite, like someone was pretending.

"I'm looking for Georgia. It's Eld. The fisherman."

The door opened. Georgia was in a housecoat. "Hello, Eld the fisherman," she said, and leaned against the door frame.

"I didn't want to bother you, but I'm in a spot. I'm hoping you can help. I need to get in touch with Mickey."

"Oh," she said, opening the door wide and stepping back into the room. "I was hoping you came here to fuck."

Eld followed her and looked around the apartment. Georgia spent her time on something other than keeping house.

"That would be okay too," he said to her back. She walked through the living room into a bedroom. The air in the apartment was warm. He wanted to open the window, and he was amazed that he could have that thought, about windows, just then, while Georgia walked around the bed and slid off her housecoat.

"It's warm in here," he said.

"Great, isn't it?" She crawled up onto the bed. "Included with the rent. No need for blankets."

Whatever else might be said of his life, and what he had made of it, he knew some marvelous women. At least one too many, in fact. Later, when he looked in her kitchen, he found she had a white steel Frigidaire instead of an icebox. He knew what those things cost, so he opened it gently. The shelves inside were empty except for a dozen bottles of beer. He took one and sat at the kitchen table. Georgia came out of the bathroom and sat across from him. She was naked under her housecoat and she hadn't tied the belt. She picked up his beer from the table and took a long pull on the bottle.

"You said you need to find Mickey."

"Yeah. I think so. See, I run over to Canada—"

"I don't want to know what you do for him."

"Why not?"

"Do you want to know what I do for him?"

Eld didn't respond.

"Exactly."

"Leon, his guy up our way, he checked out of his hotel and disappeared. I don't know how to reach him, or Mickey."

"I don't want to know what you do, but you got a boat, and I'm a good guesser. I'd guess you are getting leaned on and need help."

"Something like that. This part of the business, I wasn't supposed to be involved in it."

"Me neither, Eld the fisherman."

Georgia took one of Eld's Camels from the pack on the kitchen table and found a red glass table lighter. The lighter lit on the first try, just like the matching one in the bedroom. The house was a mess, but someone kept the lighters full of fluid.

"Mickey, sometimes he's a little boy. He thinks he can retire to something like an honest living. He's building on that island up by you, more stuff down in Florida. Hotels and nightclubs. For people who play tennis, for Christ's sake. He knows all the right people to get permits, keep the cops out of his business, that sort of thing. He's been a real gentleman putting all that stuff together, but he wasn't always like that."

"When he made me an offer, he went out of his way to tell me I could say no. Reasonable about it."

"Ten years ago, he wasn't like that. He hustled. Shot some guys. Put together a big organization, had some more guys shot, made deals with the Canadians, held off the guys from Chicago. In those days, he was smart, and he wasn't reasonable. Nobody wanted to be his enemy."

"And now?"

"Maybe not as smart. Says he's retiring. His operation, and most of his guys, now that's all somebody else's outfit, part of a deal. That's all fine, I guess, but Mickey got rich being a killer. He's no businessman, unless the business involves killing. His money was in banks that went bust, businesses that failed. You know, there's a depression on."

"Seems I read that someplace."

"Now he needs whiskey money to fund his innkeeper dream. He knows the booze business, so he kept doing it after he was supposed to be retired. That's not going over so well with his former colleagues. He's a semiretired gangster with no muscle, maybe two or three loyal guys, and a world of enemies."

"How do you know all this?"

"I thought you didn't want to know what I did for him."

"Oh. Christ."

"Don't worry, hon. He doesn't ask me what I do with my free time."

"You could have told me."

Georgia took a long drag and exhaled smoke at the ceiling. "That would have been a strange conversation, and anyway it's not your business who I spend time with."

"Do you know where he is?"

"There's a party at his house tonight. I'm sure he'll be there."

"Why is there a party at his house?"

"Because it's Friday. Not everybody is a fucking long-faced Lutheran."

"I'm not Lutheran."

Georgia took another pull on his beer and emptied it. She put down the bottle and smiled. "Want to go? You can be my date. There will be a band. We can dance. That's what I was planning to do tonight anyway."

Eld stood and went to the Frigidaire for another beer. "Dancing with you in Mickey's house seems like a bad idea, but I'm not going home without I talk to the man."

"By home I assume you mean your wife."

"Yes. My wife, my family, the people in Minden I asked to help me. They're all in the same spot, one way or another, and I put them there."

"You'll need a different hat."

"What?"

"Your suit will be okay. But you can't walk into a party at Mickey's wearing a flat cap. Everyone will think you're a boxer. A boxer or maybe somebody there to fix the toilets. You want to look like a swell that's there slumming."

Georgia had a gray fedora in her closet. The hat was too big. He looked in a mirror and saw himself in his boxer shorts with the hat down to his ears. Georgia was next to him and when she raised her arms to adjust the hat her housecoat spread open. He tipped his head back to make her reach until she was pressed against him on her toes. The hat slid off onto the floor. They stepped on it on the way to the sofa.

He woke on the sofa when Georgia said she was hungry. Then she said she wasn't much of a cook and didn't have much in the house anyway. They would need to go out to dinner before they went to Mickey's. She was pulling on stockings and talking about a chop house they could walk to when Eld interrupted.

"If I asked you something, would you tell me the truth?"

"I could, but I might not." She sat on the bed. "Oh hell, go ahead and ask me."

"Why me?"

"Why you want to know something like that for, something inside somebody else's head?"

"I don't have money. I'm no gangster. I catch herring for a living."

"I'm not the kind of girl that needs a reason."

"You saying it's random? I'm the lucky winner?"

She sat on the sofa where he was stretched out. "You really want to know, I'll tell you. You remind me of someone. Not the way you look. He wasn't handsome like you. More how you are. Not exactly quiet, but not flashy. You expect to work for everything. You're not looking for an angle."

"I remind you of someone. Someone you knew in France?"

"No. I knew him here, but he died over there. I was on the ship over when it happened. Just arrived there myself when I got a letter from his parents. I went over with the Army Nurse Corps thinking I'd find him, track him down. Silly, I know. By the time I set foot in France he was already dead. I was sent to a French field hospital for a year. Spent the war patching up French boys."

"You speak French?"

"Not really. I learned enough to ask a few questions and tell them I was raised on a farm close to French Lick, down in Indiana. French Lick. They sure liked that, those French boys."

"You're from Indiana?"

She blew smoke at the ceiling. "No."

"I wish I hadn't gone, hadn't signed up."

He'd never said that to anyone, but he knew he would be a better man if he hadn't gone. Without France he might have held on to a belief in honor, or purpose, or just enough god to keep him out of Georgia's bed. Instead he believed that all grand ideas were bullshit and the best you could do was look out for your own little corner of the world. His own little corner of the world, that's what kept him from being a nihilist.

"Really?" Georgia tapped ash on the rug. "It was the most exciting time of my life. I fell in love. Bunch of times."

"Not me. I wish I hadn't gone to France. I wish I hadn't said I would take my boat to Canada for Mickey." He put his hand on her. "Hell, I wish I hadn't done this."

She put her hand on top of his and shook her head. "No. Don't you get regretful on me. You're a grown-up. Like the man said, 'you pays your money and you takes your chances.' Besides, we aren't hurting anyone. It's just you and me, spending time together. I don't need anybody, not a church or anyone else, to tell me it's okay."

"That's maybe not how they'd feel at home."

"Your wife? I'll speak for her here, if I might be so bold. This, you and me, that starts to wear on your conscience, you just forget about unburdening yourself to her. That would just hurt her to make yourself feel better. That's cowardly and low."

She reached into his underwear. "You bear this cross all by yourself."

"Mickey asked me if I came home from France a nihilist. Did you go over there, come home a nihilist?"

"Jesus, I hope so."

TEN

After dinner Georgia used the phone at the restaurant. She said she was arranging a ride, and indeed a brand-new Ford V8 rolled out of the dark to pick them up. They were waiting inside, watching through the window, when the car pulled up to the curb. Red wheel rims matched the body color. Eld whistled when he saw it.

Georgia pushed through the door out into the street. "That's Mickey. Cars, houses, tennis clothes—anything for a first impression."

Surprise crossed the driver's face when Eld got in, but the man said nothing. He pulled a hard U-turn across four lanes of traffic so that Georgia slid across the seat leather into Eld. She stayed there for the length of the twenty-minute drive. Eld tried to keep track of where they were going, but he was distracted by the skill of the driver. After the first U-turn, the man shifted and braked so that the movement of the car was barely perceptible. In silken movements, his knees pumped as he worked the pedals and his swift arm shifted the gears of the big machine without urgency or grinding noises.

The heat in the car was dry and pleasant and the road was freshly paved. This was a version of the future. Skilled men like this driver would operate machines, and undreamed-of prosperity would be commonplace. Eld thought of Doc and Bea, how they should inherit this world, how it was his job to be sure this world arrived, and that they would share in it when it did.

In a neighborhood of stately brick houses, the big Ford turned on a driveway into a yard protected by tall hedges. There were people out on the lawn, drinking in the cold air. They drove past a man in a raccoon coat with a golf club in his hand. Two women were arm in arm, dancing. Georgia was out of the car and waiting on the steps when Eld thanked the driver for the ride.

"Yeah, sure," the driver said, and then chirped the tires as he pulled away. The driveway didn't head back to the road but went up a hill past the house and disappeared into some trees. They were outside the city somewhere. In spite of the cold, three sets of French doors across the front of the house stood wide open to a stone porch, and the music from inside spilled out onto the lawn. The building was red brick and some kind of white stone, like a library or a hospital.

"C'mon," Georgia said. "You can gawk inside, where it's warm."

There was no place to hang their coats. Eld asked someone he thought was a waiter and the man told him to throw it in any empty bedroom.

"It won't be there when you get back," he said, "but you just go ahead and take somebody else's."

Eld kept his coat on, and had Georgia's over his arm, but when he looked back she was gone. He was in a large room with two chandeliers and a carpet rolled up on one end. Couples were dancing. One of the horn players in the band was the colored man Eld had ferried to Sanilac Island. He swerved past people in a dining room and turned into a darker room dominated by a pool table. A man with a cue stick was telling a woman not to sit on the table. She was drunk and laughed in his face. Eld found an empty spot before a bookcase at the far end of the room. He hung Georgia's coat over a wing chair so he could light a cigarette. He hadn't seen Leon or Mickey, and now that she had wandered off, it occurred to him for the first time that without Georgia he didn't have a way out of there. That seemed like a mistake.

The man with the pool cue asked him if he wanted a game. His tie was pulled open and his shirt unbuttoned at the neck.

"Thanks, but I'm not staying. Just waiting to meet somebody."

"Well, we can play while you're waiting." The man was racking the balls. "You'd be helping me keep that drunk floozy off the table."

"Okay. You break."

The man broke and sank four balls in a row. Eld missed his shot and the man ran the rest of the table. Eld watched the man play and smiled.

"You've done this before," Eld said.

"Every day. Another game?"

Eld stood near the doorway and scanned the crowd for Mickey. They played for half an hour. The man never looked up from the table and every game went the same way. He made bank shots, and he could use English on the cue ball so that its path bent around other balls in the way. Eld watched and laughed.

"What do you do for a living, friend?" The man was racking the balls again.

"I'm a fisherman. Herring mostly, up in the thumb. You?"

"I'm a pool player."

Eld laughed. "Sounds nice."

"I told Mickey to buy this table, and he did. So I come to his parties and play." On the break he sank two balls, then chalked his cue. "This life is very pleasant. Night like tonight, I would like to live forever. This is a Brunswick competition table. Top of the line. If I didn't play on it, nobody would. Drunk floozies would spill their drinks on it and have it all to themselves."

"You know Mickey?"

"Sure."

"Do you know where I might find him? He's who I'm waiting for."

"Tell you what. You sink one ball this next game, I'll take you to him."

The man didn't sink anything on the break, and Eld sank the fifteen ball. He leaned his cue against the bookcase.

"Let's go," he said.

The man looked up from the table. "You don't want to finish the game?"

Eld followed the pool player through a large and busy kitchen, out a back door, and across the lawn. Fallen leaves scattered in the wind as they walked and Eld felt acorns through the soles of his shoes. He was glad he still had his coat on. They came to a swimming pool with a tarp pulled over it. On the same brick patio as the pool was a stone structure that Eld thought was a garage, but as they got close he could see it had large picture windows facing the pool. Inside, the well-lit room was occupied by a matching set of leather chairs and sofas, woven rugs, and half a dozen men. Leon was there with Mickey. A grand fireplace, six feet wide, was blazing at one end of the room. Eld looked over the occupants of the room as he entered behind the pool player. It wasn't obvious who among them was capable of building that fire.

"There he is."

It was Georgia. Eld hadn't seen her. She was sunk down into a sofa with her stockinged feet up on a coffee table, a rocks glass in one hand and a cigarette in the other.

Mickey looked up at Eld, and then to Georgia.

"Is that my hat? You gave my fucking hat to the fisherman?"

"You weren't using it," Georgia said, "and he needed one. From those according to their abilities to those according to their needs. Or some shit."

Eld remembered the day in Canada when he thought he was going to be shot. He thought for a long moment about whether he should take off the hat. He knew from his time in France that this feeling was something you did not get used to, but if you ignored it, put one foot in front of the other, you could make it through to the other side. He always had, anyway, but probably those other guys, the guys who died, they thought that too.

"I didn't know," Eld said. He kept the hat on. If he was going to be shot, it would be standing up.

"There's nothing to know," Mickey said.

Georgia turned her gaze from Mickey to Eld and smiled.

"Come on in and sit down," she said. "We were just talking about you. You and your friends up in Minden. Unfortunately, I now know all about Mickey's latest misadventures and how you are in a jam."

There was whiskey in her voice, and she looked terrific. Eld had had her twice that afternoon, and even now he wanted her again. Probably every man in the room did.

Mickey threw the butt of his cigar into the fireplace. "Leon tells me that you got a visit from the state police."

"That's right," Eld said.

"Seems our little endeavor is no longer a secret."

"They told me to shut the operation down. I didn't tell the other captains. Far as I know, they are still going across."

"Jesus," said Georgia. "The Purple Gang warned you, which we can assume is a professional courtesy, because they usually don't warn anybody—they just turn up and shoot everyone—and you guys left the fucking Lutheran fishermen up there to deal with it on their own. They don't even know they are in trouble."

"Two-thirds of the liquor in this country comes through Detroit," Mickey said. "They can afford to let me ease out of the business. My guys, it's just a trickle. A retirement plan."

Georgia turned to Eld. "You thought you were going to work for General Motors, but really this is a mom-and-pop operation. Just the people in this room. You and your friends up in Minden, you are on your own. There's no cavalry."

"Now you've hurt my feelings," Mickey said. "Saying stuff like that about me, like I have no morals whatsoever. Maybe I made a mistake, got our fisherman here in hot water, but I'm not going to leave him with his dick out in the wind."

Leon spoke up. "We got five guys, Mickey." He pointed a finger at Eld like it was the barrel of a pistol. "Not counting the fishermen. What do you want to do?"

"We are going to ride to the rescue," Mickey said. "Right now. Whatever Georgia might think of me, I'm going to take care of my guys."

"What if you just picked up a phone?" said Georgia. "Told your old pals it was a misunderstanding and that you would put a stop to it right now. No hard feelings."

"No. We are going to drive up to Minden. Tonight. All of us here. I'm going to see to it personally."

"I thought you wanted to be an innkeeper. Maybe an architect. Not a gangster anymore."

"I've never run from a fight. Not going to start now."

"You might try it," Georgia said. "We could all just say sorry and run away. I like that idea."

Mickey was headed for the door. He walked past Eld without looking at him. He wore a bow tie and wingtip shoes, the two-tone kind where the toes were brown and the uppers white.

"Georgia," Mickey said. "You're coming with us. I want you to see me make this right. Maybe you'll think better of me. We can stop by your apartment if you need a bag." He looked at Eld. "And anything you left there."

The other men left with Mickey and walked toward the big house. The pool player nodded at Eld on his way out, leaving Eld and Georgia alone.

"I usually like a nice drive," she said, "but four hours in the dark, a car full of men, and these gimlets make me pee."

"You could have told me it was his hat," Eld said. "That you were his girlfriend." He was finished with her, finished with Mickey, finished with all the surprises this new life had brought.

"The hat." She looked up at it, sitting on Eld's head. "Right. Well, truth is the hat slipped my mind. And I'm not his girlfriend. I'm his sister."

He took a full stride toward the door before what he'd heard brought him to a stop. Sister. He thought about things Georgia had said to him, and things she hadn't.

"I don't think I belong here," he said.

"You don't. That's how come I like you."

Georgia was struggling to put her shoes on. They had buttons down the front where Maggie's shoes had laces. Georgia was having trouble with the buttons. Eld looked both ways before he dropped to a knee to help her. The shoes had a sturdy heel. When he grabbed one and put it on his leg just above his knee, Georgia exhaled and collapsed back into the sofa. When he finished buttoning the second shoe she was smoking.

"Seems you are useful for more than just the one thing," she said.

Eld pushed her shoe off his leg. "Your name. Georgia. A phony name. Why?"

"Mickey's idea, but not all his ideas are bad. See, I like Detroit, but only at night. At night, and maybe Hudson's during the day. If you are the kind of person who likes to go out at night, and it says in the *Free Press* that your brother is an underworld figure, then maybe you don't advertise your family ties. Mickey has a lot of enemies, as you have discovered. I didn't want his enemies, so I picked a nom de guerre."

She put her cigarette in the corner of her mouth and held her arms out. "Voilà. Je suis Georgia."

Eld pulled her up out of the sofa and she stumbled. He held her up and took the cigarette from her lips. He could smell the gin and cigarettes on her, but there was perfume too. She laughed and Eld looked down into her open mouth. That particular view reduced her charms considerably. He wondered for a half second if the trouble men and women have with each other couldn't be solved if everyone took a long hard look into each other's mouths. Inside a person, where it was pink and wet and smelled of recent meals or Chesterfields or what have you, it wasn't something you loved, or even particularly wanted. Yeah. That would cure you, get your head straight and send you back to your wife and a steaming plate of cabbage.

They were halfway across the backyard when the music stopped. One of the waiters came out the back door and ran past them toward the woods. He wasn't wearing a coat. Eld was watching the waiter duck into the tree line when he heard a gunshot, and then another. He turned and saw on Georgia's face that she recognized the sound for what it was.

"Oh, Mickey," she said, and ran toward the door.

Eld grabbed her from behind and pulled her down to a crouch against the rear wall of the house. The real shooting started then, a single shot or a burst of a few, every ten seconds or so. The sound went on for at least a minute. Besides gunshots there were screams and crashing noises. Eld imagined falling bookcases. He watched the back door and thought about what he might do if anyone came out. Probably what he would do was get shot with Georgia in a gangster's backyard so that his family could struggle along without him. There were a few more shots, with long spaces between. Someone was shooting bodies, to make sure.

When the back door finally swung open a cluster of party guests ran toward the driveway where it dipped into the woods. Georgia shouted at them, but they didn't stop or answer her. Car doors slammed and someone stepped on the gas. Inside the house a man shouted to call the ambulance service. Someone else asked where the phone was.

Eld stood and positioned himself between Georgia and the back door. He moved slowly along the wall until he could bend and peer into the kitchen. The room was empty. Georgia followed him into the house. They found the pool player first. He was on his back near the pool table. There were two more men face down. Blood had saturated their suits and was pooling under their bodies. One of them had been shot in the forehead so that the back of his skull was missing and the inside of his head was open to the room, like a melon that had been scooped out. Eld could see inside the man's head, right through to the oak floor planks through the open mouth. Eld took off his hat and covered as much as he could.

Georgia knelt by one man and felt his neck. She rose without speaking and ran off to the ballroom in the front of the house. She was too far away for Eld to grab, and he didn't shout because he didn't want to make any noise. He followed, but at a distance and as quietly as he could manage. The front door was wide open and cold wind came through the house. Drinks were spilled on the floor and a table was overturned. Eld wondered at ice on the floor, and then he saw it had been on the table under banks of oysters. Oysters were on the floor too, and overturned ashtrays and pots of cocktail sauce. He had never had an oyster and it seemed clear he had missed his chance.

The rug was still rolled up at one end of the room, but there was a man sprawled over it now, propped up by the carpet under the small of his back. He was dead too, just as obviously as the pool player and the other men they had passed. That was four now. At the end of the ballroom, where the band had been, Eld went up a stairway to the second floor. Leon was at the top of the stairs, a revolver on the floor next to him. That was five.

Eld thought of quiet horses. Whenever he had seen this many dead there had always been horses. A horse is a large animal, much stronger than a man, and harder to kill. Often, after a shell, all the men were dead immediately, but the horses took time to die. Compared to men, horses made little noise when dying. Eld had come upon more than one that was still alive when that didn't seem possible, given their wounds. That gave him a fear of horses he hadn't had before.

There were no horses in Mickey's house, but Mickey himself was at the end of the hall, in a large bedroom with a big oak bed. Mickey was in a chair with a plaid scarf in his hand. He had put on a wool overcoat since Eld had seen him last, and he had been shot in the face with a shotgun. Georgia was sitting in a matching chair a few feet away. She was crying quietly, her eyes on the floor. While Eld watched, she looked up for a moment, took in her brother, and her chest heaved before she looked down again.

Hearing voices, Eld looked out the window. The lawn below the bedroom was as crowded as the house was empty. He pulled Georgia up from her chair and walked her back though the hall. On his third pass through the ballroom that evening he saw the head of a bull elk mounted high on one wall. He kicked glasses and ice buckets out of the way as he moved through the room, towing Georgia behind him. He snatched an unbroken Seagram's bottle off the kitchen floor and went out the back door, over the lawn, breaking into a trot when he reached the long driveway.

"Is there a garage?" he shouted at Georgia.

She was jogging to keep up with him. He let go of her arm.

"Yes. Yes. It's back here."

He was glad for the cold air in his lungs but it reminded him he had left her coat somewhere. He thought to offer his, but he didn't want to stop. When the house lights grew distant, they were on a narrow lane in woods of black trees. They could have been anywhere else in Michigan, and Eld wished they were.

The drive curved and dipped and soon was so deep in woods that Eld thought Georgia was mistaken, or drunk, or too shell-shocked to know what was happening. When he slowed, she kept on, running in her buttoned-on shoes.

"It's here," she said, in gasps. "Another hundred yards."

The stone walls of the garage matched the pool house. Plank bay doors were closed but unlocked. Eld pulled up the door and loud metal groaned. He worried but didn't stop. The door swung up past his head and revealed the red Ford V8, the first car of four in the dark garage. The driver's door was unlocked, but the key was not in the switch. Eld thought about where the driver might be, and if he might be going through the pockets of a dead man when the police arrived.

Georgia got in the passenger side. "Keys," she said, and pointed.

Eld followed her finger to a nail in the wall holding a key ring.

He drove slowly, without the headlights. When they got to the end of the drive there were still groups of guests on the lawn, and more had wandered down the road in clusters of five or six. Eld wanted to know what happened, but he wanted more to be somewhere else, so he didn't stop. When he turned the big Ford out onto the road and switched on the headlights he saw the band walking on the side of the road. Among them was the colored musician he had spoken to on his boat. He was carrying a trumpet case and looking over his shoulder at the big Ford.

"What are you doing?" asked Georgia.

"I know that guy, the horn player. We are going to get him out of here."

"I know all these people. They got here somehow on their own, to drink my brother's whiskey. They can get themselves the hell out of here."

Eld ignored her and pulled over where the band was walking on the side of the road. Many of them carried their instruments without cases, as if at any moment they might strike up another tune to accompany the evening's events. When the car pulled off the asphalt onto the gravel shoulder most of the musicians backed up, but a man with a trombone stood his ground. Eld wondered if that was a musician's instinct, to cling to the thing that made him who he was, even in times of crisis. Had the band on the *Titanic* held on to their instruments too? Could they be found on the bottom of the Atlantic, even now clutching tubas and French horns? Eld had nothing like that to cling to, except maybe a herring, and that was his own damn fault.

He rolled down the window and called to the horn player he had met on his boat. The man eagerly jumped into the back of the Ford. He looked from Eld to Georgia and sat back into his seat and took a breath.

"Did they kill your brother?" he asked.

"Why hello, Claude," Georgia answered without turning around. "Yes, my brother is dead. No more parties for you, I guess."

"I was afraid of that. I'm sorry. He was always fair with me."

Eld stepped on the gas too hard and the big V8 spun the rear tires. They fishtailed out into the road. His hand was jittery on the gearshift and his joints seemed over-lubricated. He wanted a cigarette. He knew this feeling from France, and he knew for him it always came *after* something terrible. He was grateful for that. He had seen men who panicked *during* something terrible, and that was worse. They couldn't function, sometimes they screamed, and they were called cowards, usually by men who were never asked to do what others had done. The fact that Eld didn't feel it until it was over, that was just the way he was made. Like his eyes being blue. If other people wanted to say that was courage, well, he wouldn't stop them, but he knew better.

They were a mile from the house when Eld got a cigarette lit. "What in hell just happened?" he asked. "Who did all that shooting?"

"I surely don't know," said the horn player Georgia had called Claude. "But I thank you for the ride out of there. You can drop me anywhere in the city."

Georgia turned around. "You didn't recognize them?"

"They had paper masks on. At least they did by the time I noticed them. Hoover's face."

"How many?"

"Five or six, I think, but I was praying, not counting. One of them looked right at me and kept going. They knew who they were after, and it wasn't me."

Georgia was saying something, but Eld spoke over her. "Did they speak to you? Say anything?"

"It's not like that," Georgia said. "There's nothing to say. They went to Mickey's house to kill him because he went back on his word. Simple. Just like I told him. Christ, Mickey."

"What about the other men that were shot?"

"Leon, the other guys, they were what was left of Mickey's muscle. They had to go, to show everyone that taking sides against them was a losing proposition."

"You told Mickey all this?"

"Many times. He told me that I worried too much, that the Purple Gang wouldn't begrudge him a little retirement sweetener. Seems he was wrong."

Eld took his eyes from the road to take in Georgia's profile. She had a beret on. He thought he knew all about her, how she was heartbroken by a war and threw herself at men, but it turned out he knew nothing important.

"He thought he would get a warning," Georgia said. "A kind of professional courtesy."

"Well, he did. State troopers came to see me in Minden, and somebody paid a visit to Leon."

"Yeah. He didn't tell me that until tonight."

"What did you do for him, exactly?"

"Mickey was fearless, and he had big ideas, but he wasn't the smart one. That's me. I whispered in his ear. Kept him alive, made him rich. At one time he had a lot of money. That meant a lot of women around. Beauties, all of them, but all of them just, just—poison." She spat the last word. "They couldn't tell him anything, and even if they could, they wouldn't. My job, as the only one who still loved him, was to tell him to go sniff his own shit from time to time, to check if it still stank."

"Anywhere along here is fine," Claude said from the back seat.

Georgia finally turned to look at Eld. "Where are you going?"

"Your place."

"Best not," Claude said from the back seat. He spoke quickly.

"Christ," Georgia said. "The horn player is better at this than you."

"You think they are there, after you?"

"Maybe. Maybe after you. Anybody who worked for Mickey would be wise to lay low."

"I don't work for anybody. I'm independent."

"We run into them, you can try to explain that."

"You could just pull off right here," Claude said. "I'll hop out, walk home."

"They warned me right in my front yard," Eld said. Georgia didn't respond. He was looking through the windshield, but he saw his reflection too. Fool.

"Claude, where do you live?"

"Black Bottom. Close to Chene, but you don't need to take me there."

"Next left," said Georgia. "Take the next left."

Eld looked over to Georgia and turned the wheel. "Claude, you have a gun?"

"I do appreciate the ride," Claude said, "but I'm a horn player, not a gangster. You can just let me off here."

"He'll pay you for it," Georgia said, without turning around.

"You married, Claude, you got a family?"

"No."

"He does," Georgia said. "Wife and at least one kid I've seen. A little boy. I've seen them at Mickey's pool in the summer."

"What do you want?" Claude asked.

"I'll take you wherever you want," Eld said, "but I need a gun. I want to buy yours."

"Damn it, I don't want to be in your business. Why didn't you just pick one up before we left the house? They were laying all over."

"I wasn't thinking about it."

"Don't you have one?"

"It's on my boat, and I'm not going there."

"*Sell* him your gun, Claude," Georgia said. "No one is going to know it came from you. If he has occasion to use it tonight, he probably won't live to tell anybody where he got it."

Claude sank back into the seat and folded his arms across his chest. "I got a shotgun," he said. "Double barrel. Sawed off so it fits in a horn case. It's at my house. Price is fifty dollars."

"Jesus," Eld said, "that's—"

"Done," Georgia said. "My treat." She pulled up her skirt and retrieved folded bills from the top of her stocking. When she peeled off a fifty-dollar bill and held it over the seat toward Claude, he didn't take it right away.

"If it helps," she said, holding the folded bill between her fingers, "consider it a parting gift from Mickey. Your patron. A patron of the arts."

Claude directed Eld through a series of turns until they pulled up in front of a wood-frame house with a porch that ran the length of the lot. The neighboring houses were close, but the house was large and had been painted recently. Eld was counting windows and trying to guess the number of rooms when the front wheel jolted over the curb and into the lawn. He worked hard all his life, and until recently had been honest, but somehow a negro horn player for the mob was doing better than him. He ground gears finding reverse, and when he backed off the curb the chassis bottomed out on the big car's springs with a resonant boom.

Claude cursed as a light came on inside the house. "Turn off the headlights but keep the motor running. I'll be back in a couple minutes."

When he was gone Georgia lit a cigarette. "What kind of a wife do you think he has?"

"I'd guess she's colored too, don't you think?"

Georgia snorted. "Not that. Do you think she's going to be scared, or she's going to yell at him? It's going to be one or the other."

Eld watched her closely as she tapped her cigarette ash onto the car seat. Not twenty minutes ago the woman had seen the inside of her brother's head. She wasn't making a lot of sense, but she wasn't screaming either.

"Are you okay?"

"Fuck no."

"You know where I'm going?" he asked her.

"If you're smart, we'll go to a hotel. You'll call your wife. Tell her to get out of the house, meet you somewhere tomorrow."

"We don't have a phone. Nobody in Minden does. They haven't run the wire that far north yet." Eld thought for a moment about the next question he asked, knowing the answer wouldn't change what he was doing. "Whoever it is that killed Mickey, you think they went up to Minden, went to my house looking for me?"

"I don't know. Probably. That's the way they do things. The way Mickey did things too. It's what I would tell him to do. You move all at once, so the other side doesn't have a chance to hit back. You being down here, that was just lucky."

"I'm driving up there tonight. Right now, soon as we get Claude's gun."

"I know. I'm going with you."

He wanted to say no, but he didn't know where to stash her where she might be safe. He had put enough people at risk already. He also didn't look forward to the four-hour drive to Minden by himself. Georgia was drunk, but she would sober up on the drive, and she knew these people. She knew better than he did what they might do next. A pretty woman in button-up shoes would be hard to explain when they got to Minden, but everything he had done would come out in the wash anyway. He would have to take the consequences. The thing he had to do now, the only thing, was make sure that nobody he was responsible for, not the other fishermen, not Georgia, and especially not his family, would get hurt on account of things he had done.

Claude came out on his porch and looked both ways before he crossed the lawn to the car and opened a rear door. The shotgun was wrapped in a towel. He set it on the back seat and unfolded the towel so Eld could see. He held up a pillowcase with something in the bottom.

"Shells," he said. "About a dozen. All I had." He closed the door and stood by Georgia's open window. He had a thermos that he held out for Georgia.

"Coffee. From my wife. It's a long drive up to Minden."

Eld pulled the car away from the curb but didn't turn the headlights on until they were down the block. Georgia had been wrong about Claude's wife. The woman hadn't yelled at Claude or been scared. She had been kind. She'd made coffee for strangers on a long drive at night. Maybe Georgia wasn't as smart as he thought. Maybe the people who killed Mickey weren't on their way to his house where his wife and kids were sleeping.

ELEVEN

Two hours north of Detroit and Georgia had polished off all the coffee in the thermos. When she asked, he pulled over so she could pee by the side of the road. They were midway through a dead-quiet acreage that had been plowed under for the winter, lit up by a full moon set in a sky clear as vodka. A few months ago the barren furrows would have been verdant ranks of beans or sugar beets. As a fisherman, Eld shared with farmers a primitive and unspoken theology born of suffering the whims of a vicious Mother Nature. The bright moon and cold naked earth reminded him lean times were always coming. He had a bad feeling.

Georgia opened her door and frigid air blew up Eld's pant leg past his knee. He recognized the high-pressure weather pattern that would end the season for herring and anything else that required open water free of ice: clear, still, and jarring cold. Georgia was in his mirror, lit by the taillight, squatting with her hand on the fender. Steam rose from the growing puddle.

The Ford was a thrill. On the way to save his family from gangsters they didn't know were coming, and Eld couldn't help but admire the car. There wasn't anything good to say about Mr. Ford, but Eld liked his machines, and this one commanded particular respect. He had the car up past sixty on straightaways, and when he dumped the clutch after a stop sign the rear tires squealed. The heater blew air off the big V8, filling the car with warmth and the gentle scent of motor oil and exhaust. When Eld cracked his window to stay awake, Michigan air came in biting cold off the lake. They were almost to Christmas. Yesterday, leaving his house when he was already thinking about Georgia and not where he was, Maggie had asked him, now that they had money, about a Christmas tree.

Georgia stirred at the sign announcing they were at the Minden town line. "Your wife," she said. "What is she going to do when she sees me?"

"She won't. There's a hotel in town. I can drop you there and drive home."

"I should go with you. Maybe they are already there, or been there and gone already."

"If that's true, what are you going to do?"

"Tell you what to do."

Eld considered that and decided it couldn't hurt.

"We only have Claude's shotgun," he said.

"You keep the shotgun. My aim's not great when I've been drinking. We park a few blocks away, around a corner so they don't see us coming. We go to your house on foot, try to get a look in the windows, see if there is anybody waiting for you. See them before they see us. You going to have any trouble pulling the trigger, if that's what's required?"

"No," Eld said.

"Okay. Have one more cigarette with me." She fumbled with the pack before tearing the paper. Her hands were trembling, but she managed to light one and hand it to Eld.

"It's easier," he said, "if you don't think too much. Just put one foot in front of the other, do what you need to, and then you're out the other side. Or not."

"That supposed to be encouraging?"

"Either way, it's over."

"That's what got you through the war?"

"Yeah." Eld turned off the highway onto a street of tidy yards and small wood-frame houses. "The only way out of this, for me anyway, is out the other side." He parked the car and took the cigarette. "You could leave now, though," he said. "Take the car, go wherever you want. I'm grateful to you, but saving my family, that's my job."

Georgia opened the car door then stopped to answer. "Mickey was my family. He didn't know it, but I'm all he had. The rest of them, those people he thought were his friends, they were in it for a paycheck or a good time. There's nobody to mourn Mickey, nobody to be angry, nobody to get even for him. Just me. If it comes to it, I want to do it now before I lose my nerve."

Eld carried the shotgun in the towel as they walked through a dozen dark front yards and turned a corner. The yards were moonlit and the smell of woodsmoke from banked stove fires pooled over the houses. When Eld's house came into view he stepped behind the trunk of a chestnut tree and motioned for Georgia to join him. The lights in his house were out, like every other house on the street.

"Around the back. My son's room is there. If we don't see anything wrong, we'll go in the back door and wake him up."

"You have the keys?"

"No keys. It's never been locked."

He bent at the waist and proceeded at a jog. The last twenty yards he slowed and dropped the towel. The shotgun at his waist, he looked behind him and saw Georgia walking upright, like she was headed into Hudson's to buy a new hat. At the side of the house he stood beside a window and paused to listen. Georgia caught up with him.

"They're not here," she said, not whispering. "At least not anymore."

"How do you know?" Eld was whispering.

"The lights would be on. They would be making noise. These guys, they make themselves known."

Eld looked through the window until he thought he could make out a coffee cup on the table. Maggie would have sat up with the crossword. They walked to the back of the house and Eld went in with the shotgun pointed chest high. When he blinked the rolled-up carpet and overturned tables of Mickey's house painted the backs of his eyelids. He left the lights off and ducked into Doc's room off the back hallway. He put his hand down on the bed and grabbed a handful of blankets. The bed was made and Doc wasn't in it. Panic rose in Eld's throat and Doc's name came out in a gurgle. His took three strides to the living room, bent at the waist with the shotgun in front of him. His eyes skipped from object to object even before he turned on the light. Maggie's coffee cup was on a folded copy of the *Free Press*. The drying rack next to the sink held clean dishes.

Nothing overturned or broken. No oysters scattered across the floor. This was Maggie's house after dinner. The air smelled of ham. Somebody upstairs got out of bed.

Georgia came through the back door at the same time Bea came down the stairwell. The girl stopped and looked at Eld without speaking. Georgia was next to him when the hem of Maggie's housecoat came into view at the top of the stairs. Eld couldn't quite believe that, of all possible lives, he was living this one.

He lowered the shotgun. "Is there anyone here?"

"What do you mean? It's four in the morning." Maggie had reached Bea. She sat on the step, gathered her housecoat around her knees, and looked from Eld to Georgia and back again. Somehow he had called a meeting of all the women in his life.

"Did anyone come here looking for me? Did anyone at all come here? For any reason?"

Maggie was looking at Georgia. "Are you going to introduce us?"

When Eld said nothing, Georgia spoke up. "I'm Georgia. The man your husband works for is my brother."

"Where's Doc? Tell me quick now."

"Eugene came by to see you yesterday morning, but you were already gone. He said he was going to miss a pickup because there'd been a fire on his boat. He left word for you to do the trip instead. After Eugene left, Doc said he could do it."

"You didn't let him," Eld said, hoping to make it so.

"There's no telling him anything. He left early this afternoon. Said he would spend the night in Grand Bend, be back in the morning."

Eld had to sit. He backed into a kitchen chair and his legs folded under him. He rubbed his finger on his upper lip where he had once grown a mustache.

"Charlie," he said. "Charlie's boat."

Maggie stood on the step. "Beatrice, you go on back to bed." She continued down the stairs, walked past Georgia, and lit the stove. In the quiet of the kitchen she made up a pot of coffee and slid it on the burner. When she sat across from Eld he didn't look up. She took a cigarette from a pack of Chesterfields on the table and motioned at Georgia to take an open chair.

"Okay," she said. "Tell me."

TWELVE

When Eld knocked on Charlie's door, he had two packs of Chesterfields, Claude's thermos full of fresh coffee, and two hundred dollars, but no food. The sun was coming up and the Ford was idling behind him on the street. Georgia was at the wheel, Maggie and Bea in the back. The shotgun lay across the passenger seat.

Charlie's wife, Marie, answered the door. The lower part of her face was wider than the top, and her lower lip was as big around as a man's thumb. Part of that lip was stuck to her teeth in a snarl that was no less intimidating for its inadvertence.

"Eld," she said, "it's not even six in the morning."

"Is anyone here, Marie? Besides you and your family, I mean."

"No, but Charlie's still in bed. What do you want?"

Eld tried to squeeze past the woman, but Marie's hips took up the doorway and she moved to block him. He tried to duck to either side of her, back and forth twice, but in the end he had to lay hands on her and push her inside. She was shouting as he closed the door behind him. He ignored her and turned to wave at Georgia through the window. The rear wheel of the big Ford spun on Charlie's lawn, sending clumps of grass through the air.

Marie stopped shouting to watch the violence done to her yard. "Aw, fuck," she said.

"Charlie!" Eld shouted. "Get up! I need your boat."

Bedsprings creaked, and then footfalls on an upstairs hallway. Eld looked around. The house was small like his, but the home made by the inhabitants was not the same. An overflowing ashtray sat an inch from an uncovered stick of butter. A stack of soiled plates on the counter were topped with a pot. Someone had collected dirty silverware and placed it in an upturned beer mug, but that's as far as they'd got.

Marie was talking, something about how last night was card night, when Charlie came down the stairs in his boxer shorts.

"Eld? What the hell."

"Mickey is dead. Somebody killed him, and they might come up here after us too. Doc went over yesterday in my boat, alone. I mean to get after him this morning. I need your boat."

"Mickey is dead? You sure?" Charlie looked at his wife in a way that made Eld think he might know something.

"Yeah."

"Why go after Doc?"

"Mickey was killed because we were running whiskey. If they want to stop that, they'd come up here too. I think they torched Eugene's boat."

"That's just your hunch."

"No. They warned me too. Sent the state police a couple weeks ago."

"*Warned?* Eld, why am I hearing this just now?"

"I told Leon, but I should have told everybody. Anyway, the warning was for me specifically. Now Doc is in my boat, out there alone."

Charlie took a moment before he spoke. "Cold last night. There will be ice in the harbor and chunks out in the lake."

"Yeah. I'll be careful with your boat."

"What if he's already on his way back? How you going to find him?"

"He'd dead reckon across. If we do the opposite there's a good chance we'll spot him. It's cold, but visibility is good."

"Suppose you're right, and somebody is out there trying to stop him. What are you going to do?"

"I need your shotgun too."

"Boat doesn't leave the dock unless I'm in it," said Charlie. "I'm going with you."

Charlie was a careless man, bordering on stupid, and Eld's instinct was to talk him out of this. The world might find it acceptable to make Charlie pay for his carelessness, but Eld didn't. He considered for a moment the time it would take to convince Charlie to stay home, and the effort involved. While he considered this he saw Marie look at her husband. He expected annoyance, or even disgust, but he saw instead that she admired Charlie. Marie saw the courage in her thick-fingered man, jumping without thought into someone else's trouble. Maybe she was right. Maybe she and her husband and their dirty kitchen deserved his respect. Maybe he didn't have time to argue with this idiot.

The cabin of Charlie's boat looked like the inside of his wife's kitchen. Chunks of frayed line littered the deck. Tin cans, labels still attached but emptied of their original contents, stood lined up in rows on most available surfaces. The nuts and other fittings they contained did not appear to be categorized by size. A bowl that had once held somebody's lunch was now home to half a dozen fouled spark plugs.

Islands of brittle ice spread from pilings in the harbor and clung like a skirt to the hull. Another day of this cold and the entire harbor would freeze over, thickening by the hour until it could support the weight of a man. All the boats still in the water would be hauled out for winter storage. Fishing and smuggling were just days from closing for the season. Mickey had almost made it. Eugene, Eld, Georgia, all of them had almost made it.

Eld stood on the bow with a boat hook until they got out of the harbor, ready to push away any floating chunks of ice, but none materialized. The air wasn't moving but it was cold enough to make the back of his knuckles burn. He alternated hands that held the boat hook and stuffed the other one into the pocket of his mackinaw. When he got back to the wheelhouse Charlie bumped up the throttle. He was drinking coffee. Claude's thermos was open to the cold and steam rose. Eld poured some into a dirty cup and resealed the bottle.

Charlie stayed on a heading of eighty-six degrees, almost due east. Eld had been too long a captain to make a good passenger, but this was Charlie's boat. He kept his mouth shut and swept the horizon with Charlie's binoculars. When Charlie asked, Eld told him everything about the warning from the state police and the scene at Mickey's party. He told Charlie everything because here Charlie was, on this errand. He told Charlie everything with the exception of Georgia. If Charlie knew, his wife would soon, and Minden was a small town with a long memory. Maggie didn't deserve that. Of course, she didn't deserve any of this, but maybe he could spare her whispers behind her back about a wandering husband.

Charlie poured the last of the coffee. "Marie's cousin," he said. "He knows Mickey. He put me up to it, said this would be easy work for a few months. I'm sorry if it was me who got us all into this."

Eld hadn't thought of that, and for a second the idea that everything was Charlie's fault was a relief. A moment later and he knew that wasn't right. It felt good to have another man share responsibility, but Eld knew better.

"No," Eld said. "It was me that got the other boats involved. I offered Mickey a way to scale up. That's what got the attention of the competition."

"Maybe, but to be honest, I admired your ambition. We all made more money, and I wouldn't have done that without you."

Eld picked up the binoculars and made another sweep. He didn't want to think about his ambition and how it had put him in Dutch with gangsters, gotten out in Charlie's boat this late in the season, out looking for his only son. He knew better than to look at events for lessons, or even meaning, but he understood that he should have been content with his life. He could have caught a few herring, stayed poor, stayed in his wife's bed, and inherited the earth. If he hadn't coveted, if he hadn't wanted more, well, maybe he'd be home with Doc now, planning to cut ice after Christmas.

A white speck. He swept past it but swung the binoculars back. It might be ice, but if it was, it was the only chunk they had run across all morning. No. It was the bow of a boat. He told Charlie and passed the binoculars to him.

"It's a boat, all right," Charlie said, "but not yours. It's too fast, and too white."

The boat got closer. At half a mile Eld recognized it as the cabin cruiser he had seen with Doc. He ducked into the cabin to load Charlie's shotgun, the third shotgun he had handled in the last week. The sixteen-gauge double barrel was really a pheasant gun, but Charlie had some buckshot shells. Eld leaned it against the inside of the door frame before stepping out on deck.

The cabin cruiser altered course to intercept them, and at one hundred yards it throttled down. Charlie put his boat in neutral and joined Eld out on the deck as the cruiser slowed and came alongside. There were three men on the deck, one more than there were barrels on Charlie's shotgun. They wore matching wool jackets that looked new. Eld thought for a moment that they might be in the uniform of hired crew for some auto magnate's pleasure craft.

One of them called over. "You guys work for Mickey."

"Who's Mickey?" Eld shouted back. "We're fishing. What are you doing out here? Cold day for a cruise."

"We're out looking for boats working for Mickey, and we're finding them."

"I don't know any Mickey," said Charlie. He was grinning, enjoying his courage.

Eld was thinking about the word *them*. Plural.

One of the men was struggling to unbutton his new wool jacket. It might have been that his hands were cold, or maybe that the new fabric around the button holes was still stiff. Eld was already moving for the shotgun when the man's jacket swung open. The pistol was aloft in a stubby-fingered hand, then pointing at Charlie. Charlie's face was sorting things out from top to bottom, so that the eyes were all frozen terror but the mouth was still set in a smile, and then the top part of Charlie's head was gone. He stiffened then, so that his toes came off the deck as he fell backward. He made a long grunting noise as he fell.

The sound and the smoke were familiar and Eld knew to stop thinking. He had the shotgun to his shoulder and was on one knee. He put the bead on the man's face and pulled the trigger. Without looking to see what happened he swung the barrel to the other man and shot him in the back as he ran. The third man made it into the cabin. The engine of the cabin cruiser roared as Eld reloaded two more shells. He fired at the spot in the cabin where he thought the wheel should be, but the prop wash rocked Charlie's boat and his shot was high. He fired the second barrel at the same spot, but the cabin cruiser kept on and was quickly out of range.

In the wheelhouse Eld used Charlie's binoculars to search the horizon. He put the boat back on course to Grand Bend before he went out to deal with Charlie, hoping that the body could be cleaned up. It couldn't.

He covered Charlie with an empty net bag and went back in the wheelhouse. He didn't know what Marie would see, looking at Charlie. He saw France. The natural state of savagery was right there, impossible to deny. For some reason the savagery had bubbled up here, on this icy morning in the middle of a glass-calm dark lake, on the imaginary line between two places with names made up by men who had different rules about drinking potions made from fermented grains. That savagery had erupted, burning through the curtain, leaving mangled corpses, widows, orphans, what have you, and Eld had been its deacon, ushering it into the world. That's not what he had wanted to be.

Two hours of empty water and the Canadian coast was well into view. Maybe Doc had encountered some hassle with the whiskey and got held up in town. Maybe the Canadians wouldn't give it to him because he was a kid, or maybe Doc was off looking for breakfast somewhere. He was not by nature an early riser. Eld was thinking that neither of them should come back across the lake in a boat. He would find Doc in town and leave both boats there. They could catch a ride down to Sarnia and take a ferry across the river back into Michigan. Together he and Doc would gather up the rest of the family and they could go west. Drop everything. The house. His boat. Like those Okies headed to California, but they would go to Oregon instead. There was good fishing there. Salmon. They would take Mickey's Ford and all the whiskey money. He looked forward to the drive and the feeling of how warm the Ford got when he turned on the heater. He would spend time being a father to his children, maybe teach Doc to drive along the way. Or they could go to Canada. He'd read that three years' residence and they could apply to be citizens. Be almost English, with all that shit about the king. What the hell. No Canadian had ever pointed a gun at him.

He wasn't looking for his boat anymore, so he was startled when it came into view not five miles off Grand Bend.

It was low in the water. Doc had overloaded her with too much whiskey. He could get away with it in this weather, but Eld was already thinking about what he would say to Doc in way of warning, how wind and swell on the lake came up fast, especially in winter. Doc knew that, would smile and nod, maybe say *I know, Dad*, proud of the way he had brought over so much on one trip.

The *Nancy* wasn't moving. It was adrift. Eld had the shotgun up and was saying *Doc Doc Doc* over and over as he closed the distance. He was shouting it when he got close. He backed off the throttle, then shut down the engine, still shouting. Nothing moved, but the engine of the *Nancy* was idling. Eld heard himself and stopped shouting.

He jumped across without tying off, the shotgun in one hand. He landed on a heel and slipped, the back of his head hitting the rail as he went down. Eld couldn't see for a few seconds because his field of vision was crowded with streaks of light and colors. He slipped around in something, struggling to get upright. His arms slid repeatedly and the white streaks faded from his vision. The colors he saw were red. He stood and saw it was blood. There was a puddle of blood on the deck and he had landed in it.

He ducked into the cabin of his boat, where he had made his living for years. Doc had used the French binoculars without returning them to their case. Half a store-bought sandwich was on the shelf near the wheel. The shape of the roll was unfamiliar. It hadn't come from the bakery in Minden. Doc must have bought it in Grand Bend just a few hours ago. He'd left a bag right where someone might trip over it. Eld recognized the cloth bag from home. It had wax paper bundles in it, wrapped by Maggie and tied with string. Five or six seconds passed, the kind of seconds that once they tick past you can't ever go back to where you were.

Eld had been wrong about Mickey, wrong about Georgia, wrong about rum-running, wrong about risks. Most of all he'd been wrong about himself. He wasn't the man who could take care of his family and lead them to a better place. He was a fool, and he'd brought them here. Just like in France, somebody else had come out and met the fate Eld had made for himself. This time it was Doc.

In every direction the water was glassy. He shouted for Doc and listened in the cold for an answer.

PART II

THIRTEEN

Maggie had forgotten about the chocolate until Bea came into the office a little after four, but she was pleased to see the girl's reaction. Mothering had taught Maggie that the child in a person didn't leave all at once, or even at a steady rate. First the adult flickered unexpectedly, by way of some offhand comment, or, in Bea's case, pursed lips and rolled eyes. The adult flicker increased, more every day, until a person more reserved and distant became the norm and the child became only an occasional flicker. The child in Bea's eyes lit up when she saw the chocolate. Maggie said no, but she was relieved to see that at least a little of the girl she knew was still in there.

The heap of chocolate bars was four feet across, corralled into a corner of the waiting room where visiting food company executives would see it and know the commissioner meant business. Usually the pile was made of foodstuffs less appealing to a fourteen-year-old girl. Commodities like sacks of flour or jars of pickles were more common, and this close to

Thanksgiving the department was focused on turkeys, but the inspectors had returned from a rat-infested warehouse with a trunkful of slightly nibbled chocolate bars.

Georgia had pulled the big Ford up to the curb at four, right on time, and Bea got out of the back seat, making it clear to her waiting mother that she was old enough to go straight home. The girl was annoyed at being ferried around by Georgia, and waiting an hour on her mother in a meeting room at the Michigan Department of Agriculture did not improve her mood. This Friday-night ritual, including Bea's growing petulance, was the low point of Maggie's week. She had considered asking Georgia to hang on to Bea a little longer, but Georgia already did so much for them. Maggie would not intrude on the Friday nights Georgia spent on the town with her various admirers, even if the town was only Lansing.

Maggie was reasonably sure that the chocolate had not been touched when they packed up to leave her office. In her warnings to Bea, she had used the words "rat shit" injudiciously, after checking to be sure none of her colleagues were in earshot. The untouched pile was reason to smile. Bea had listened, taken a warning to heart.

"The good lord gave my daughter sense enough not to eat rat shit," she said.

Eyes rolled.

The bus driver looked up when Bea walked past without paying, but he said nothing. Maggie never paid the fare for Bea. She thought the bus drivers probably approved, out of solidarity with other working people, but she didn't give a damn either way. When they first arrived in Lansing she couldn't afford the fare for both of them and was terrified that a driver might call her out. After almost a year on the state payroll she might be able to afford it, but now she refused on principle. Two years of working every day and she would be happy to argue the point with any bus driver in the city. She worked all day long for the government, paid taxes to the government, and moved her family around town on buses so she could keep working for the government. The government could damn well cover the cost of getting Bea home once a week. She dropped a nickel in the fare box for herself and walked to where Bea had found a seat.

Sitting had little appeal after a workday typing and answering phones, so Maggie stood in the aisle and held the grab rail. Bea looked out the window, ignoring her mother. She had recently become tall for her age, growing out of school clothes at an expensive clip. Bea clearly enjoyed her recent growth, and getting older in general, carrying herself in a way that made others assume she was even older than her fourteen years. Showing no sign of the crippling shyness Maggie remembered from that time in her own life, Bea often spoke up to shop clerks and other adults before her mother had a chance. On those occasions Bea spoke clearly and with confidence, though always in a cheerful way. The exchanges began with Bea's practiced but sunny exclamation of "Good evening," a phrase not commonly heard in Michigan four years into the Depression. Standing in Bea's wake, watching a charmed butcher or waitress smile and respond, Maggie felt the tug of annoyance and the warm glow of pride at the same time.

"We're getting off at the next stop," Maggie said.

Bea looked up.

"Been a long week, and I'm not in the mood to cook dinner. Let's go to the diner."

"Cobbler?" Bea asked.

"Yeah, what the hell."

Two older women in the seat behind them looked up when Maggie cursed. She stared them down.

They had to wait for a booth, and when they sat down the end of the table was sticky from sugar. Theirs was the only table without an adult man.

"Know why the Friday special is always fish?" Bea asked. "Because of Catholics," she continued, without waiting for an answer. "They think they go to hell if they eat meat on Friday."

"Is that right?"

"I'm not sure about the hell part, but I think they are not supposed to eat meat on Friday. What kind of fish is it? The menu doesn't say. Just says fish."

Maggie smiled. "That's the question of a fisherman's daughter. These people," Maggie gestured at the crowded booths and the counter, "city folk, they'd eat carp. Don't know any better."

The waitress didn't know either, but she went to the kitchen to find out. She came back and said it was yellow perch from Canada. Maggie smiled and ordered the fish, hoping her little family might enjoy a small moment of unity, until Bea ordered a bacon sandwich with tomato soup.

"We're not Catholic," Bea said by way of explanation when the waitress left.

When the food arrived, Maggie grabbed her daughter's hand. Before she bent her head, she saw Bea look in both directions. "You don't have to say anything out loud, but we got things to be thankful for, and a long list of things to ask for."

"No one else in here is praying."

"No one else in here is missing a daddy and a brother," Maggie barked, louder than she had intended.

Silence dropped over their section of the diner and a few seconds passed before conversations picked up again. Maggie exhaled and looked down into the table. Her instincts with her children, the instincts that had told her when to hold them, when to make them something sweet, when to spank their behinds, had become useless. Bea wasn't a baby anymore, and Maggie feared she was failing her. That feeling would ruin her fish, but it was too late to leave the diner.

Maggie bowed her head and prayed alone, moving her lips without speaking, rattling through a rote thanks to Jesus for absolving her sins and for the food they were about to eat. She looked up to see her daughter staring at the table, embarrassed for her. She slowed and formed thoughts with precision. She asked for strength, and asked, as she had every day for nearly a year, for an answer. She didn't ask for the return of her men. Such a miracle made her prayer an absurd plea whispered into a void. A return was too much to ask, but she felt she deserved at least an answer.

When the perch came she managed to eat half her plate. Rising anxiety and anger with Bea had taken the edge off her appetite, but she ate the fish because it cost money, and because she wanted to confirm her memory of the taste. Eld was a herring fisherman, but sometimes a school of perch blundered into his net. Perch were not easy to sell, so he sometimes came home with bushel baskets of the pretty foot-long yellow-banded fish. The arrival of so much fish, fish that would spoil in a day or two, swept away every other workaday priority and called for an immediate feast. These events had taken on the character of spontaneous festivals with neighbors and friends. Perch bubbled in oil on the stove and beer batter stuck in clumps to her whisks. Doc cleaned fish while Eld coached, and her kitchen filled with other fishermen and other wives, clinking beer bottles and exhaling a blue haze of cigarette smoke. That was all gone now, but the perch on her plate had the same delicate, nutty flavor. That much in the world had stayed the same. The fish didn't care what happened in her life.

She had promised cobbler, and after the dinner plates were cleared, she asked for an order to share. The wait for tables had increased since they arrived, and the waitress did not try to hide her annoyance. More than half the bodies that waited inside the door were men. Men with boots wearing work clothes, some with wives and children, but many in groups of three or four. Maggie could feel them hovering there, hungry and waiting, and the waitress shot a look over her shoulder at the line when Maggie asked what kind of cobbler they had. Without enthusiasm the waitress reported peach or blueberry. Maggie didn't expect to eat much, but she asked for peach because she knew from bitter experience that a single errant blueberry would irreparably stain school clothes.

She left Bea with money to pay the check and went to a machine by the bathrooms to buy cigarettes. She didn't smoke or drink in public, but she enjoyed both habits at home and she knew the pack of Camels in her kitchen drawer was near empty. When she returned Bea was standing and had her coat over her arm. They were outside and down a short flight of concrete stairs when the waitress appeared in the door behind them.

"Was there something wrong?" the waitress called. The crowd of waiting diners watching from behind her now included a policeman. Maggie's stomach sank and she gripped the fresh pack of Camels in her coat pocket.

"No," she answered.

"You always stiff the waitress? I got rent too, you know. You took one of my tables for most of an hour, had dessert in my Friday rush, and didn't tip me a dime."

Maggie looked to Bea, but Bea had taken several steps away from her mother, out of the light thrown from the steamed-up diner windows. Maggie sighed and began to formulate an apology. She took a step back toward the stairs and was reaching for the quarter in the bottom of her coat pocket when the waitress spoke again. This time she had all those men behind her watching. She spoke like she knew that.

"I know your kind. Yell at your kid and stiff the waitress, but you make a big show of praying, don't you?"

In the quiet moments that followed a handful of snowflakes landed on Maggie's overcoat. The men in the doorway were all watching. They were on the side of the aggrieved waitress. Maggie would have been too. The policeman was looking at the legs of the waitress visible below her uniform. This was all lined up against her, but Maggie had a little money in her pocket, a warm apartment where the rent was paid, and she knew there was whiskey in her kitchen cupboard.

She gathered herself and put her shoulders back. "Fuck you," she said.

They were walking fast and had made the end of the block when Maggie spoke.

"Guess we aren't going back there," she said.

Bea stopped. "Why do you do things like that? That waitress wasn't wrong. You go to church on Sunday but shout curse words at a diner full of people."

Maggie turned to look at her daughter. The lights of the diner were visible down the block. She grabbed Bea's arm and pulled her along.

"A Christian woman doesn't go around shouting curse words in the street," Bea said.

"Oh no? Well, this one does. And how would you know what a real Christian does? All we have here is phony ones. You think those people were Christians, standing there ready to judge me? I don't think Jesus gives a tinker's damn whether we forgot to leave a tip, or what kind of language I use, and anyway he knows I need to make the occasional curse if I'm going to raise you up by myself with all these phonies around."

In the building's stairwell Maggie followed Bea and wished again they had a fireplace, or even a coal stove like the one they'd had in the Minden house. The apartment had only a steam radiator that hissed and boomed at night, but it was just below a window that looked out over the street. After Bea went to bed Maggie pulled up a chair, an ashtray, and a bottle of Seagram's with a glass over the bottle top. She watched the cone of light under the streetlamp and looked for a swirl of snow. Maggie knew from experience that three Seagram's would have the desired effect, but she also knew that the desired effect would leave her indifferent to the prospect of a hangover, so three inevitably led to five or six. She had learned to confine her drinking to Friday for that reason. Up to four drinks and she could remember that they had a roof overhead and money coming in the door, no small feats and more than many could manage in a depression, but after four drinks her thoughts inevitably settled on what she had lost. Long choking sobs would wake Bea, so Maggie trained herself to recoil from thoughts of Doc like the red-hot handle of a skillet left on the fire.

Her husband was gone too, but that loss was easier to bear. She often thought of Eld when she was drinking, because she could never get to four drinks when he was handy. He was a lean and handsome man, and three drinks was enough for her to get ideas. Sometimes at night in the Minden house, if she'd had a couple, she might say she heard something, or forgot to turn off the stove, just to get his naked body out of bed where she could see him in the moonlight. He'd check downstairs, and finding nothing, return to find her naked and focused on something else. Her mother said he was good for nothing, but she was wrong. Eld was surely good for that.

But Eld was gone, so Maggie sailed through three Seagram's on her way to six and a nasty Saturday morning hangover. Sober, she could convince herself she had loved him, but a few drinks and she knew that wasn't true. She appreciated Eld and his steady habits, his strength. She liked the look of him. When he was naked, and he turned in the dim light so that she saw the muscle in his arms and back, she wanted to touch him. More than that, she wanted to be touched by him. After four Seagram's, in front of the radiator in her housecoat, it was hard to think of anything else, but she knew she hadn't loved him. She knew because she had something to compare it to. She'd known the real thing.

Doc's father had not been anywhere near as handsome as Eld. He was four inches shorter, dark, and he didn't have Eld's head of wavy hair, but he was funny. He said his family was Maltese and from upstate New York, though when she met him he was on loan to a Minden farmer from the boys' reformatory down in Ann Arbor. He didn't seem to care what anyone thought of him, so for three months Maggie thought of little else. From the night she met him at a Knights of Columbus dance until the day he shipped out, she saw him almost every day. She gave herself to him willingly the first time he tried, and with enthusiasm every time after that, mostly in the barn on the farm where he worked. The farmer's wife chased her off twice, and on the second occasion called her a dago's whore. He didn't care about being called a dago, so Maggie didn't care about being called a whore. He was gone a week when she wrote him, with plans for a life of travel and adventure, marriage in a Maltese wedding far from small-town Michigan. She learned by return mail that he had died of the Spanish flu at an army hospital somewhere in New Jersey.

She had attended every church dance and club social for miles around, nipping from bottles offered by boys shipping out, and welcoming even the faintest overtures at romance. She might have been trying to get something back, or maybe a dead lover was something that could be cleared out only by more of the same. Eld was not the first, or even the most memorable, but his letter was the only one she received from any of them. By then Maggie knew she was pregnant, and knew from the timing that the father was a Maltese boy dead in New Jersey. When she wrote Eld that she was pregnant, he said he would marry her. Apparently it didn't occur to him that he might not be the only candidate. That he thought of her that way seemed a good reason to accept his offer. Later, when Eld came home from France and met the boy he thought was his son, she wondered if the particular throes of her grief had been guided by divine providence, or even some subconscious instinct. They married in the Methodist church, with Doc in her mother's arms in the first pew, it being understood that the Kaiser had prevented a more discreetly timed ceremony.

Maggie emptied her fifth drink and gave the bottle an eye before deciding to call it a night. She had rolled over the logs of her own bad decisions enough times to bore even herself. She crushed out her cigarette and emptied the ashtray before creeping into Bea's room. She couldn't see Bea's face in the dark, but a blanket-wrapped form was visible and the warm air in the room was sweet with her breath. Maggie watched the blanket rise and fall for a long moment before continuing down the hall to slip under her own thin blankets. Whether she had loved them or lied to them, or both, all her men were gone now. She was, almost, alone, between her girl and all the horrors of the world. *Almost* alone.

    She fell asleep thanking god for Georgia.

FOURTEEN

Peameal bacon was sizzling in butter when somebody knocked on the door. Maggie stood by the stove, spatula in hand. She looked to the apartment door but didn't move. Peameal bacon was expensive and she wasn't going to leave it alone to char. She looked to Bea, but the girl showed no inclination to budge from the sofa.

"Oh hell," Maggie said softly, then, "Who is it?" loud enough to be heard through the door.

A voice answered from the hall. "It's Clyde Barrow. Here to relieve you of the Canadian pork products I can smell clear out here in the hall."

"Georgia," said Bea, smiling. She stood from the sofa and ran to the door.

Maggie looked back to her pan and flipped a slice of the bacon. Georgia drank and smoked more than Maggie, she swore often in public, and she told racy stories about her many hapless suitors, but she never got a scold from Bea. Georgia wasn't here when Bea brought a stomach flu home from school and shat on the bathroom floor, and Georgia didn't do Bea's laundry or talk to her teachers, but Georgia got unreserved affection. Maggie owed Georgia, but in her weaker moments, Georgia's easy way with Bea was an annoyance. She didn't look up when Georgia came in, but she heard the rustle of shopping bags. The woman came bearing gifts.

"This is for you," said Georgia, "but this bag is for your mama."

Bea took a bag from Georgia's outstretched arm and sat on the sofa without a word.

"My date last night," said Georgia, "he puts something greasy in his hair that smells like old ladies, but he's a buyer for Arbaugh's. He took me in after hours for a tour"—here she shot an eyebrow up—"and let me buy on his discount. Might have to jog him around the track a couple times, at least until I get my Christmas shopping done."

There were gift-wrapped packages inside the bag, wrapped in different paper. Such presents were common enough that Bea didn't ask the occasion before tearing off the paper. The package contained a large candle, the expensive kind that came sheathed in amber glass and smelled like vanilla. Bea ran for matches. Georgia had an unerring sense of what would appeal to the girl. Objects like candles that suggested adulthood and a certain controlled femininity, but also a degree of danger. Maggie would have bought mittens.

"Your mother is getting ready to say it, so I'll beat her to it. Never leave a lit one alone. You don't want to burn the damn building down."

The scent from Bea's candle rose in the room and wrestled with the smell of the bacon.

"Had breakfast?" asked Maggie.

"What am I, a farmer? It's ten o'clock on a Saturday. Of course I haven't."

"Closer to eleven. Pull up a chair."

Bea made toast and used more butter than was necessary, though Maggie said nothing. They ate and talked about Georgia's date and the snow that had finally come after midnight. Georgia said the streets were already plowed when she drove over.

"There are a few benefits to living in a government town," Georgia said. "The men are boring and the women are a bunch of officious bitches, but the potholes get filled."

Maggie's present was a Pendleton blanket. She took it from the box and knew immediately she would drape it over her legs while drinking and looking out the window. It was perfect.

Impatient to hear whatever it was that Georgia had come to tell her, Maggie sent Bea out to buy cigarettes after breakfast. Bea understood her banishment was a pretext and resisted. The conversation was brief, ending up where all participants knew it would. Bea's defiance was limited to a refusal to wear mittens. Instead she borrowed her mother's gloves.

When Bea was gone Georgia lit a cigarette and blew smoke at the ceiling. "So, I saw the judge last night."

"I thought you had a date at Arbaugh's department store."

"A woman can't have more than one appointment on a single day?"

"Lord, you are a slut."

"Getting better at it every day. The judge looks good, by the way. He hasn't gotten fat, and he grew a beard for the winter."

"You know I don't give a damn what the old fool looks like, so why did you come over this morning? Bad news?"

"Maybe. Well, not good news, anyway. The judge told me they're moving to Florida. He's finally retiring on all the money my brother paid him over the years. Unless they're getting divorced, and they're not, Nora is going with him, though she doesn't know that yet. That means your patron and his wife, your boss, are about to leave town."

"Aw, hell. Nora's good people. I like working for her."

"I know. The judge doesn't know who your next boss is going to be, but you can bet he isn't going to be like Nora, understanding when Bea is in your waiting room or letting you slide in late from walking her to school."

"Right. Shit."

Maggie took in her kitchen, the sofa in her living room, the remnants of the breakfast they had just consumed. She had made a home for her and Bea. They were doing okay, if just barely, but all of that depended on her job.

"Not like you're goldbricking now," Georgia said, "but that job is about to get harder. I figured you'd want to know, in case you wanted to get started finding another one."

"Another job? You read the papers? There aren't any jobs. I wouldn't have this one if it wasn't for you putting in the fix with the judge. They're lining up for soup out there. No, seems we're making our stand right here in Lansing, on a state paycheck."

"What about the WPA?"

"Sewing? Serving food in a prison? No thanks. I like working in an office. I'm going to stay. We'll just have to adjust."

"Maybe Bea can go to school on her own."

When Maggie didn't respond, Georgia added with a smile, "She sure thinks so."

"I'm not going to be here forever, and she will be on her own soon enough. Until then, my remaining child is out of my sight for more than a few minutes only when the law demands. If I could go to school with her, I would."

Maggie stood and walked to the window. The small park across the street had filled with children playing in the snow.

"Nobody is after you," said Georgia, "or Bea. It's been a year. The people Mickey did business with, they're mostly dead or in prison. They were probably never after *you* in the first place."

"So you've said. But that leaves the rest of the world. The rest of the world is still out there."

They finished another cup of coffee and a cigarette apiece, talking, once again, around Maggie's lost men. Bea was returning as Georgia got up to leave. She thanked Georgia again for the candle. Georgia was out the door in the hall when Maggie called to her.

"Guess I'll see you in church."

"That's right. I'll be sitting by the window."

FIFTEEN

The night she saw Eld for the last time, Maggie put her daughter in Georgia's big red Ford. They dropped Eld with Charlie, then drove to her mother's house. That was really the only decision Maggie had made. They drove four miles, covering all the places on this earth where Maggie had ever lived, and most of the places she had ever set foot. Everything after that decision, after that drive, was forced on her by the decisions of somebody else.

This woman, this Georgia, her brother had been killed by the same people who were after her family, so Maggie didn't ask questions. The questions she might have asked included where a woman went to wear shoes like that, with heels and buttons down the front, or how she knew her husband. But Maggie had seen the look on her husband's face and understood that night was a time to be practical, so she didn't ask, and instead got in the Ford.

Eld and Doc were two days missing when Maggie made Christmas cookies in her mother's kitchen. Her mother kept the sugar in the same place it had been when Maggie made cakes for her Maltese boy. The house was just a few miles from town, but Maggie was an infrequent visitor. Her mother never seemed quite happy to see her, and the house echoed with too many of Maggie's mistakes for her to find solace there. When the cookies were warm and her effort had floated a momentary sense of comfort on cinnamon air, her mother asked if Bea was getting a little plump. Bea was right there, a cookie in her mouth. She spat it out.

The old woman had never been kind, exactly, but Maggie thought she could count on a certain low-grade civility that was part of her mother's sense of propriety. She was wrong. The years of solitude had soured the old woman on her daughter, made her cruel. Gray haired but still vigorous, she skulked around the house and said nothing encouraging about Eld and Doc. On the third morning with no word, it took Georgia and Maggie together to convince her to go to the police and ask about Eld.

"Taking care of men is part of life," she said. "I took care of mine until the lord saw fit to take him from me. Now you take care of yours."

Maggie swallowed her temper. "I would, but I got Bea to look after. For a few weeks, we don't want anybody to know where we are."

"What did that man get you into that you can't walk the streets of your own town? That you need to hide out in my house?"

"The sooner we get Eld back," Georgia said, interrupting, "the sooner we are out of your hair."

On the first day in her house, in a quiet moment alone, Maggie's mother had whispered to her that Georgia "must be some kind of prostitute." Now she looked across the kitchen table at Georgia and nodded.

"If getting my house back requires a visit to the town hall and a talk with the police, I will do just that."

The old woman returned at noon with a bag of groceries. She dropped hints about the cost of groceries until Maggie put a five-dollar bill on the kitchen table.

"What do the police know?" she asked.

Maggie's mother looked at the bill and then at Maggie.

"I told them Eld and Doc were missing. They didn't seem surprised. They said somebody shot Charlie McCallister. His boat was frozen in shore ice on the Canadian side with Charlie still in it, shot dead. He was frozen stiff, so the Canadians don't know how long ago it happened. Marie told the police Charlie left with Eld, but Eld wasn't in the boat. The police in Ontario asked around Grand Bend, but nobody remembers seeing him." She looked at her daughter. "Or Doc."

Maggie started to say something, but Georgia cut her off. "That doesn't mean anything. They wouldn't tell the cops about their American customers. Did the police ask about Maggie?"

"Yes. I told them she was staying with friends. They asked where. I said I didn't know. They wanted to know why Maggie didn't come herself, looking for her husband and her boy. I told them I wondered that myself."

"Maybe they stayed in Canada," said Maggie. She wanted someone to say that was probably true, but the women she was with weren't the kind to say things they didn't believe. Georgia said nothing, but the old woman looked at them both in turn, then spoke.

"You could have seen this coming, could have stopped this. You always liked your men too much. Let them run wild. This is what you get."

The words in Maggie's mouth melted away and she put her head down on the kitchen table.

Georgia gave Maggie's mother a hard look. "Let me give you some advice," she said.

"I'm not accustomed to taking advice from uninvited houseguests."

"Just the same. I give good advice, and you are getting it for free. Your daughter is missing her son, her husband. She's pretty rattled and hiding out with you only because she has to. She's not going to stay here for long. You might want to make sure she wants to see you again."

"My daughter? Are you telling me how to talk to my own daughter?"

Maggie stood up from the table and took the stairs slowly, her hand on the wall. Georgia followed her to the bedroom, where Bea was sitting on the bed, listening. Maggie told Bea to pack her things.

"Where are you going?" asked Georgia.

"We are not staying here another night."

"Sure," said Georgia, "but where are you going?"

"I don't know." Maggie put a dirty sock in a pillowcase, then sat on the bed. "I don't know, but I was hoping you could give us a ride."

"Indiana."

"What?"

"Indiana."

Bea returned to the room with a blanket. Georgia put her hand on the girl's head. There wasn't much to pack.

"Call themselves Hoosiers down there, and even they don't know why. Every Hoosier I ever met was a jack pine savage. Every one. Put ketchup on a steak. But that territory belongs to Chicago. Nobody from Detroit will come looking for us down there. They could ask Chicago to look for us, as a favor, but we aren't important enough for them to use up a favor."

"Do you think anybody is still after us? After you?"

"Probably not. Probably never were. But it's not worth taking the chance either. We can lay low down there for a couple months, just to be sure. By then whoever set out to shut Mickey down will know they succeeded and have something else occupying their mind. These guys aren't diligent. They get a big idea, wave guns around, act all at once, and then nobody follows up. They'll forget about us, or they'll be dead, or in prison."

"I'm betting my family on them doing a half-assed job?"

"Half-assed is a safe bet. Safe as you'll ever see."

After forty-eight hours with the woman, Maggie understood why Eld had brought Georgia to their home in the middle of the night. Georgia knew something about the people who were after them and she didn't get excited. She hadn't cried once since they'd met, even with her brother shot dead. Just then Maggie didn't want to be making all her decisions alone, and Georgia seemed like good counsel. Besides, Bea had taken to her, and you could never tell where that girl was going to come out on people. They were packed in a few minutes. Maggie's mother was still in the kitchen as they left, sitting at the table with her coat still on. On her way out the door Georgia took the bag of groceries.

Georgia drove the big Ford and Maggie smoked her way through a pack of Chesterfields. She wasn't crying, but she was quiet. She didn't think she could manage more than a few words without breaking down. When she closed her eyes she saw Doc in a diaper, a naked baby Doc marching across the floor with a serious look on his face, Doc asleep with his hands over his head. She tried not to close her eyes.

When they stopped at a diner in Port Huron, Maggie ate though she wasn't hungry. She ate Michigan bean soup with soft rolls because she thought she might need her strength, and because she wanted to eat something from home. She had never been out of Michigan before and didn't know what the jack pine savages might eat down there in Indiana. Georgia bought an orange Faygo and a map at a gas station before they swung west across the state. She handed the Faygo over the seat to Bea, who inspected the bottle before asking for a straw.

"Sorry kiddo," said Georgia. "We're on the lam, which is traditionally a no-frills operation. You go ahead and gun it. Right outta the bottle."

Bea seemed to take in that notion before upending the bottle and chugging its contents. Less than a minute passed before she emitted a thunderous belch.

"That's the spirit," said Georgia.

The farmland that spread out from the sides of the highway was flat and gray, except where white snow filled the low places. Occasionally blocks of woodland or a creek interrupted the quilt of cow pastures and fields, and every ten miles or so they passed through a small cluster of homes around a church and a general store.

"You get out of Detroit," said Georgia, accelerating out of such a town, "not a lot going on in this state."

After dark they stopped at a tiny hotel. The man who took Georgia's money answered the bell with a napkin in his hand and something he was chewing in his mouth. He took Georgia's cash and said nothing when she registered under the name Roosevelt. Maggie and Georgia each took a bed, and Bea curled up on the small sofa. The room was cold all night and they left without breakfast in the morning. Georgia drove until they hit Lake Michigan, then turned south along the shore. Just after noon they crossed the Indiana line.

A filling station outside Michigan City had a sign in the window that said COTTAGES FOR RENT, but the boy pumping gas knew nothing. He made a phone call and told them the owner would be there directly.

The boy invited them in out of the cold, and the four of them filed into the garage where the boy sat when he wasn't working. The concrete floor was swept, but the only place to sit was a rear bench seat scavenged from an old car. The two women and Bea squeezed onto the bench, and the boy took his stool before them.

"Good afternoon," said Bea.

It had been quiet for a few moments, and her voice startled the boy. He stood from his stool.

"Me?" he asked.

Bea nodded.

"You too," he said. "Are you here for the holidays?"

Georgia laughed, but Bea answered brightly, saying they would be here until after the New Year, perhaps longer. Maggie noticed the boy had clear skin and his hair was wavy. The patch on his coveralls said CARL. She looked back at Bea.

"Carl, is that your name?" Maggie asked.

"Yes, ma'am."

"Is there a place near here to get lunch and buy groceries?"

"Most people here drive on to Michigan City, two miles down the road. They'd have anything you need there."

"Do you live here?" asked Bea.

Carl looked around the garage.

"In this town, I mean."

"Yes," said Carl. "I go to Michigan City High. I play football. In the fall, I mean."

"Oh," said Bea. "I like football."

"Oh brother," said Georgia. "Here's our landlord, not a moment too soon."

A pickup truck pulled into the station, and a bearded man got out of the cab. When he entered the shop he stamped his feet on the concrete floor. He looked around the room and turned to Georgia before speaking.

"Most of my cottages are just for summer, but I got one year-round house I can show you. Is your husband going to join us?"

No one answered for a few seconds.

"He got held up," Maggie said, "but he'll be along in a few days."

"Well, maybe you should book into a hotel and we can go look once he gets here."

"That won't be necessary," said Georgia.

The bearded man hesitated.

Georgia stood up. "We'll pay up front."

When the man didn't move, Georgia produced a roll of bills from her pocket and held it up.

The man smiled and snapped his fingers. "Right. In the absence of your husband, Mr. Green will do just fine. Let's go take a look. I can take the two of you in my truck. The girl can wait here with Carl. It's not five minutes away. I'm Vincent, by the way."

Bea had gotten up, but before Vincent stopped talking she had dropped back down on the bench and slipped out of her coat. Maggie looked from Bea to Carl and back again. She didn't want to leave Bea alone with a stranger, but the boy was no more than sixteen, and she could see Bea was going to put up a fight.

"Fine," said Georgia. "You can tell us about the place on the way over."

The house was the largest in a row that had been put up for the season. It was bigger than they needed, and right on the beach. Maggie saw two stories and a coal furnace and was ready to say yes.

"I'll tell you ladies up front," Vincent said, "it can get tricky here in the winter. The rest of the houses on the street are empty until June. You'll be on your own. Plow comes late after a storm, and if the power goes down, Edison takes a while to get here."

The kitchen was big, and there was a Frigidaire. A sofa in the living room faced two armchairs, and there was a card table.

"It's fine," said Georgia. "We'd need it for two months, maybe three."

"No problem," said Vincent. "Nobody looks to rent these houses until June, earliest."

Georgia looked at him. "You do a lot of negotiating, do ya?"

"Bank owns these places, not me. Foreclosed on the mortgages and now they're stuck with them. They pay me to take care of them. The houses, that is. The bank, it can take care of itself." When he laughed his breath was visible in the cold air. "So you see, I don't care what you pay."

They walked through the house and ended up out on the porch. There were wooden chairs, a bench, and a table. Brown grass ended at a low fence, and after that sand stretched down to the water. Chunks of ice were piled up at the water's edge.

Georgia was looking at walls. "The bank won't spring for a fresh coat of paint?"

"I told them not to bother. At least not till June. In a winter storm, the north wind comes down off the lake, been blowing over that water for three hundred miles, it picks up the beach sand and scours the paint clean off."

Maggie thought about that, about cold dark nights and what was left of her family in a house sandblasted by icy winds.

"Your place," Georgia said, "the filling station. Must get pretty slow in the winter."

"We do all right."

"Hardly seems like there'd be enough business to keep it a going concern."

"Don't see how that's any business of yours."

"Any chance you trade in anything besides gas?"

Vincent didn't say anything.

"Maybe you could sell us a couple of quarts?"

"For your husband?"

"That's right."

"Might be I could find you a jar at that."

SIXTEEN

By the time the school bell rang Maggie had already dropped Bea and was walking to the bus stop. She didn't make New Year's resolutions, but any success in January, even one as small as delivering a scrubbed child to her school on time, held possibility. Maggie wanted this morning—a rent-paid, bathed-and-fed, on-time morning under a clear sky—to portend a happy and efficient 1934. Officially, she did not believe in such things. She was a Christian woman, and future telling was silly pagan bullshit, but she arrived at her office smiling nonetheless.

She was still smiling an hour later as she packed up the last of the office Christmas decorations. Nora had watched her looping tinsel around her hands and boxing it but hadn't said anything. When she took the job as Nora's secretary, Maggie couldn't type. "You'll learn" was all Nora had said, and she had, at least to the level of proficiency necessary to do the job. Maggie didn't mind the occasional personal task, and she didn't mind making coffee and cleaning up around the office. Something about the way Nora asked for things made it tolerable. Maggie couldn't say no, but she appreciated that Nora asked.

In the weeks that had passed since Georgia dropped by with her news from the judge, Nora had said nothing. It would be a first, but maybe Georgia had it wrong. Maybe the judge had changed his mind, or Nora had convinced him to stay in Michigan. Whatever the reason, Maggie was pleased. She wanted her life to stay the way things had settled. Not easy, but not a crisis either.

"Maggie? Can you come in for a minute?" Nora pulled her head back inside her office door without waiting for an answer.

Maggie hopped down from the step stool she had been using with a wooden angel and tinsel in her hands. She was still holding those items when she sat in the chair before the expanse of Nora's desk. The desk was large, green, and steel. Maggie had filled out the requisition paperwork and happened to know that the desk was made in the Raiford Prison workshop. Three men in coveralls had complained loudly while moving it in, but Maggie had paid them no mind. She respected Nora and tried to protect her from the picayune dramas of state bureaucracy. She tried not to think about how the judge had put in a word for her, and why. Her little family's survival in the midst of a depression depended on her ability to live with certain unpleasant contradictions, that being one.

"How's Bea?" Nora asked. "She happy to be back in school?"

"Not as happy as me."

"Right. Well, I asked you in here to let you know I'm leaving. Bertie wants to retire, and he says we're moving to Florida."

Maggie raised her eyebrows, which was as much surprise as she could feign.

"You don't sound thrilled," she said.

"Been to Florida? Miami's all right, but five miles inland and it's a swamp full of alligators and hillbillies. Bertie keeps saying 'god's country,' like god is a mosquito."

"It'll be warm at least."

"Yeah," Norah said. "I suppose. You know, they have these huge cockroaches down there, inch and a half long, but they call them palmetto bugs, like a pretty name is going to make them any different."

"I'll be sorry to see you go. When do you leave?"

"My last day is the end of the month." Nora sat up. "They got somebody lined up to be my replacement. Somebody in the governor's office is backing him."

"Do you know him?"

"Yeah. His name is Honeycutt. Dan Honeycutt. He's from over on the west side of the state. Muskegon. Lot of Holy Rollers over there, and he's one. I'm telling you this because, you know, *I* hired you to be my assistant. He didn't."

"Am I losing this job?"

Nora leaned back in her chair and crossed her arms across her chest. "Not yet. He'd have to let you go once he gets here, to replace you with his own pick. The thing is, he's KCR. They look out for their own."

This was information Maggie didn't already have. She leaned in. "What's KCR?"

"Kingdom of Christ the Redeemer. It's a church. Mostly out west, Nebraska, Kansas, but some here too. He might put one of his own people on your job."

"Can he do that?"

"Maybe not officially, but he could always come up with a reason to fire you, make room for a new girl. You know I don't care if you come in a little late, or if Bea does her homework in the waiting room, but he may not be so inclined."

"Well, shit," Maggie said without thinking. "Sorry. It's just, no jobs out there, and anyway, I like this one."

"Yeah. I know. That's why I'm warning you. I looked around in the department for you, but there's nothing open. Everyone is hanging on to these jobs. It's tough."

Leaving Nora's office, Maggie resisted the temptation to immediately call Georgia, but when she picked up Bea from Georgia's apartment that night, she accepted the invitation to come in for a drink. Bea was bent over a textbook doing homework. Maggie was worried enough not to bother sending her out of the room.

"Ever heard of the KCR?" she asked Georgia.

"What? No. What's the KCR?" Georgia was reaching for a bottle in her cupboard. There was nothing else in the cupboard. No flour, no sugar, no spices.

"It's a church."

"You're asking me about a church? Not my department."

Maggie accepted the offered glass. It was a real rocks glass, thick-bottomed and heavy, made for good whiskey. The woman had excellent whiskey glasses, but no flour.

"You were right. Nora told me today she's leaving at the end of the month. My new boss, after Nora leaves, is some churchman from Muskegon. Name's Dan Honeycutt. He's KCR."

"Never heard of him. But you go to church. Maybe you can chat about your shared love of Jesus, or whatever."

"Thing is, he may want to bring in his own secretary, and I can't lose this job. There's five hungry souls out there looking for every open job."

"It comes to it, you know you can come to me. I can cover your rent. For a while anyway. I still have a little left from the days when Mickey was flush. The stuff the banks couldn't find."

"Thanks, but I'm hoping I don't need to take you up on that."

Maggie took a sip of Georgia's whiskey. She had spent the day at work coming up with a plan. Her plan was dishonest, or if not quite dishonest, at least phony. She wanted to lay it out in front of Georgia, but she was ashamed at the level of her scheming.

"I was thinking," she said, "that there probably aren't that many KCR churches in Lansing. What if I found this guy's church and joined?"

Georgia had lit a cigarette with a kitchen match. She stopped without waving it out and looked at Maggie for a long moment. "You interested in their particular brand of theology?"

"I'm in church every Sunday. Not all that particular where. I figure if I'm in his church, this KCR, maybe I volunteer for something, make a big noise about me raising Bea on my own, he can't very well fire me. It would look bad."

Georgia blew out the match before raising her glass at the living room where Bea was doing homework. "Bea, honey," she called.

Bea looked up.

"Your mama, she can take care of herself. She can take care of herself and has enough care left over for other people too."

"I don't know anything about these KCR people," Maggie said, "but I need to join right away. I can't look into it while I'm at work. I was hoping you could help."

"You want me to go to church? Start caterwauling and singing and all that shit?"

"Couldn't hurt." Maggie paused. "But no. I'll do that part. Starting this Sunday. But I need to know which church to go to. Can you sort out where the KCR churches are in Lansing, and which one this Honeycutt fella goes to?"

"I'll start with the phone book."

SEVENTEEN

The offices were state property, so alcohol was not officially served at Nora's farewell party, but more than a couple coffees were fortified discreetly. Maggie had had three, and was wondering why she didn't drink whiskey in her coffee more often, when Dan Honeycutt stopped by.

Nora introduced him to the dozen or so employees in attendance, and he gave a short speech with a fork in one hand and a plated piece of cake in the other. Maggie had seen him twice already, on the preceding two Sundays, but mostly she had looked at the back of his head. She got a long look now. He was square jawed, not fat, and his dark hair was thinning only at the very top of his head. All of the ingredients were there, and in the right proportions, he just didn't manage them quite right. He wore suspenders, and the plaid of his suit clashed with his necktie. She decided that on balance he was not an ugly man.

"We have a mission here," he said, putting his cake down on the conference room table. "A mission for the governor, to be sure, and a mission for the people of the state of Michigan, but also a godly mission." When he said this, he held his hands before him palms up, like he was beseeching something. "I take that charge seriously, and I want you to as well. I intend to run this office according to biblical principles. By that I mean we will set an example. In this office we will strengthen the ethical and moral foundation of Judeo-Christian principles in government."

Maggie followed his words, hoping to snatch and hold some principle she could spout back to him, but all she could imagine was the inspecting of foodstuffs according to Judeo-Christian principles. She had worked out that his words might not mean anything at all when Nora motioned her over.

"Dan, this is Maggie, my crackerjack secretary. Makes everything around here run on time."

Dan looked at her shoes for a moment, and Maggie had to stop herself from looking down at them herself.

"Well, it's nice to meet you, Maggie," he said. "How's your shorthand?"

Maggie had never taken shorthand for Nora and didn't know how. She started to stammer something, something that might have turned into *Oh, fuck it*, but Nora interrupted.

"It's after five, and it's Friday. No shoptalk."

"I like to dictate—"

"Do I recognize you from somewhere?" asked Maggie.

"I don't know. Do you?" Dan was looking down at her and smiling. Standing this close, she appreciated that he was tall. Maggie recognized his smile as the special kind worn by a man who has been the recipient of too much female attention. She asked him where he lived, and where his kids went to school. When this line of inquiry did not produce any overlaps, she delivered, as evenly as she could, the question she really wanted him to focus on. He was nodding and turning away.

"Where do you worship?"

"I'm a deacon," he said, turning back to her. "Kingdom of Christ the Redeemer."

"The one on Saginaw Street?"

"That's right."

"*That's* where I've seen you. I just started there. Been going the last few Sundays."

Maggie was ready for his questions. She had taken a stack of literature and read all about the KCR theology. She was ready to say she appreciated KCR's commitment to missionary work, taking the word to those poor buggers in the jungles of the Amazon and Africa, condemned in their ignorance to eternal hellfire unless saved by the intrepid youngsters of KCR. She would explain that she had taken a copy of *The Path* but had been busy at work, preparing for his arrival, and hadn't yet had a chance to go over it.

"That's great," Dan said, turning away again. "Guess I'll see you on Sunday, then."

Maggie would have stayed, to send off Nora properly, and to have added a few more fortified coffees to her count, but she saw value in delivering herself in small doses. She had promised Georgia that her conversion with Dan would be attempted with subtlety.

When she got home there was a note from Georgia on the kitchen counter. She and Bea were at Shanghai Palace. Without removing her coat Maggie was back out the door and on the street in front of the restaurant within a few minutes. She faced steamed-up storefront windows, but her family was not difficult to spot. Bea was on one side of a booth, talking, Georgia on the other side, already smiling. Bea put her hand to her head as if she were saluting someone, and then the two of them were laughing. No food was visible, but there was a pot of tea on the table, and room for Maggie in the booth next to Bea. She smiled, standing out in the cold, but didn't go in straightaway. She soaked in the feeling for just a moment, while it was still pure. Soon she would be inside and Bea would say something cutting, or Georgia would share something a little too grown-up, but while she was outside, this little moment of her life was worth the effort.

When she got to the booth, she had to maneuver past the waitress delivering platters and bowls of rice. Maggie asked for another plate.

"Good," Georgia said. "We ordered enough for three."

Maggie took the seat next to Bea and slid out of her coat. They seemed to be waiting for her to say something. She smiled but stayed quiet. She wanted them to start laughing again.

"How was Nora's send-off?" asked Georgia.

"Nice. Good cake."

Maggie looked over the platters. They hadn't ordered any fish. Christ only knew what kind of fish they use in Chinese food, but she would probably have ordered it anyway, out of some loyalty to their old life. She decided then not to order any more fish. The practice didn't solve anything, and maybe it intruded on their happiness. She should always be striving for that, for more happiness, and not letting a thing like fish get in the way.

"Do we still have to go to that KCR church again this Sunday?" asked Bea.

Just like that and the feeling was gone.

"Is it so bad?" asked Maggie.

"It's longer," Bea said.

"I'm not one to encourage churchgoing," said Georgia, "but in this case your mom's reasons are pretty good. Why don't you just bite the bullet once a week for an hour?"

"Hour and a half," said Bea.

Maggie served herself some rice and then spooned something from another platter over the rice. The steam that rose from the food smelled of oranges. There were other places in the world, places where hot food smelled of oranges. She might live there, with her husband and boy, but she didn't. Maybe those places had even worse things in store.

"I'm starved," she said.

Bea followed her mother's lead, but Georgia only sipped her tea.

"Maybe I'll come along too," she said.

Maggie had a mouthful of rice, but Bea asked, "Come along where?"

"To your new church."

Maggie swallowed her food. "Why?"

"Couldn't hurt, right? And I'd like to get a look at your new boss."

"Why?"

"Maybe I know him."

"You spend time with churchmen from Muskegon?"

"Not as a rule. Maybe I've been missing out."

"I doubt it. I met him tonight. Not your type. Straight off the cob."

"Would sure make things easier, though, wouldn't it?"

Maggie looked from Georgia to Bea. Bea stopped eating, something round and deep-fried speared on the end of her fork. She was watching Georgia. She understood. Maggie thought for a moment about how to be the mother she had hoped to be, but she didn't have that kind of family anymore, and the short path to continued happiness, for both her family and Honeycutt, might well lead up Georgia's skirt. Bea would understand whatever she understood.

"I suppose it would. But I couldn't ask that of you," Maggie said.

"You didn't, and anyway, we're a long way from picking out china."

EIGHTEEN

Maggie was still in the bathroom when Georgia arrived at the apartment to pick them up. The more attended of the two Sunday services, when Honeycutt and his family made their appearance, was at nine thirty. Knowing Georgia's cavalier attitude toward punctuality, she had told her the service started at nine. The sound of conversation drifted through the door. When she turned off the faucet, she could make out the words.

"What?" Georgia was saying.

"It's just, well, that's a little minxy for church," said Bea.

There wasn't time for this, and they couldn't arrive late. Maggie was thinking of a sweater she had that could cover Georgia's bare arms, or cleavage, or whatever expanse of flesh she had thought to bare in a house of worship. She left the bathroom at a clip and retrieved the sweater from her room.

Georgia was in a black dress with a shawl but no sleeves. "Turns out I don't have any frocks made from a fucking bedsheet."

"Language," said Maggie, arriving in the door frame of the living room.

"We're not there yet."

"Here, pull this on over top."

Georgia caught the sweater Maggie had tossed and made a face. Maggie was pulling on boots.

"Look, these people, we're not trying to impress them with our fashion sense. We want them to see a young girl being raised by a fisherman's widow."

When Maggie said "widow" both Bea and Georgia looked up, and Maggie paused for a second. She had never used that word to describe herself. Her husband, her son, they never came home one day. That's all they knew. That didn't make Eld and Doc dead, and it didn't make Maggie a widow.

"Right," Georgia said, holding up the sweater. "Camel wool over a black dress. Brown over black. We needn't concern ourselves that our style will intimidate."

They were at the church in time to see Honeycutt arrive with his family. He greeted other men and shook their hands as he walked up the aisle, trailing his family by a few steps. His wife entered the pew first, followed by three young children. She was a heavy woman in a broad-brimmed hat. The pews between the two families were still empty, as Maggie had hoped, and Dan saw them as he turned into the pew after his kids. Maggie nodded at him in recognition, but remembered not to smile. Dan nodded back and touched two fingers to his forehead.

Maggie let her mind wander for the next half hour. She stood when everyone else did, and sang when she heard the organ, but her thoughts were not on the proceedings. She had spent time in the churches of Methodists, Lutherans, and Baptists without ever really considering herself one of them. So far as she was concerned, the KCR service was unremarkable, and, it must be noted, the music below average. Someone in the choir, and it sounded like an older woman, was dramatically off-key, to a degree that no one could pretend otherwise. The voice was distinct from the others, a high warbling falsetto delivered with enthusiasm. When that voice missed the first note by a hair-raising mile, Bea looked up from her hymnal and Georgia shot a wide-eyed look at Maggie, but no one else in the congregation registered surprise. After the third or fourth verse it occurred to Maggie that maybe the congregation, or some of them anyway, took their Christianity seriously enough to not care what the choir sounded like.

The pastor was the same young man who had officiated the preceding Sunday. He was not out of his twenties and had a noticeable curve at the top of his spine. Not quite a hump but it caught Maggie's eye, and though he hadn't mentioned it yet, she thought there had to be some Christian mileage in his condition. He apologized for the cold air of the church, but said he was enjoying it. He called the cold air "bracing," a word that Maggie understood but had never used, reminding her that she was not in one of the churches in Minden. The pastor spoke of the cold and then explained to his flock that soon he would be hot all the time. Not in hell, he hoped, but in Africa. The congregation dutifully chuckled. He explained again that he was going to Africa to take the good news of Jesus to the dark corners of that continent.

Housekeeping out of the way, his sermon started slow and meandered a little, lingering too long in descriptions of the Nebraska wheat fields where he was raised. The picture he painted sounded inferior to the woods and blue water of Michigan and Maggie again started to tune out. The pastor continued, pacing back and forth as he spoke. Bored, Maggie looked down to the hymnal and took note of the local advertisements on the back cover. A bakery offered cheesecakes. A pharmacy delivered. She heard the sound of the pages turning in her hand.

The room had gone dead quiet.

The pastor stood stone still and silent. For thirty seconds he didn't move, completely mute. Maggie looked around. The man in the pew in front of her had his hand hanging in the aisle where she could see it. His hand tightened into a fist. She heard breathing.

"In this world!" The words boomed from the young pastor in a voice Maggie had not heard in a lifetime of Sundays, and nothing at all like his delivery in the preceding weeks.

The pastor stabbed a finger in the air as his words echoed and his voice rose to a shout. "Yes. In this world. Yes. Yes. We are all of us in this world, but not of it."

Some of those gathered murmured, but some answered him with a clear "Yes."

"Not of here. Not of Lansing. Not of Africa. Not the sweet fields of Nebraska. Love not those places, or the things in them. Friendship with this world is enmity with the lord. You cannot love this world and still love the father. Those earthly places will pass away, and with them their pleasures. We are here today, but our true place is with the lord."

He stopped again and stood with his arm held out in front of him.

"Our place is with the lord," he shouted. Droplets of spittle hung in the air before him. "With the lord, for eternity."

He stood silent for a few moments more and then his arm fell. He seemed to collapse into himself a little, dropping his chin to his chest. A deacon rose and helped him back into a chair. With that, the sermon ended and the service reverted to a proceeding more or less identical to the many thousands Maggie had seen before. Minutes passed and the rawness of the sermon's end faded into commonplace singing and chanting, standing and sitting. Maggie wondered if she was misremembering what had happened, but when the service ended, Georgia leaned over past Bea and whispered in her ear.

"What the hell was that all about?" she said. "I thought for a minute they were going to eat us."

They filed out of the church into bright winter sunshine and a gaggle of smiling congregants. The shuffling crowd pushed them apart and Maggie was soon separated from Georgia and Bea. The current of bodies pushed her out toward the street until she backed to the edge of the sidewalk, surveying the crowd.

Maggie saw them then. Georgia and Bea were smiling, chatting with the young pastor and Dan Honeycutt. The four of them were looking at her, and Georgia was waving her over. She concentrated on keeping worry off her face and started toward them. Surely the pastor and her new boss would have questions, and her scheme to keep her job was an obvious one. A careless word would put Dan Honeycutt on the scent. Georgia was looking up into Dan's face and smiling like it was the best day of her life. Bea said something to the pastor. He laughed and put the back of his hand to his mouth. She didn't have to worry. Her little tribe was good at this. Of course, that fact was another reason to worry, as it suggested they were all liars in peril of eternal damnation, but she could work on that some other time.

The pastor insisted Maggie and her family join him for lunch in the church hall after the service but he wandered off after leading them there. Maggie passed through the buffet line and took servings from three different potato salads. There were many ways a person could add mayonnaise to potatoes, and the three beige clumps on her plate were solid evidence that the ladies of the Lansing KCR had most of them covered. Maggie was talking to the pastor's young wife, who seemed terrified at the prospect of going to Africa, when Honeycutt's wife appeared with a plate. Maggie introduced herself and said she was new to the congregation. The woman said her name was Fran. She had short fingers. Maggie saw she hadn't taken any potato salad.

"We're not for everyone," Fran said. "KCR, I mean. We're not afraid to hear the spirit."

"I think I noticed." When Fran didn't respond, she added, "That's okay by me. I'm not ashamed of being Christian."

"My husband tells me you work in his new office, that you were the secretary to his predecessor."

"That's right. Nora. She moved to Florida."

"Too hot for me, but I guess it beats Africa."

The pastor's wife excused herself. Fran and Maggie watched her walk away.

"She's not cut out for that life," Fran said.

"Maybe she'll grow into it. People can surprise you."

"Some people, they think they know what they want, they spend their life trying to get there, and they find out it's not for them. Then it's too late. There's a lesson in that."

"True enough. Some people, they never get what they want in the first place, and some get it, only to lose it. I try to remember it's all a part of god's plan." Maggie said that and immediately thought she was putting it on a little thick.

"You can't blame everything on god," Fran said. "Knowing yourself, that's not god's job." She looked at Maggie's plate. "If you start coming here on the regular and you go to these potluck lunches, you'll notice there's only one or two meat dishes. The wives, they'd say it's because there's a depression on and meat's expensive. Anyway, if you get through the newcomer class and you stick it out with us, you'll never want for potato salad."

"There's a newcomer class? First I heard of it."

"There is. In fact, Dan's in charge of it. Usually he waits until there are at least a couple new families before he starts a class. You must complete the class before you can be baptized."

"Is the class for kids too?"

"How old?"

"Fourteen." Maggie scanned the room and found Bea. She had looted the dessert table and was sitting on a piano bench with a plate. "That's her over there by the piano."

One of the potato salads Maggie had served herself had mustard in it. The others seemed to rely entirely on salt for seasoning. She saw that Fran had filled her plate with chicken and dumplings.

"When it's your turn, what do you fix?"

"Fish," said Fran. "I make fish. I grew up in Muskegon. On the lake."

Maggie thought about how you might make fish for a couple dozen people so that it kept warm and would taste all right after sitting a few hours. Fried fish wouldn't keep. Not even for an hour.

"Chowder? Do you make a chowder?"

"That's right. Or a casserole. With rice in it." Fran hadn't taken her eyes off Bea. "Your girl, is she good with kids?"

"Sure," Maggie said. She had no idea.

"Sometimes Dan and I go out at night, and we need a babysitter. We'd use girls from the neighborhood, but they're all Catholic. I think Dan would be willing to go out more if we could leave the kids with a girl from the church."

"I'm sure Bea would love that," Maggie said, though she wasn't at all sure. She was sure that if Bea were babysitting his kids, it would be that much harder for Dan to fire her.

Fran smiled for the first time. "I'll work on Dan to get that newcomer class started. You shouldn't have any problem."

"I hope not. I hope we've found a new home here. Spiritually speaking."

"Some of the teachings take a little getting used to. We take the word literally. It's not what you would find with the Lutherans, but if you do have any problem, Dan will be right there to ask for help. With you working together, you'll be spending almost as much time with him as I do."

Maggie smiled, and the two women scanned the hall until they found Dan. He was across the room, talking to Georgia. She touched his arm twice while they watched. Dan was gesturing, making some point that Georgia evidently thought was insightful and funny. She tossed her head and laughed, and Bea was looking too. Maggie entertained a moment of pity. All these women watching him, all with plans for him, but the look of guiltless satisfaction on his face made sympathy impossible. They would all work their angles, and he would do as he saw fit. Hell, he might even be dumb enough to do something none of them wanted.

Maggie gathered Georgia and Bea to leave early. They had made their presence known, their determination to join the KCR church clear, and she had made some modest inroads with Fran. Lingering over cookies could only endanger these successes.

It was cold in the car, and they were quiet until Bea spoke at the back of her mother's head.

"Are you going to stop smoking? And drinking?"

Georgia turned back from the wheel. "Why in the hell would she do that?"

"The church. The pastor told me. KCR doesn't permit smoking or drinking. No coffee either."

"I know," said Maggie. "I read the literature. I'm working on it."

"You need to stop before you can be baptized," said Bea. "The church wants you to show some commitment before they invest in us."

"Speaking of commitment, my new boss needs a babysitter. What do you think?"

"For the Honeycutts? Would I get to keep what I earn?"

"Sure, but then your spending money comes from what you make. You go to the movies with your friends, you pay for it."

"You don't let me go to the movies with my friends."

"I spoke to Dan Honeycutt for some time," said Georgia. "I learned some things too. That church is not altogether normal. Even besides that weird spell the pastor had, with all the shouting."

"Like what?" asked Bea.

"Well, they have all the regular Jesus-y stuff, but some old-timey stuff too."

"Like what?" This time it was Maggie who asked.

"He said that in some of the churches, especially the old ones out west, the men have more than one wife. I got the feeling he was accepting applications."

Bea looked up. "Do the women have more than one husband?"

NINETEEN

Those early days in Indiana, in the sandblasted house on the receiving end of a fierce north wind that had whipped down three hundred miles of frigid lake, the three women mourned three men, and they did so without much discussion. They spent days without mention of why they were there. They filled hours by playing board games and euchre. Maggie couldn't go back to Minden. Georgia couldn't stay in Detroit. Neither of them had anyone else. They had both known Eld, but then each had their own unshared loss that the other didn't know and didn't mention.

Maggie saw Georgia was good company. She had a dark and easy sense of humor, and she knew how to navigate the world beyond small-town Michigan without making Maggie feel like a hayseed. For a start, Georgia knew that a lawyer in Michigan City should be one of their first visits, and that, once retained, he would let them use his phone. Maggie never asked Georgia how she came to be at Maggie's front door that night, standing behind Maggie's handsome husband. Eld's explanation, given hurriedly across a kitchen table while planning to go after Doc, was that they were thrown together by violence and death. Initially that seemed plausible. Georgia seemed like the kind of woman who would turn up in those circumstances. But Maggie had seen enough of Georgia—her clothes, her legs, the way she spoke to men—to know better than to ask more. Eld was nowhere to be found, and Maggie understood the need to be practical.

They walked the beach and collected driftwood. Maggie made pies during the day. Georgia admitted to no skills in the kitchen, so she bought a Philco radio in town as her contribution. They listened to Fred Allen or Jack Benny while Maggie cooked. After dinner Bea liked to tune in to *Amos 'n' Andy*, though Georgia said that they didn't sound like any colored people she knew.

"You know colored people?" asked Bea.

"Yeah. Sure."

"My class went to Port Huron once and we saw a negro." Bea was smiling, pleased to show off her worldliness.

"Well, that's exciting," said Georgia.

"He was an old one."

"Did he bite you?"

"He was on a stool. Didn't do much of anything."

"Bet you stared at him anyway, the whole time."

"She was just curious," said Maggie, defending her child from her new friend and benefactor.

"Right. Sorry, kiddo. Feeling cooped up."

"My Sunday school teacher said colored people are inferior," said Bea. "That it says so right in the bible."

"Mighty Christian of him to make that observation," said Georgia.

"Oh hell," said Maggie. "Your teacher was Gina Dawson. She's Minden born and raised. She doesn't know the first thing about negroes."

"I know something about negroes," said Georgia. "Known quite a few, starting with some I met in France. They were all from the South. I wondered what they were doing over there, but they didn't strike me as inferior to white men." She paused to nurse her drink. "Sadly, they weren't any better either."

The nearest town of any size was Michigan City, named after the state they were running from. On one of their resupply trips, Bea went to the library and came back with the news that Michigan was a Chippewa word for "big water." Bea was plainly pleased with herself, but Maggie was a little disappointed in the Chippewa.

"That's it?" she said. "Big water?"

Bea's face fell. "Yeah. That's what the book said. What did you think it meant?"

Maggie was expecting a name more descriptive of her time in the house on its shore.

"Maybe 'lonely winter' or 'mourning water' or, Christ, I don't know, 'desolate frozen waste' or something."

They bought ground beef at the butcher and that night Maggie made meatloaf and mashed potatoes. There were no electric lights in the dining room but Bea had found a hurricane lantern. The room was dark outside the ring of their faces.

When everyone had eaten their fill, the food was only half gone.

"Dad loves meatloaf," Bea said. "Your meatloaf. Not just any old meatloaf. He says the meatloaf at the Pontiac tastes like it has sand in it, and that the gravy is orange."

"Doc liked it too," Maggie said, surveying the table. She had used the past tense. "I made too much. Like they were going to be here. I bought the same amount of meat I always do. Boiled the same amount of potatoes."

She started to cry then. Quietly at first, but after a few seconds it got away from her and grew louder.

"Meatloaf makes great sandwiches," said Georgia. "You can grill the bread so it's crispy and the meatloaf is just warm. I dip mine in mayonnaise."

"You make grilled meatloaf sandwiches?" Bea asked. It was clear from the struggle in her voice that she was trying not to cry.

"Well, can't say I have," Georgia said. "You got me there."

Bea snorted.

"But there's a diner on Woodward Avenue, Jackson's Teepee, where it's the special on Wednesdays. I used to go there a lot. They have cigar-store Indians standing around and old Indian artifacts in glass cases."

"I wonder," said Maggie, but then she didn't finish her thought.

"Wonder what, Mom?" asked Bea.

"The Indians who lived here. The ones who named Michigan."

"The Chippewa," Bea said.

"Right. The Chippewa. They lived in this place too, and they had people who disappeared out in that water. That water, or nature, or god, or whatever, has been taking people like that for thousands of years. Just happens it was our turn."

"Does that make you feel better?" Georgia asked.

"No. But it makes it seem inevitable. Like there was nothing we could have done."

The Indiana house and its driveway were obscured from the road by an overgrown hedge, though the hedge did nothing to stop the elements. There were a few dustings of snow that December, but heavy snow held off until January. By then Georgia had begun driving the Ford into Michigan City two or three times a week. She used the phone at the office of the lawyer she'd hired, cagey about who she was calling, while Maggie took the opportunity to buy groceries and supplies. Sometimes when Georgia was finished they caught the noon matinee at the Huron Theatre, though sitting in the near-empty theatre made Maggie nervous. It was well past the Christmas break, and she hadn't worked out a believable excuse for why Bea was not in school.

The night before *The Mummy* opened in town it snowed. Maggie made coffee and watched the sun come up to reveal drifts up to the running boards of the Ford. She stepped out on the long porch and took a deep breath. Holding the cold air to the count of ten cooled her from the inside. She put the temperature at about thirty degrees before checking the thermometer to find she was under by one. It would warm up when the sun got high, and much of the snow would melt off.

She lit a cigarette and waited for her house to wake up. They would need breakfast and someone to lead the process of digging out the car. After that they would need a grocery list, dinner, and then a plan to get them through the next two months of winter. Bea would need her, today and most days, for the next few years. That was all work worth doing. It was true what they said about work. There was salvation in it.

Georgia came through the door with a cup of coffee and asked for a cigarette.

"I'm paying that lawyer," Georgia said, after smoking most of her cigarette in silence. "An hour of his time every day, just to use his phone. He's pretty dumb for a lawyer, but not so dumb that he isn't curious. I'd guess he knows we are hiding. He might try to use that information to his advantage."

"What does that mean? Do we need to leave?"

"We came here together, to godforsaken Indiana, of all places, because I couldn't stay in Detroit and you couldn't stay in Minden, but I don't want to be here forever. Indiana, it's the most Southern of the Northern states. Even up here, just a few hours from Chicago. People eat grits. You ever eat grits?"

Maggie ignored her question. "Are you leaving?"

"I don't know how much Eld made, or what happened to it, but I'm guessing you're not fixed for life."

"Mostly he paid off our debt on the boat, back mortgage payments, money we borrowed from my mom. Eld gave me two hundred dollars before he left. I've still got most of it."

"That's a start, but it won't keep the wolf from the door for more than a few months."

"I've got the house."

"No." Georgia shook her head. "The house is gone. You can't risk sticking your head up back in Minden. When you don't make the mortgage payments the bank will foreclose on the house and sell it. Probably at a loss." Georgia finished her coffee and let the cup swing by her finger from its handle. The last few drops fell to the porch.

"What you got is two hundred dollars. The calls I've been making, I've been asking around for you. For a job."

"A job? What would I do?"

"There's a depression on. I think you do whatever the hell you can."

"I didn't mean—"

"Mickey, he was all I had and I worked for him. Everyone else on the payroll, they were all Mickey's friends. I've been calling them, looking for help. Most of them, seems their loyalty was a dollar wide and now they won't take my call."

"They're probably scared. I know I am."

"The life they chose, it takes courage. They were happy to take money from Mickey when times were fat, and they were fat for a long time. It would take only a little courage to help me out, but seems that now all those men are fresh out of courage."

"None of them would help?"

"One. There was one exception. He's a judge who used to do favors for Mickey."

"Is he going to get the police to help us?"

"Oh, Christ, no. You should hope you never talk to another policeman as long as you live. Mickey helped the judge move up in the world, to a higher court, in Lansing." Georgia turned to face Maggie. "The judge says he can get you a state job. His wife's a bigwig. Needs a secretary. State payroll."

"Is that safe? Going back to Michigan?"

"It's Lansing. The governor lives there. You shoot up a house party full of gangsters in Detroit, you might get away with it, but you don't shoot up the state capital. The people in charge, they don't like it when somebody shits where they eat. Mickey kept a low profile in Lansing, and so did his competition." Georgia tossed her cigarette butt out on the lawn.

"We'd be safe there?"

"Probably. Maybe. But that's the only job I could find for you, so either way, that's where we're going."

"You're coming?"

"Don't you want me to?"

"Sure I do. We need all the help we can get, but we're no kin to you. Why help us?"

"It was my brother who got you in this pickle, and he was kin to me. My only kin. I took care of him, until he wouldn't let me, and now I'm on my own." Georgia choked out the last few words, and that was as close as Maggie ever saw her come to crying over her brother.

"Anyway, turns out I like kids," said Georgia, recovering. "Not so much babies, but once they are old enough to talk back and fetch cigarettes. I could be an auntie to Bea. Counteract all that churching up."

Their cigarettes burned out and coffee cups empty, the two women stood in the cold and regarded each other across the space left by the dead men who put them there. Without speaking it out loud, they reached an understanding.

"Okay," said Maggie. "Lansing."

"Besides," Georgia said, smiling, "the judge, he's sweet on me."

When Bea woke and joined them, Maggie told her she would have to dig out the car if she wanted to go see *The Mummy*. Maggie was chopping up leftover baked potatoes for a hash breakfast when she heard Bea head out the door. She had melted the lard into a cast-iron skillet and grated half an onion into the potatoes when Bea came back in.

"That was quick," said Maggie. "You sure that car is all dug out? The plow went by early and pushed up a drift. I figured it would take the three of us—"

"The police," said Bea. "The police came down the road. They stopped and asked me about the car."

Georgia called out from her bedroom. "Are they gone?"

"Yes. I think."

"What did they want?"

"They asked me about the license plates. If they were Michigan plates."

Georgia came into the living room not completely dressed. Maggie and Bea stared.

"Where does a woman even find underwear like that?" asked Maggie.

"Oh hell," Georgia said. "The cops, what did they say?"

"Only one of them spoke. He asked if our car had Michigan plates. He didn't want to get out of the patrol car and dig into the snow because he wasn't wearing boots."

"What did you say?"

"I lied," said Bea. "I said they were Indiana plates."

"Good girl. Did he say anything else?"

"He asked me who owned it." She looked at Georgia. "I said it was my aunt's."

They were packed and on the road before nine o'clock. On the way out of town Georgia pulled into the same filling station they had visited when they arrived. She turned around in the front seat and spoke to Bea.

"That boy, the boy that works here?"

"Carl."

"Right. If he's here, I want you to ask him a favor. I want you to ask him to put Indiana tags on this car."

"What if they don't have any?"

"They sell whiskey here. They'll have some spare tags around."

"If he asks why we need them, what do I say?"

"He probably won't, but if he does, say whatever you want. It can sound stupid and it won't matter. Just make out like you are in a jam and need his help. Here he comes, now go."

Maggie watched her daughter meet Carl halfway across the lot. Bea's back was toward the car, but she and Georgia got a clear view of Carl's face. He looked concerned, and he was nodding. His first step back to the shop was a bound. When Bea shut the car door behind her, the two older women looked at her over the back seat.

"You were right," Bea said. "He said they have a stack of plates. Figures they can spare a couple."

"Now that wasn't so hard, was it?" Georgia said.

"No," said Bea. "He's a nice boy."

Georgia snorted. "Don't worry. There's lots."

With a full tank and new plates, Georgia swung a wide turn out onto the road. She was driving slow, but even so the Ford slid sideways on the glassy veneer of compacted snow the plow had left behind. Maggie inhaled sharply and put her hands on the dash until the tires found purchase again. No one spoke for the next twenty minutes. At the Michigan state line, Maggie looked over the seat at her daughter.

"When the police asked you about the license plates, why did you lie?"

"I don't know," said Bea. "Seems that's what we do now."

TWENTY

Along with fourteen other potential converts, including Maggie and Bea, Georgia attended the first two newcomer classes in the KCR church hall. The classes concerned, as Georgia described it, more or less regular Jesus-y shit. She took only very irregular notes, but on several occasions during the first two classes she attempted to engage Dan Honeycutt in private conversation on topics beyond theology. His responses were cordial, but his thin smile betrayed annoyance. Maggie was surprised at the subtlety of Georgia's maneuvering, and even more surprised at Honeycutt's evasions. Perhaps he was a better man than she had suspected.

The third newcomer class was at the Honeycutts' home. The fifteen candidates had by then dwindled to eight, and as Dan Honeycutt had explained at the previous week's class, they were on their way to becoming family. He felt that the intimacy of a family dinner table was more fitting, now that the subject of the classes would turn to the history of the KCR. The class didn't learn that Mrs. Honeycutt was in Nebraska with the Honeycutt children until they arrived to find Dan alone in the big house with cardboard boxes of jam doughnuts.

Maggie and Bea arrived early. Dan seemed pleased and offered a doughnut. When Bea opened the box there were two vacant wet spots, each with a kiss of jam where doughnuts had previously been parked. Maggie imagined for a moment Dan Honeycutt alone in his house with a box of doughnuts, unable to resist, not once but twice. Yet this same man had somehow been immune to Georgia's obvious charms. In a flash of bitterness Maggie thought unbecoming, Georgia had said she thought Dan might be a little light in his loafers. Maggie looked at the greasy silhouettes in the doughnut box and worried. If that were true, she had nothing to offer his appetites.

She smiled and declined the offered doughnut. She explained that Georgia would not be attending the third meeting as she had decided to continue worshipping elsewhere, for the time being. Dan listened with his head at an angle.

"Maybe it's a different path for her," Maggie said.

"No," Dan said, with an air of finality. "There's only the one path. Bible is clear. Anything else is just what we tell ourselves. We want everyone to be saved. It's a natural impulse, but it just isn't so."

"Georgia is a handful, but I don't think she's going to hell."

"It doesn't matter what we think. People we like, people we think are good, little old ladies and kids and pastors from other churches, truth is none of them will be saved. They're all going to burn. That's what the bible says."

"That's a little hard to swallow. Georgia is my friend. She's practically family."

"That's why we discourage friends outside the KCR. You try to get them to hear, to save them, but they are deaf to the truth. I knew this would happen. I could see right away Georgia wasn't one of us."

"Well, she didn't say it was permanent. She might come around yet."

"I don't think so. You, on the other hand, you and Bea, I think you have a home with us." He touched her arm and smiled. The gesture might have been sincere, but Maggie thought about Eld just then, about what he might have done. She tried to imagine Eld laying his hands on another woman. That turned to a thought of Eld putting his hands on her. She hadn't been touched by any man since Eld. Dan was not a man Maggie would choose, and she didn't like the turn his teachings had taken, but his touch wasn't entirely unwelcome.

When the other candidates arrived, Dan sat them around his dining room table. They started with a doughnut, then a prayer, and finally Dan said he thought they were ready.

"Up to now," he said, "everything we've covered is more or less traditional Christian doctrine. It's all stuff you know from the bible. You would get close to the same teaching from the Presbyterians or the Methodists down the street. That's the stuff that appears in our publications and that we talk about in church on Sunday."

One of the other candidates, a middle-aged man who attended every class in the same tweed jacket, shifted in his chair and leaned forward. The man had told Maggie that he was a widower. His wife died before they had children and he had never remarried. His story was sad, if commonplace, and, unlike her own, his interest in KCR appeared genuine. Still, there was something about the man Maggie found suspect. His eagerness now, his apparent desire to hear secrets, cemented her opinion.

"I heard that there is an off-the-books part of KCR." The smile on his round face, parked under stripes of scalp exposed by thin hair, struck Maggie as a leer.

"Secret stuff," he said.

"Well," Dan said, "there's nothing that's secret. The core of KCR isn't secret, it's sacred. We don't put it on flyers that just anyone can pluck from the church hall. But you aren't anyone. Everyone here has shown some commitment. Enough, anyway, to share in the good news of the first terrace."

No one around the table said anything in response. Maggie wondered what he meant by terrace. She knew a terrace was a kind of porch that they had on plantation houses in the South. She was thinking about terraces, and the people who lived in houses that had them, while Dan got started. He asked everyone to put away their notebooks, and then he spoke for most of an hour. The things he said made her a little queasy and she considered reaching for a doughnut. When Dan was done, the man in the tweed jacket got up to leave.

"That's a little much to swallow," he said. "I'll need to think about this."

"Sleep on it," Dan said. "And I'd ask you to keep what you heard here in confidence."

"I figured ghosts or something, but I didn't count on . . . Well, I guess you are saying you got a whole crop of new Jesuses."

"Prophets," said Dan. "Not Jesuses. God didn't just abandon us two thousand years ago. He sends prophets, and if we listen, if we keep our hearts open, they find us. They show the way to him."

"Right." The man was at the end of the table farthest from the door. It took him a few seconds to gather his notebook and hat. He walked around the table and stopped by Dan.

"I got a hard time believing Jesus is out there somewhere in Wayne County, driving around in a Buick."

"We're not for everybody," Dan said, "but you sleep on it. And again, we expect you to keep what you heard here to yourself."

"It's a free country."

"It is. And you are free to violate our trust. But we have friends too. Some of them work at GM, same as you. Maybe higher up than you even."

"Is that some kind of a threat?"

"You know, James, James Waller of Seneca Lane, employed by General Motors since '31, I don't think I need to make threats. I think you are an honorable person who knows better than to betray a confidence."

"Oh hell."

The man in the tweed jacket, James Waller apparently, left the door open on his way out. A current of cold air came into the room and blew the doughnut box to the floor. Dan tried to field questions for a few minutes, but the other candidates were mostly silent. As they were filing out, Dan asked Maggie and Bea to stay for a moment.

"Half of them won't come back," he said after the door closed on the last one. "It's always that way."

"It's not something you hear every day," Maggie said.

"What do you think?"

"I'm not sure. But I'm keeping an open mind."

"Bea," Dan said, looking at the girl, "could you clear off those the dirty dishes for me, wash them up in the sink?"

Bea already had her coat and mittens on and looked to her mother. Maggie nodded at her and then started to help.

"No, Maggie, let Bea," Dan said. "I need you to come with me up to my office."

Maggie followed him up the stairs and noticed he was a little wide in the hips for a man. There was a threadbare spot in his sock where it met his shoe. In the hallway she passed the open door of a bathroom and saw the counter around the sink was crowded with toiletry items. Some of them were tipped on their sides. They arrived at a room at the end of the hall and he gestured for her to enter. She walked through the doorway, deciding she was as far away from the kitchen downstairs as she could get and still be inside the house. She heard the door close behind them. There was a wooden ship in a bottle and a bust of a man she didn't recognize.

She wasn't a girl anymore. She knew what was likely to happen next, and an hour ago she would have been okay with the idea. She needed her job, and if she were honest, she had spent the night with lesser specimens. She had been alone for a long time, he was a man, and that was almost enough right there. But the gangs of Jesuses, possibly driving around in Buicks, the wide hips, the hole in his sock, the ship in the bottle, and his bathroom trafficked by family had now accumulated to dampen her mild enthusiasm for the project. And she was terribly sober.

When she turned around he was on her. She backed away but didn't say anything. He followed and put his arms around her, pulling her to him. He was apparently having some kind of a moment, because he said nothing and kissed her. His kiss was the better part of the next few minutes. Sugary breath was followed by lips and a tongue that tasted like doughnut. He groped around until he found her ass and then squeezed it. Maggie wasn't thinking about him so much as she was waiting on a physical response in her own body. She let him get to the point where he was trying to pull her dress up before she stopped him.

"That's enough," she said, and pushed him back.

"Did I make a mistake?" he asked. His face was flushed and his erection was obvious. "I'm sorry. I thought—"

"That's enough for now." She didn't want to have a conversation. She wanted to take her daughter and leave. She managed to force a smile, which became a real smile because he was almost panting, and she stopped before she laughed.

"You are a married man."

"Oh, if that's what's troubling you, I can put your mind at ease on that score."

"I met your wife. I don't see how I could be at ease."

"We are a KCR family. Both us were born in KCR. I'm fourth terrace, and she's third. That's as high as a woman can go. The church doesn't pretend. It understands how god made men, and so does my wife."

"I'm not sure what that means."

"I knew from the first time I saw you that this would happen. I knew you were right for the church, and right for our family. Your friend, Georgia, she's pretty, but I could see right away she wasn't right for us. She's not earthy like you."

Christ. Her plan, such as it was, seemed to be working, but she did not quite believe what she was hearing. Georgia was the earthiest woman she had ever laid eyes on. And my god, did this man think that was a compliment? She hadn't been desired since Eld, and she liked to be desired, but to be considered *earthy*? She would rather conspire with Honeycutt than manipulate him, but it occurred to her that he might be too dumb for that.

"I'm going home now."

She walked around him and out the door. Dan followed her. When they got to the top of the stairs Bea was waiting with her coat on. Maggie remembered Dan's erection and stepped sideways to block her daughter's view. She knew then, hiding this man's penis from her daughter, that she was going to be at least a little complicit. She needed to be careful, but there was a bargain to be struck here. Giving this man what he was after would mean she could keep her state paycheck. She had been party to worse deals—deals with banks that took her house, deals with men who left her alone in the world.

"Thanks for your help," Dan said.

"Of course," said Maggie. "And I'll think about what you said."

"I sure hope you do, and if you have questions, I'll see you in the office."

TWENTY-ONE

Monday morning of the following week, Dan introduced his new assistant to the rest of the office. The new assistant was a fresh-faced boy named Timmy. He might have been twenty.

Dan had called all the staff, sixteen people, into the conference room without explanation. Maggie's face flushed when Honeycutt made the announcement, but she stayed in her chair and said nothing. She should have let Dan pull her dress over her head. How would she cover the rent next month? The groceries? Her next move wasn't clear, but she knew she had to think. Losing her dignity here, shouting or crying, in front of her colleagues, didn't seem like much of a plan.

"Now, you all know Maggie has been with this office for going on a year," Dan said from the end of the table. "She was my predecessor's assistant. I inherited her, so to speak." Dan smiled. Maggie made up her mind to go ahead and lose her dignity.

"And you all know she has been a diligent employee who earns every cent of Michigan taxpayer money that she takes home every week. But what you don't know is that there was a little more room in the budget this year than we thought. Room enough for another inspector. I can't think of a person more deserving or more qualified, so as of right now I am promoting Maggie to the position of inspector."

Maggie caught up to what had happened only as her colleagues were applauding. Many of them were more qualified than her, and most of them were more senior. She took in their faces. There were smiles, but also a few stunned looks. They would hate her now, scrutinize her work, watch her for mistakes, bad-mouth her whenever possible. She smiled and stood.

"Well, this is a surprise," she said. "I can only say thank you, and that I won't let you down."

Dan disappeared to his office and returned with a large rectangular sheet cake.

"Fran made this," he said. "It's got pineapple rings on the top."

He needn't have said that, because the rings were obvious. There were even red cherries in the middle of each ring. Dan handed her a knife, so it fell to Maggie to cut pieces of the cake. In so doing she spoke to all who wanted a piece, which was everyone. The person who most obviously should have gotten the promotion to inspector smiled, took a piece, complained it was too big, and congratulated her. He had been with the office a long time. He would be there longer still. His face said he accepted the capricious way that bureaucratic plums were distributed. He would endure. His day would come.

Maude was another matter. Maude was hired before Maggie, but only by a few weeks. Maude was competent and hardworking. Maggie rarely thought of Maude at all, but when she did, the word "mousy" appeared at the front of her mind, unsummoned. Maude lingered to chat after receiving her slice, keeping up a patter while others took their piece and moved on.

"I didn't know you were interested in an inspector job," Maude said. "You could have knocked me over with a feather."

"It was a surprise to me too, Maude," Maggie said. "Maybe I should play the number today."

Maggie took a square of cake for herself. It seemed that their exchange had reached its natural conclusion, but Maude was still there.

"I heard you joined Dan's church. Just as he got here."

Maggie looked up from her cake. Maude was ready to drop the smile off her face, like you might pull a trigger, to reveal something else. Maybe mousey wasn't right after all. Maggie contemplated saying *Fuck you, Maude*, but only for a moment. She thought better of that as she tucked in her lower lip to make the *F* sound. She had come to rely too much on the phrase, useful though it was, and it wasn't well suited to every unpleasant interaction. Also, Maude wasn't wrong.

"Well, Maude, it's still a free country. I think it says in the Declaration of Independence somewhere I can be whatever religion I want."

Maude put her hand on her hip. She still had the fork in her fist. "The Constitution. It's the Constitution that says you can hustle down to your new boss's church just in time to save your job, maybe get a promotion."

Maggie was making the *F* sound again when Dan reappeared with a broad smile on his face.

"Well, anyway," Maude said, turning to leave them, "congratulations."

"Isn't it the damnedest thing? I ask Fran for it once a week." Dan looked both ways. "The pineapple rings, with the cherries in the middle, they kind of look like . . ." He held his hands up to cup imaginary breasts.

"Right," Maggie said. "Right. I guess I could see that."

"So, the new position, you get an office. All the offices on our floor were already taken, so yours is up on five. I asked them to have it ready today. Let's go look."

Maggie motioned at the square of yellow cake on her plate. She wished now she hadn't cut a piece with cherry on it.

"Take the cake," he said.

Dan ignored the elevator bank and opened the fire door to the stairwell. Air carrying the smell of dust and cigarette butts puffed out into the hall. Maggie had never been to the fifth floor, and on the way up, walking beside Dan on the wide steps, she realized she didn't know anyone else who had an office up there. On the fifth landing someone had left a couple chairs and a row of Coca-Cola bottles. Cigarettes were crushed out on the floor tiles.

"It's mostly storage up here," Dan said. "If you need to meet anyone, use the main office."

The hallway was quiet, and the peaked ceiling reminded Maggie that they were perched at the top of the building. They walked past several rows of stacked desks and packing boxes before stopping before an open door. It was a small room, almost perfectly square, with a desk, a chair, and a filing cabinet. The desk surface was bare except for a black telephone. A single window looked down over the interior courtyard.

"The nearest ladies' room is down on four," Dan said. "But the phone should be working." He walked into the office and sat on the desk.

"The position comes with a state car. Go down to the motor pool and pick one out. You will be traveling for inspections, but to start I'm putting you on canned goods. The canneries are mostly within a day's drive. Beats dairies and slaughterhouses up north in the sticks. You won't track manure home on your boots."

The man who chased her out of his house with an erection used the word "manure" instead of "shit."

"You get an expense account, but you need to keep receipts."

"I'm good with keeping book, with figures."

"I know. The salary is almost double your old position. You are KCR now, and we try to make sure our own don't struggle."

She had followed him into the little room and the angle of the low ceiling forced her to stand close to him. The floor in the office had received a recent polish and the room smelled of commercial floor wax, but as she neared Dan she smelled on him the pineapple and cinnamon from Fran's cake, which was nice.

This arrangement was not the worst thing she could imagine. She took in the room again, and the pineapple-smelling man with his ass perched on her new desk. She almost shrugged but stopped herself.

"I'm grateful," she said.

She leaned in to kiss him. He stood and put his hand on her chest. He pushed her back a foot. "No. No. Not here. Never here."

He was at the doorway in one long step and then she could hear his footsteps down the hall.

She took her seat and opened the drawers of her desk. They were filled with the same office supplies it was her job only yesterday to order. She examined a pad of preprinted yellow expense forms. There were boxes she might tick for fuel or a restaurant check, and a spot for her signature over the title *Authorized Michigan State Official*.

She was still smiling when the ring of the phone startled her. She thought for a moment about how to answer, settling on just using her name. She picked up the handset and at the last moment said "Margaret" instead of Maggie. Another inspector was on the line, calling with a lunch invitation.

She hadn't set foot in a bar since before Michigan went dry. The place was dark and a menu over the bar listed German food Maggie didn't recognize. The wood and brass and yeasty smell of beer in the floorboards recalled to her a time before Doc, or Eld, or Bea. Her fellow inspectors were all men, all at least twenty years her senior, most of them farmers who had lost their land to banks when the Depression began. They, like Maggie, had a connection that got them this job, and they didn't ask about hers. Evidently lunchtime regulars at this bar, they ordered beer from a white-aproned waiter and told stories, *war* stories they called them, about dead possums in pickle vats and packaged bread baked with sawdust. She laughed at the stories but didn't tell any of her own about gangsters and missing sons. The inspectors seemed a happy bunch, more so as the lunch hour stretched to two. A few waxed nostalgic about lost farms, but then admitted to a preference for indoor work, regular schedules, and the absence of large animals.

One of them, Max, had never been a farmer. Maggie thought of him as their leader. Max said that his public service career started with dynamiting beaver dams for the Huron County Road Department. Max explained Maggie's six-week apprenticeship to her. She would accompany Max on his inspections, and he would explain where to take temperatures and where to look for rat shit.

"I'm a farmer too," Max said. "It's just that I farm the government.

Sometimes you work hard. Sometimes you sleep in." He slapped the table. "Sometimes you fertilize."

The other men groaned, then Max leaned across the table and spoke softly to Maggie. "I don't owe any bank," he said, "and there's nothing to foreclose on. You won't get rich, and it's not glamorous, but you dig in here, young lady, like a tick, and you can be set for life."

Max presented her with a thick manual and a leather bag that looked like the ones doctors carried. The enclosed kit of tools included a thermometer, tweezers, and a stack of little manila envelopes with string closures.

"For the rat shit?" she asked, holding up an envelope.

There were laughs and she decided she liked these men, these fortunate uncles. The sauerbraten was good. Her job, the rent, Bea's future—for the moment they were all secure. Max was right. Maggie couldn't remember the last time she felt this at ease. When the waiter returned, she ordered a beer. There were several startled looks.

She gestured at the glasses on the table. "What, a woman can't order a beer too?"

Max looked at the other faces before speaking. "Oh, it's not that. It's just, I thought KCR folks didn't drink."

Jesus. She remembered then what Eld would say about someone he thought was particularly incompetent. Eld would say they could fuck up a free lunch. Here she was, fucking up a free lunch.

"Can it be our secret?" She smiled at the uncles. "I'm new to KCR. Sometimes a rule slips my mind."

The uncles accepted her transgression with seeming good humor. She was now in league with them, already in debt to the tune of one secret. On the walk back to the office she was offered a wink and a conspiratorial peppermint.

Alone on the elevator when her colleagues got off, she looked down at her shoes. She would need new shoes. Boots, in fact. Pants too. Clothes appropriate to walk cannery floors. In her office she read the inspections manual and made notes on one of her new pads. Undisturbed, she read until she reached the chapter on confectionaries and thought of Bea. It was almost five and she couldn't recall hearing a noise since she had returned from lunch.

Since she was just more than a girl she had always taken care of somebody. First Doc, Bea, even Eld, and then she was hired to take care of Nora. She answered cries and calls and fetched things and typed in the service of someone else. She looked around her new fortress with the shiny floor and realized she wasn't there to take care of anyone. Life without someone to take care of was quiet.

She would need a radio.

TWENTY-TWO

Maggie had stepped out of the car and run around to the driver's side while Georgia slid across the bench seat. She took the wheel in her hands and pulled herself forward. The Ford's hood looked bigger from there, a red plain of sheet metal that dropped off a cliff. The inside of the big car had warmed on the drive out of town, but her short trot around the front of the car was enough to remind her it was still winter.

"I don't have any cigarettes," said Georgia, "so this is going to be a short lesson."

"You teach me how to do this and I'll drive us to a store."

Georgia made a noise that Maggie recognized as a hungover sigh. Maggie had insisted on an early start to avoid traffic, and they had the Saturday morning roads to themselves, but Georgia was not at her best in the mornings. Maggie gave her friend a long look. Now that liquor was legal and gin mills were open all hours on every other block, Georgia didn't get much sleep. The bags under her eyes were more or less permanent, and her voice had developed a tobacco rasp that Bea sometimes imitated. Nobody was getting younger, but some ways of aging were harder than others. Not for the first time, Maggie thought of asking Georgia if she had a plan. Her way of life depended on men she wasn't married to, and those men would grow less interested every year.

Georgia explained what the gearshift did. She leaned over to point out the clutch pedal and the parking brake. Her breath smelled like mud from the bottom of a creek. They were in the empty parking lot behind a crate factory. Georgia pointed the car across the lot at a cornfield before turning off the ignition.

"Okay," she said. "Switch places with me and let's get started. There's nobody here, and you got plenty of room to fuck up."

Georgia took Maggie through the process of starting the car, putting it in gear, shifting and stopping. Maggie started the car and the big engine raced.

"Foot off the gas," said Georgia.

Maggie took her foot off the clutch instead. The car leapt forward ten feet and stalled. Georgia didn't lose her patience, saying only that it took time to get a feel for a clutch. After several attempts, Maggie got the car moving forward and into second gear before running out of parking lot. Georgia shouted for the first time then, and soon they were driving in a circle. Maggie got it up to third and poured on throttle. The car lurched over fissures in the lot, but she kept her hands tight on the wheel. Sweat was dripping from her underarms, droplets rolling down her sides, but she was grinning.

When Dan Honeycutt had asked if she could drive, Maggie had lied.

Like Bea said, that's what they did now. But she could learn. Lansing was full of thick-tongued idiots making vowel sounds at each other, and they all seemed to drive. She would learn from Georgia and get a license before her first solo assignment. Learning to drive was another thing she had to do. She hadn't expected it to be fun.

"Stop! Stop!"

Georgia was opening the door before Maggie brought the car to a halt. She made it a single stride from the car and bent over. Vomit splashed onto the asphalt. Georgia was coughing and spitting, her hands on her knees, when a black two-door rolled up beside them. Now between two cars on an empty plain of blacktop, Georgia retched again. The passenger door of the other car opened and a man stepped out. Maggie saw his uniform, then the gold police star painted on the car. She turned the ignition off. Georgia stood up. Maggie was looking at her back. She wondered which look Georgia wore on her face. An embarrassed smile? No. A matter-of-fact look. Georgia's arm came up to wipe her mouth.

The policeman was younger than they were. He looked at the pile of vomit on the ground and then up to Georgia.

"Ladies," he said. "You been drinking this morning, or maybe you're just going home?"

"I confess," said Georgia. "Last night. Might have overindulged. Weak stomach this morning."

"What about the driver over there?"

Maggie smiled and waved through the open door. The young policeman took a step sideways and pointed at her.

"You been drinking?"

"No, Officer. Not me."

The driver of the police car opened his door and stepped out, but he didn't move beyond that spot. He was the older of the two. He spit on the ground.

"Christ. What is that smell?"

"Lady got sick here."

The older policeman put his hand on the top of the car and drummed his fingers.

"Check the car for bottles," he said, then put his head down and spat again. There was enough liquid in his spit for Maggie to hear it hit the ground.

The younger policeman asked Maggie to get out of the car and then he looked under the seats. When he finished, he stood outside the car and shook his head at his partner.

The older policeman closed his door and came around the front of his car.

"What are you two birds doing here, driving in a circle and throwing up on private property?"

Maggie waited for Georgia to speak. Some of the differences in their skills they acknowledged. Georgia couldn't cook. Maggie couldn't dress herself in anything other than clothes that Georgia described as high Methodist. Talking to law enforcement wasn't anything they had discussed, but Maggie felt sure that was on Georgia's side of the ledger. She looked to her friend. It was cold in that parking lot, looking at two policemen.

"Funny you ask, Sergeant," said Georgia, "I was just asking myself the same question."

Georgia started to say something more and then her voice changed to a gurgle. She bent over and threw up again. The younger officer stepped back while the older one curled his lip and issued a grunt of disgust.

"She was teaching me to drive," said Maggie. "I work for the state, and starting soon I'll need to drive for my job. I asked her to teach me."

"She got a license?" asked the younger one.

"Yes," Maggie said. It occurred to her then that she didn't know.

"What's wrong with her?"

"I'm fine," Georgia said. She stepped toward the younger one. "Wanna smooch?"

His baton was in his hand in a second and then it was over his head. The old one moved fast then, stepping in front of his partner and pushing him back.

"You gonna go around bashing hell out of every canned-up bird you run across? Every drunken old whore gets a thumping?"

"I'm not old," Georgia said. She was poking at the pile of vomit with the toe of her shoe. "That right there was cuisses de grenouille," she said. "Frog legs."

The two cops looked at her.

"Heard of that," said the older one. "No wonder you're throwing them up."

When they left, Maggie admired the way the older cop eased off the clutch at the same time he applied throttle. The black patrol car rolled forward without jerking or shuddering before turning out onto the highway. They got back in the Ford and Maggie started it up.

"The balls on that cop, calling me old," Georgia said.

"He called you a drunken whore."

"There's a case to be made for that, but *old*, that shit was just gratuitous."

"Do you feel okay?"

"Yeah, sure." She was digging through her purse. "Wish I had some gum. Gum or a cigarette."

Maggie looked straight ahead. She didn't often ask for advice, and had rarely been given any when she did need it, but just now she needed some. More specifically, she needed the particular brand of advice available from a woman who drank too much and threw up in parking lots before offering to smooch policemen.

"The reason I got you out here was not just to teach me to drive, although I need that too. I wanted to tell you my plan, see what you think."

"Why didn't you tell me at home? We had to come out here in this cold weather early in the morning so you could tell me something?"

"I didn't want Bea to know."

"That's probably a good sign that it's a bad plan."

"Maybe. It's Dan Honeycutt. That's my plan."

"You gotta be kidding me," Georgia said.

Maggie cracked a window. The vomiting hadn't helped Georgia's breath.

"Out with it," Georgia said, "and keep driving. Shift and brake some more. Then we'll get out on the road."

Maggie stopped and started the car a half dozen times, then drove in circles, then turned out onto the highway. She told Georgia about her encounters with Dan, and her promotion thereafter.

"Do you think he promoted me because I kissed him?" she asked.

"Of course," said Georgia. "The thing I want to know is, did you kiss him, or was it the other way around?"

"Does it matter?"

"Hell yes it matters. Who's got which end of the leash? One way and it's you leading a man around by the spindle to get what you want. The other is him keeping you like a pet, paying you for a roll in the hay."

"What if I said it was both?"

"I'd tell you that sounds like marriage. You going to get married?"

"I was married, and now I'm alone here with a kid. I liked being married better. Especially if he's already got one wife. She can wash his socks. I'll take the paycheck."

Maggie pointed the big Ford out toward the highway and pressed in the clutch as she applied brake. She couldn't help her smile as the car stopped without a jerk or sputter. She could learn to do these things.

"I don't know how long this can last," she said "but what I'm asking you is, am I crazy? Can this work?"

Georgia exhaled. "He's not the worst-looking man."

"Oh hell. I don't care about that."

"The job, do you like it? I mean, I know it pays, but do you want it, really?"

"I'll be an inspector. The salary is nearly double. I might be able to put something away. And I'm there to make sure people don't get sick from tainted food, or ripped off, so it's an honest living, doing something useful."

"Turn out into the road. There was a town a few miles back that had a diner. I could use some coffee."

There were no cars on the road when Maggie pulled out. In a minute she had shifted through the gears and was at highway speed.

"Seems you are taking to driving," Georgia said.

For a minute it was quiet in the car. Maggie could feel Georgia looking her over and she wondered what her friend saw.

"Look at you," Georgia said. "All grown up. You and Honeycutt, it seems like a workable arrangement, at least for the time being. But I hate to see you do this. You were married in a church. You're a mother. This kind of thing, taking up with a married man for personal gain, it will make you something else."

"Yeah. It will make me something other than poor. Anyway, you were going to do it."

"Right. Better me than you. I been doing it for years. What did that cop just say? 'Drunken old whore.' You want to be a drunken old whore?"

Maggie didn't answer and drove without speaking until they reached the diner. She pulled into the lot and stopped. When she turned the ignition off a series of metallic plinks filled the silence.

"There's whores in the bible," Maggie said. "Generally, they do all right."

"Did he say anything about me?"

"Who?"

"Honeycutt."

"He did. Said you weren't earthy enough for his taste."

"You sure can pick 'em."

TWENTY-THREE

Maggie was issued a black Dodge coupe. For the last three weeks of her training period, she drove Max around to their appointments. Starting and stopping the Dodge, she remembered the way the older policeman drove. He had pulled away and accelerated like somebody who did it all day long, every day. He had worked clutch, gears, and gas pedal so that from stopped to speed there were no jerks or pauses. With that memory as her ideal, she practiced, and she read the driver-safety pamphlet issued by the state. Her hands rested at two and ten on the wheel. She kept to the speed limit. She would pull away from a stop sign, repeating to herself the words the policeman had said. The time it took to say those words was the precise amount of time it took to smoothly engage the car from a standstill. She moved her lips at every stop, uttering silently, *Drunken old whore.*

It was important to her, and with some satisfaction she became a very good driver. Max noticed and said as much. After his first ride as her passenger he announced that she would do all the driving from now on. This arrangement had the added benefit of allowing him to nip occasionally from the flask he kept in the inside pocket of his jacket. From canneries they moved on to other facilities, where Max always seemed to know someone. They were greeted, if not always warmly, at least with familiarity.

At some of the bigger facilities the inspections took more than a single visit. Max once led her around a commercial bakery every day for an entire week. She got out of bed easy that week, picked up Max from his home, and drove to a low cinder-block building forty minutes north of town. Spotless expanses of steel and painted concrete trapped clouds of moist air scented with cinnamon and apples. She followed Max as he looked under tables in storerooms and noted any workers missing hairnets. The place was cleaner than any kitchen Maggie had ever cooked in.

On Thursday Max fished an éclair out of a trash barrel in the break room. It had a thumbnail-sized dollop of amber grease on it. The offending pastry secured in a wax paper sample baggie, his steps quickened until they were at the éclair line. He demanded the line be stopped and then searched it until he found a stalactite of axle grease clinging to a gantry. A conveyer belt of pristine pastries sped below. Another foot and they were painted with a timed squirt of icing.

Max produced a clipboard and violation form from his briefcase. He stood near the line and began to write on the form. The workers nearby disappeared.

"Somebody is coming down here to argue," Max said, without looking up. "You let me do the talking."

Max and Maggie were soon joined by a man with a loosened necktie. He did not wear a jacket and his sleeves were rolled up.

"What's the trouble, Maxie?"

Max looked up for a moment, then back down to the paper. "Lou," he said with a nod. "It's a little thing, but you got foreign matter falling into the line."

"I don't see anything falling."

Max looked to Maggie. "Show him the éclair."

Maggie used, for the first time, a pair of tongs from her bag. She removed the éclair carefully, but even so the nodule of grease was now smeared.

"It was in the trash in the break room," Maggie said. "Somebody was hiding it."

Max didn't look up from his clipboard, but he stopped writing.

"That's a hell of an accusation, lady," Lou said. He looked closely at the éclair. "Looks to me like somebody with greasy fingers was helping themselves. Wouldn't be the first time an employee had a snack at company expense. Can't say I blame them. They're my favorite too. In fact, might have been me, now that I think about it."

Maggie saw the lie, and she thought she knew what to do next. "And how did it end up in the break room trash?" she asked.

"I don't know. Maybe they were about to get caught. Maybe they decided to go on a diet."

Max had stopped writing. "Lou," he said. "You promise me this gets fixed, and maybe we can work something out."

Lou shook his head. "Yeah. I saw you come in on Monday, I went to the bank. Come up to the office." He pointed at Maggie. "Without her."

While they were gone Maggie stood near the gantry and watched éclairs speed by. She waited, but the grease didn't fall. There were a lot of éclairs there, so many it was hard to believe that they could all be sold. She had never purchased one in her life. The sweet doughy smell of them reminded her of Dan's breath the night he kissed her in his house.

Max returned without Lou.

"We're done here," he said. "Let's go to lunch."

Maggie started the Dodge and drove back toward Lansing without saying anything. The violation notice was still on Max's clipboard. He balanced it on his knees, drew a single line across the page from one corner to the other before returning it to his briefcase.

"The fine on a violation like that, it's a small thing to the company," Max said. "Sometimes, a case like this, we just settle it off the books. They don't want the record, so they'd fight it. We'd win in the end but waste a lot of time in the fighting. If they pay the fine straight to us, there's no record. Nothing for them to fight."

"They paid you?"

"Paid *us*."

Max took an envelope from his inside coat pocket and shook out two fifty-dollar bills. "One's yours." He folded one of the bills in half and tucked it into Maggie's inspection bag. She looked back to the road. Fifty dollars was more than her salary for the week.

"That's not a fine," Maggie said. "That's a bribe."

"To-may-to, to-mah-to," Max said. "There was axle grease on the food. That's a real violation. I don't make up phony violations just to get a payoff. Some guys do, you know."

Maggie pulled out on the highway. Max was turned toward her, but she kept her eyes on the road. She liked Max. He was competent, and he didn't talk down to her. Sometimes he was even kind. She didn't want to believe he was a bad man. A whiff of alcohol reached her and she knew he had his flask out. The cap swung on a hinge and made a metallic clink when he tilted it up for a nip.

"The real dirty places," he said, "the genuine risks to the public, I write them up, report them. Go through all the channels. Maybe even shut them down. But a place like this, a big outfit with lots of money, a minor violation like that, they will fix it right away. The public is protected. The only difference is that we don't waste months in hearings fighting them."

"There's another difference," Maggie said. "Your way, we get the fine instead of the state."

"Well, that too. And as long as we work together, anything we get, you get half. If Honeycutt transfers you to work with somebody else, they might not offer you anything. They think because you're new and you're a woman that they can't trust you. They won't tell you what they are doing, and they won't give you your share. You make sure they give you half."

Maggie looked over. Max was settling back in the seat and pulling his hat down over his eyes. Maybe he wasn't crooked, just slightly bent. Or maybe he was crooked, but only when he was chiseling a few bucks off the bosses and the big trusts. Like he said, the public was never in any danger. She knew she had to make a decision, right now, on what she was going to do next. She wasn't sure, but she figured taking the money was a crime. She was sure that she would lose her job if Honeycutt found out. She tried to imagine herself in Honeycutt's office, the one in his house, trying to tell him that his inspectors were taking bribes and that Max had given her fifty dollars. She remembered Honeycutt's erection and his breath that smelled of doughnut icing.

"Max," she said. He didn't answer. She took her hand off the gear shift and poked him in the shoulder.

"What?" he said from under his hat.

"Where do you want to go for lunch?"

TWENTY-FOUR

After the first time, Maggie made a point of turning the lights off. Honeycutt's frame didn't bulge at the middle and he could look smart in a suit, but he was a little fleshy without his clothes on. The attention of a man was welcome, but Maggie had spent too much time with specimens more chiseled than Honeycutt to find his naked appearance exciting.

She invariably brought their encounters to a close by getting on her hands and knees, then dropping to her elbows, and finally reaching out to the edge of the mattress. Honeycutt thought this was earthy, and, regrettably, said so, but Maggie assumed that position so she could put her face in the sheets and conjure visions of Eld, or her long-dead Maltese boy. This sometimes worked, but afterward she knew it was 1934 and she was now old enough to be mother to the boy who died of flu in New Jersey in 1918.

Honeycutt had appeared in her office doorway and given her a key in a folded scrap of paper. An address was written in pencil on the paper. There was no one to hear them on the fifth floor, but Honeycutt had said nothing. He handed her the key, turned on his heel, and left. After work she drove to the address in her black Dodge and let herself in. There were two bedrooms, but only one had a bed. There was no alcohol in the place to warm up with, and no cigarettes to reflect with after. The icebox was empty, and she couldn't get the radio to work. She found linens and made the bed, brought the heat up, and still had to wait at the kitchen table for an hour before Honeycutt arrived. She was thankful she didn't know his invitation was coming, as otherwise she would have spent the hour in the impractical underwear Georgia had insisted she buy for this occasion.

When he finally arrived, Honeycutt smiled and sat at the table. He started talking about the KCR teachings on marriage. Maggie didn't want to hear it, and didn't want to be embarrassed by what she didn't know. Attendance at the weekly newcomer classes had dropped off to Maggie, Bea, and four other students. Maggie spent the time trying to look as if she was following along, but she hadn't understood much of anything for weeks. There were a lot of old names. Malachai. Ezekiel. Various people smiting each other. A fair amount about marriage, from which Maggie understood that men in the bible had many wives. She didn't care. The classes, this interlude, this was her job. She didn't need convincing.

As Honeycutt spoke, she understood that his speech was not only for her. He was looking at his hands, which he had placed palms down on the small table. Honeycutt was not the worst man in the world, but he could stand a dash of boldness. Maggie wasn't going to listen to him talk himself into this arrangement. She stood up and pulled her dress over her head. Honeycutt stopped talking. She walked to the bedroom and he followed.

After that first time there were no more discussions of theology, although, to her surprise, Maggie's part in the act had for her an unexpected religious flavor. She believed in her sacrifice, that her willing defilement was the going rate for material comfort. That bill paid in full, she told Bea that their newcomer classes were completed.

She learned to drive in snow. The first time was freezing rain. It was early and she was on her way to pick up Max. A panel truck blew through a stop sign, the driver waving frantically as it passed. She saw his wheels were locked. Panic shot roaring blood in her eardrums. She stomped on the brake, unable to stop herself though she knew what would happen. The tires lost their tenuous grip on the icy road and the car spun out of control. Her little Dodge slid through the intersection gliding past the rear bumper of the truck with a foot to spare. The houses that drifted by the windshield were stately and well kept. The car came to rest against the curb with a hard bump that sent her across the seat.

That was the trick to be learned. Never slam on the brake. Pump it only slightly, and only if all else failed. Instead, she remained alert behind the wheel, making adjustments in trajectory only to the degree necessary to avoid collision. She got better. Inches from a bus shimmying on blacktop coated by freezing rain, or following in the tracks of a snowplow after dark, she drove fast, yet so smooth that Max rarely had reason to look up. He said she was fearless. She was not. She could imagine the sound of breaking glass and collapsing sheet metal, and it terrified her, but she remained calm. The heavy objects and powerful forces around her, whether she had set them in motion or not, had to exhaust their energy on their own. This didn't end when she stepped out of the car.

She raised her daughter alone. She took money from Max. She attended church in the pew three rows behind her boss. Twice a week she put her face in the sheets. The rent was paid.

Honeycutt decreed that her training would end on April 1. Maggie learned this from a staff memo circulated by his new assistant, even though she had been with him in the little house on Stanton Street just the night before. Despite their physical intimacy, Honeycutt remained an odd and inscrutable figure. She thought she didn't need to understand him. What he wanted seemed clear enough, as old as every story in the bible, and what he was offering seemed a fair exchange.

The uncles took her to lunch again at the end of her training. In a short speech she thanked Max for his patience and instruction. They drank beer in the same tavern as her first lunch and Max told stories of her driving over sheets of glare ice. The uncles laughed and seemed pleased to have her join their ranks, although they seemed more interested in their lunch than anything she had to say. A third round of beers had been delivered when Max leaned across to her.

"I spoke to Honeycutt this morning. He told me you are on sugar this year."

"The beet refineries?"

"Yeah. There's two within an hour of here. They're big operations."

"They smell."

"Yeah. They stink like money."

Maggie saw him drink every time they worked together. He never got sloppy, but sometimes he showed off what he knew.

"The thing is, they run round the clock during the campaign, from the time the first beets come out of the ground in September till they are all processed. They had a bumper crop this year, and there's still piles of beets the size of football fields at the refineries. If it gets warm the beets start to rot, so they are running to beat the band."

"Okay. I'll be on my toes."

"Look, I'm telling you this because they can't afford a violation, a lost day. They need you to give them a clean bill of health, no matter what. You find something, anything, they are going to want to make a deal. A good deal."

"Oh. Right."

Maggie liked the regular cash Max's negotiations had provided. She spent less than her salary every week, and together with the cash from Max, she had been growing a healthy nest egg. Maybe it was a down payment on a house, or tuition for Bea, or maybe it was just freedom, but she liked looking at her bank book. She hadn't decided yet whether she was going to continue to solicit on-the-spot resolutions to minor infractions. That was the kind of thing that came naturally to men like Max and the other uncles. They would know how to initiate that conversation, probably with a company man who knew it was coming. Maggie had never been in the room when Max made the ask. She was afraid that under pressure she might say something stupid, like *Bribe me*.

"Last year," Max said, "I worked the sugar plants. A few nitpicky things. Doors propped open to let steam out. A dead mouse. But one, I came in and found a backed-up toilet. The guys were walking through it, tracking shit all over the plant. I raised hell and they fixed it right then, cleaned it all up, even tossed some of the sugar."

"And?" Maggie knew what was coming.

Max sat back in his chair.

"I bought a new car last year. My wife, who does not have your talent for operating machinery, wrapped it around a telephone pole, but for a few months I had a sleek Packard roadster. Top down on a sunny day, I'll take that Packard over a chicken in my pot."

It was Maggie's turn to lean over the table. "How do you do it? How do you ask them?"

"Well, I've been at this awhile. I almost never see someone I don't know. Everyone I deal with, they already know the drill. They've seen me before. If they want to avoid the paperwork and the hassle, they cough up. I hardly say anything at all. But you're new, nobody knows you, so you don't have that luxury. They are going to be cautious."

"So what would I say, exactly, to someone I never met before?"

Maggie knew what she was asking, and she knew that the woman she was just a few months ago could not have had this conversation, a conversation about how to solicit a bribe. But she had shared in easy money that didn't seem to hurt anyone and she wanted more. Banks were failing. People were out of work. Every time she saw men lined up in front of steaming cauldrons for a free dollop of whatever there was, she was reminded that her own position was precarious. She understood why Eld had taken a chance.

"That's the tricky part," Max said. "Try not to be explicit. Say something wishy-washy, like *If you can promise me this gets fixed right away, I could see working this out right now*. If you had to you could explain that away."

Maggie tried to imagine herself saying that to some man in his office over a factory floor. Her skepticism must have showed.

"Look," Max said. "You don't have to ask. You don't have to do anything. You could just play it by the book. That's the safe way. But, you know, fortune favors the bold."

Maggie drove Max to three more inspections before her apprenticeship was complete. Their very last inspection together was a cavernous warehouse adjacent to a rail yard a few miles north of town. The warehouse was quiet the morning they arrived, and so cold that Maggie kept her coat on when they entered. A small handful of workers wandered around with clipboards. The foreman waved to them from a booth at one end of the cavernous space. He had a phone in his hand, but he put it down and called out to them.

"Hey, Max," he said. "I got a lift truck threw a chain. Trying to get hold of a new one. If you need me, I'll be in here, but you go wherever you like. I'd eat off the floor in here."

The building was sheet metal and windowless cinder block, with large hanging doors that slid on tracks. Bulk sacks of sugar, wheat, oats, and other dry goods were arranged in long rows, like the furrows in a cornfield. Lights hung from the ceiling in steel cages at intervals far enough apart to create a twilight at the point midway between fixtures. Maggie saw something there, some animal, moving fast. A dog. Two. Diminutive terriers with wiry coats. Max saw the dogs and sighed.

"You see those dogs, you're not gonna see a rat. A place like this, they don't make anything. Just boxes and cans piled up. Rats chew holes in boxes. You got to admire them. They survive. Wolves, bears, mountain lions, they all used to live around here and we wiped 'em out in no time. But rats? Not even close. Mankind has been more or less at war with rats for thousands of years, hell-bent on their extermination, but most you could say for us is that we fought them to a draw."

"Okay, so no rats. That's good."

"Right. See, those dogs, they're tiny but they're vicious. They don't even eat the rats. They just grab them by the neck and shake them until they're dead. A rat smells them, he heads the other way. Rats survive because they're careful."

Maggie watched two of the little dogs work together, each working one side of a row of pallets stacked high with gunnysacks of potatoes. Any rat that bolted would end up in the jaws of one or the other. Maybe she was a terrier. Her job was to ensure that the people of Michigan could count on a supply of wholesome food. Food that wasn't contaminated by rat shit or anything else. She believed in that mission, and though she took a few dollars to expedite certain minor matters, she worked hard and thought her work served some purpose. She watched the dogs work deeper into the warehouse. They were alert. Relentless. They froze from time to time, if for only a moment, then resumed frantic movements. They did not rationalize. They did not let little things go.

She stood and watched, and realized she was pulling for the rats.

TWENTY-FIVE

Bea was frosting a cake when Maggie got home. A wet dish towel to wipe up errant powdered sugar was on the countertop. When Bea started cooking, Maggie had told her to clean up after herself. Now Bea cooked almost as often as Maggie, and left the kitchen in better shape. Maggie once watched for five minutes while Bea scrubbed the inside of the sink.

Bea's interest in cooking seemed genuine, but she didn't make the weeknight dinners that were the hardest for Maggie to keep up with. Bea made projects: elaborate cakes, sauces she read about in a magazine, jams. Nothing that would relieve Maggie's quotidian burden, but when she was done with her projects, the kitchen looked to Maggie like the inside of Eld's boat. Spatulas with spatulas, mixing bowls nested in one another. A place for everything, and everything in its place. Eld could be seen everywhere in the girl, but Eld was easier to live with.

Maggie turned sideways to push past Bea in the narrow kitchen and opened the cabinet where she kept the Seagram's.

"What's with the cake?"

"Newcomer class tonight. I told them I would bring a cake."

"You know, you don't have to go."

"I don't mind."

"What does Honeycutt say about you going without me?"

"He hasn't mentioned it. There's only three of us left now. Everyone is pretty dedicated. We talk about theology."

"You too? Are you dedicated?"

"I don't mind."

That wasn't an answer, and the words annoyed Maggie. "It's bullshit, you know. All that stuff that's not in the bible. They are just making that part up."

Bea didn't stop frosting the cake. "If you feel that way, why did you join? Why do you keep going on Sunday?"

"The world is a complicated place. There's a depression on. Dan is my boss."

"So you joined the KCR because you thought it would help keep your job?"

Maggie poured an inch of Seagram's and didn't answer the question. She left the kitchen and sat in her club chair by the radiator. When Bea appeared she had her coat on, and the cake was in a box.

"How are you getting over there?"

"You don't have to drive me. I'll take the bus."

"Georgia is coming tonight. I thought we'd go out. You don't want to skip class, just this once?"

"I'm bringing the cake. I promised."

"Okay. Tell Honeycutt I wasn't feeling well."

"He won't ask. But if he does, I'm not going to lie."

When the door closed behind Bea, Maggie lit a cigarette. Bea was enjoying the untested certainty of youth. Unsullied by the dirty bargains mothering required, Bea could frost her cake and talk about Studebaker-driving Jesus. Maggie's instinct was to let Bea enjoy that certainty, but maybe it was her job to warn her too. You could be certain of a Maltese wedding in the sunshine yet end up with your ass in the air and your face in the sheets.

Georgia called through the door from the hallway.

"It's open."

She came in and looked around. The Seagram's bottle was on the floor next to the chair.

"Where's Bea?"

"Not coming. She's at Honeycutt's KCR class. Just you and me tonight."

Georgia looked from the bottle to the ashtray on the arm of the chair.

"So I'm driving?"

They went to an Italian restaurant where Georgia had been on a date. The dining captain led them to a table at the back of the crowded house, far from the front window and the bar. The tables at the front had men at them, and younger women in shorter skirts. Maggie passed those tables and understood.

"He was a dud," Georgia said, describing her date. "Tried to make out like he was a hood. He used the word 'underworld,' but he didn't know who I was. Nobody does anymore. I guess I should be thankful. Turns out he figured he was a hood because he knows a bookie who works out of a barbershop. So he was a phony and a dud. But this place, they make a kind of Italian tomato pie, with cheese on it. Call it a pizza. It was in the paper."

The waiter was civil, but not indulgent, his smiles more polite than genuine. He looked over his shoulder when Georgia ordered the wine. While they waited for the pizza, Maggie explained that she had started doing inspections on her own.

"Well, there you go," said Georgia. "It's amazing what a little knowing will get you. In the way Adam knew Eve."

"Honeycutt would like that. The knowing."

"Of course he would. He likes knowing. Men do."

"I meant the word. Funny enough, the actual knowing, that's only once or twice a week. And he doesn't mention it at work. Just asks if we can meet at the little house he rented."

"Count your blessings. He could be all over you at the office, come by your apartment unannounced."

"He wouldn't do that. He would consider it rude. Immoral even."

"He's committing adultery. You think he's worried about morality?"

"I don't think he sees it that way. He thinks it's okay, since I joined his church. Sometimes I get the feeling it's more about the church than it is about his jollies. They read all that *knowing* in the bible to mean it's okay for them to be putting the wood to more than one woman at a time. Maybe even required."

"You think he's shacking up with you out of religious obligation?"

"I don't know. Maybe. I don't want to know."

"That's right. He's a gift horse. Don't look him in the mouth. Take what you can get. While the getting is good."

"Right. That's part of why I wanted to see you. I'm not sure how long this situation is going to hold. I'd like to get a little insurance against a rainy day."

Maggie started to explain how Max had conducted the on-the-spot negotiations and the resulting gifts when the pizza arrived. They stopped speaking while the waiter placed it on a wire stand in the center of the small table.

"The guy who took me here," Georgia said, "he just ate it with his hands. Said that was the right way. But he was a phony, so I'm using a knife and fork. We're not in Indiana anymore, for Chrissakes."

The waiter nodded and said, "Of course." He withdrew without commenting on how the pie should be consumed.

"So you are taking bribes now?" Georgia said. "Given your position I can understand a certain ethical flexibility, but do you think maybe you've taken this fallen-woman thing a little far?"

"This job, the promotion, Honeycutt, Max's little side deals, together they are too much good luck. I'm making more money than Eld ever did chasing fish. This streak can't last. The next time I'm left flat on my ass I want money in the bank. The getting *is* good. Time to get mine."

"Isn't that what you are doing?"

"Yes, but maybe there's a way to get more. Much more. And I was hoping you could help."

Maggie explained that she would soon be inspecting sugar plants, and she told Georgia what Max had said.

"Okay. So, the sugar plants, they're a fat chicken. What do you need me for?"

"I've never asked for a bribe. Max always did it. You know about that sort of thing. Mickey paid off lots of people. Cops, judges, whatever."

Georgia sawed at her pizza. "I've never been a public official on the take."

"You dated a whole crew of them."

Georgia had put a piece of pizza in her mouth, so she didn't answer, but her eyebrows shot up.

"If you came with me, pretended to be an inspector, you could make the ask. You give a phony name. If it all goes sideways, nobody knows you, and there's nobody to fire. We split the money."

Georgia swallowed her food. "Why do you think I need the money?"

"It's been more than a year since Mickey died. You've never had a job. You're still driving the same Ford."

"I have generous men friends."

"Less of them than you used to. Less generous too, I'd bet."

"You know how to hurt a girl."

"That's just it. You're not a girl anymore. You're thirty-eight. Me neither. I'm thirty-five. What are we going to do in five years? Ten? We need to think about our future. This is our chance."

"A life of crime. Like Bonnie Parker. Or maybe Ma Barker."

"Ma Barker killed people. She had shootouts with the police. We aren't going to hurt anyone. We take an envelope of cash from big companies that will never miss it."

"How much money?"

"Max said he got enough to buy a new car."

"What does a new car cost?"

"He said he bought a Packard. They're fancy. About two thousand dollars fancy."

Georgia whistled and then looked around. The candles on the table lit her profile. She was still a handsome woman, but there were crow's-feet where there hadn't been. Maggie knew to be careful here. If her friend thought she was doing this for her sake alone, she would decline, claim she didn't need it.

"You think you could get that much from a sugar company?" Georgia asked. "I'd be afraid to ask for that much."

"A man wouldn't be afraid to ask for that much. Max wasn't afraid to ask for that much."

"Easy, Susan B. I'm already voting, which is fucking inconvenient. What more do you want?"

"There's three plants on my list. If we get a grand from each of them, and we split it, that's enough to keep me and Bea in the black for a year, if it comes to that."

"You really need this right now?"

Maggie sighed. "I don't know. This opportunity, it might be here next year, but it might not. Maybe Honeycutt gets bored of me. Maybe he moves on and the new boss cleans house. I'm not counting on some man to keep a roof over my head. You shouldn't either. You especially ought to know that."

Maggie didn't say that every day that passed the angle they were playing got harder. She didn't say that neither of them was getting younger. But they weren't.

"Taking bribes, it's not the same as selling whiskey. A lot of people, especially a lot of cops, they thought smuggling whiskey was harmless fun. If you got caught, you could get a slap on the wrist, because the judge was probably doing it too. Nobody thinks that about taking a bribe. Even if the judge is doing it, he sure as hell isn't going to look the other way. He has to throw the book at you."

"Okay. I thought I would tell you about it, in case, you know, you wanted an out."

"Could I use the money? Sure. Since the judge left for Florida, I've been paying my own rent. Never done that before. It takes a bite. The money I had when Mickey died, I got maybe a year left. I've been hoping a prospect would come along. A widower would be nice. Say about sixty. With a taste for travel and no kids."

"Right. And handsome too."

"Handsome is nice if you can get it, but not essential."

"Speak for yourself. I'm tired of sleeping with less than handsome men."

"Handsome, at sixty?"

"I'd settle for distinguished. Distinguished and doesn't stink up the bathroom."

They were both smiling now, and Maggie steered the conversation to familiar subjects they had laughed at before. She was ready to let her plan drop. The scheme had never seemed realistic, and Georgia's reaction had let the remaining air out of the idea. She had asked her worldly friend, and that was all the effort she was going to put into extracting bribes from big sugar companies. Even the thought now seemed ridiculous. She thought of herself as a basically honest woman, cornered occasionally by circumstances into a legally questionable activity. She really didn't need the money. She was doing okay, making a little more every month than she needed, salting away her extra pennies. They finished the pizza and ordered dessert. When the waiter left Georgia leaned across the table.

"Leave it alone. I don't like the smell of it. Those good old boys got something going to feather their nests, you let them. Doesn't mean you need to get in on it. Like I used to ask Mickey, what if you did nothing? You got a good thing going. If you do nothing, maybe you miss out on a big payday, but you keep putting money in the bank, sleep well, and you don't worry about getting caught."

TWENTY-SIX

The first facility Maggie inspected without Max, a jar factory, didn't have anything edible on the premises. She walked around with her clipboard for half an hour, in the staggering roar of machines and ringing glass, before anyone asked her what she was doing. A young man wearing leather gloves up to his elbows approached to ask if she was looking for someone. She flashed the badge issued to her by the Michigan Department of Agriculture and he shouted a reply she couldn't make out over the din. When he jogged away, back toward a furnace the size of a two-car garage, she followed. His jog, the ways his arms swung, from behind she could have been looking at Doc.

Maggie followed the young man as far as she could, but a dozen yards from the machine she was stopped by waves of heat. The young man kept on until he was close enough to shovel coal through open doors into a bank glowing crimson and orange. The roar in her ears, the greasy smell of burning coal, and the blast of heat submerged her. Surrounded by men, machines, and movement, she walked the factory in manufactured isolation. Red-hot ingots of molten glass shot by in chutes and dropped into molds, air blowers whined, and jars moved past on a conveyor belt. She completed her inspection quickly, finding nothing amiss beyond a few broken jars.

Maggie went back outside and leaned against the Dodge while she filled out the inspection form. Her ears still ringing, she didn't hear the young man approach.

"All done?" he asked in a shout.

Startled, Maggie dropped the form. He bent and retrieved it for her.

"Yes," she said. "It's sure loud in there. I don't know how you stand it."

"Yeah," said the young man, "but it's a job. Even shoveling coal beats going without." There was still a lot of boy in his face, and he was grinning. Teenage boys could be awful people, but they could be wonderful too. Like Labradors who spoke a few sentences of English. Maggie couldn't help but grin back.

"Do you need to talk to the boss?"

"Not if you can take him this form. You guys were pretty clean. Just watch the broken glass in the boxing room. We can't have it getting in the undamaged jars."

The boy looked both ways. "Lady, you sure?"

When Maggie didn't say anything, he continued.

"Every inspector comes through, they all get something. They expect it. You might as well too."

Maggie looked at this boy, telling her about her own corruption. "I'm sure I don't know what you mean."

"You talk to my boss. He's in there right now, waiting for me to come get him. He has an envelope for you with a hundred dollars in it."

Maggie hesitated.

"Maybe you don't need the money, but I can tell you I sure do. My wife is pregnant. I'll go ask for it, if you give me fifty."

Maggie heard her own voice say okay, and saw the boy jog off. The boy who was himself a husband and father, and who was learning from her to cheat and lie and sell your integrity for fifty dollars, disappeared back into the plant. She got in the Dodge and backed out of her parking spot. She was turning around when the boy returned. He wasn't wearing the gloves anymore and he rapped on the fender with his knuckles. Maggie stopped but she didn't roll down her window. She didn't want to look at him, so she stared at the center of the steering wheel. When he rapped again she turned the handle that lowered the glass.

"Here," he said, holding an envelope through the open window. "Are you all right?"

Maggie took the envelope, looking up at him when she did. She eased off the clutch and the car rolled away. She was out on the road, the cold wind coming through the window, when she understood that what she was feeling was a desire to cry. She resisted all the way back to her office, where she spent the balance of the afternoon filling out expense reports.

Most of the reports were for gasoline or meals she'd had with Max. Max liked diners with thick menus where he could order open-faced sandwiches of turkey or beef, gravy ladled over the top, or dark bars that served grilled hot dogs and cold beer. Max was old, he drank, and he took bribes, but Maggie smiled at the thought of him anyway. He went out of his way to try to help her, even if his brand of help was lessons in how to be crooked, and he told funny stories. Looking for a way to be in the world, you could do worse than Max.

For three hours the phone didn't ring, but just before she left for the day the other man in her life appeared in her doorway.

"I've got a lot on this week," Honeycutt said. "I can't make it tonight."

He might have been saying that he ordered new letterhead for the office, or that someone was coming to polish the floor. Nothing in his demeanor suggested that he was canceling their clandestine yet regularly scheduled episode of sexual congress. Of the two men in her life, she preferred Max.

This cancellation was another reason she might cry, though again she resisted. The urge, the welling in her chest, it came not so much because she was looking forward to the act, but because it left her with nothing to do for the evening.

The apartment was dark when Maggie got home. She had brightened during the last few steps to the door at the prospect of cooking something, maybe breakfast for supper, with Bea to help. Her call for Bea got no answer. A note on the kitchen table said she was attending extra bible study with a KCR group and would get her own dinner.

Maggie ate cold chicken from the Frigidaire. She buttered some bread, each clink of knife on china a surprise in the silence. The bread had sat too long and was dry, so she scraped it into the kitchen trash, reproaching herself at the waste. She had become a city person. Two fingers of Seagram's in a coffee cup and ashtray at her feet, she sat at her window. The tally for the day was all failure. Moral, sexual, familial. If she didn't act, her day would close on a one-sided rout in favor of the world. She smoked and sipped until the door opened. She was ready.

"I think you are spending too much time with them."

Bea looked up, startled. She walked into the apartment and closed the door behind her.

"With who? Our church?"

"Don't you have friends at school? Somebody else that you want to spend time with?"

"My friends are at church. I like the church. I think you made the right choice when we moved."

It was Maggie's idea, the church she had picked. Maggie's fault. Bea was a clever girl. There was no denying that. Bea would need that cleverness, and under other circumstances Maggie would have encouraged its development, but seeing it used on her, in her own house, rendered her momentarily silent with rage.

"They are serious about their religion," said Bea.

"And you are too?"

"I think so. I try. Aren't you?" Bea was taunting now.

"I'm not sure any one church has all the right ideas. I try not to take any one of them too seriously."

"Well, I'm learning a lot."

"Where? Where are you learning a lot?"

"At church, at the Honeycutts'."

Bea approached her mother. Her skirt had been rolled over at the top, raising the hem to her knees. Maggie smelled perfume.

"Where were you tonight?"

"I left a note. We had bible study." Bea entered the galley kitchen and was out of sight.

"Where?"

"At church hall."

"Was Mrs. Honeycutt there?"

"No. Just Dan," Bea said over the sound of the faucet.

"Right. Did you stay there the whole time?"

Bea appeared from the kitchen with a glass of water. "Why are you so interested all of a sudden? You were the one who decided to stop coming to class."

"Where did you go?"

"Dan gave me a ride home. We stopped to have ice cream."

"Who's we?"

"It was just us."

"Who's us?"

"Me and Dan."

Maggie stood up. Her chair fell backward to the floor. She was quiet for a moment, watching her child. She thought about the words she would say next. She wanted equally to shout at her child and to say nothing at all on the subject ever again.

"Who was at the bible study? Was it just the two of you?"

Bea met her mother's stare. "And what's wrong with that?"

Maggie spoke, in a slow cadence, with an even tone. "That's the last time you attend anything KCR without me."

Bea threw her shoulders back. "You can't stop me. You're never even here."

"I can stop you. And I will. As long as you live under my roof, I make the rules."

The last time Maggie had heard those words spoken aloud they had been uttered by her own mother. Maggie had ignored them. She was losing this argument, but there seemed no way to win.

"Rules?" said Bea. "What rules? That you smoke and drink and then lie about it? That you join a church to keep your job? That you take a man's job?"

Maggie heard another voice in Bea's words. The practiced thoughts about how Maggie lived her life had rolled off Bea's tongue. The girl had been thinking, listening to someone, inching away while Maggie's attention was elsewhere.

"A *man's job*? Where did you ever get that idea?"

"If you didn't have that job, a man would have it, and he could take care of his family."

"What the hell do you think *I'm* doing?" Maggie realized she was shouting. She had a drink in one hand and a cigarette in the other. This last little battle wasn't going her way either.

Somehow the conversation had stopped being about Bea, and her time spent with the KCR. Bea had a knack for that, which Maggie resented. Every little spat somehow became an exploration of Maggie's shortcomings as a mother. Christ knew there were plenty of those, but it was grating. Bea never seemed to be on her side. Half of her was from Eld, and whatever his mistakes, Maggie and Eld had always been a team. The two of them against the world. The world had turned Bea somehow, and she now led the chorus of Maggie's critics.

"Look, you are getting close to being an adult. Part of being an adult is understanding sometimes you do things you don't want to. I didn't want to lose your dad, or run from mobsters, or cling to my job any way I can, but them's the breaks. We are one stroke of bad luck away from joining a breadline, so I'm playing every angle I can. I'm your mother, but I gotta be your dad too. The KCR, it's more cult than Christian, but I need Honeycutt on my side. *We* need Honeycutt on my side."

Bea was crying now. "You go to his church . . . and tell him you believe, but you don't."

"You don't know what I believe. What I believe is between me and the lord."

"Your faith is a lie. Your job, your whole life is a lie."

"I'm not the point. I don't want you spending time with Honeycutt when I'm not around."

Bea turned without answering and walked to her bedroom.

TWENTY-SEVEN

In the morning Maggie got to work earlier than usual. She camped on the sofa outside Honeycutt's office with a Seagram's headache to remind her of her failings. The slow throb only made her more resolute. Honeycutt was uncharacteristically late, leaving Maggie time to pour coffee on her sour stomach and make excuses for her presence to the staff.

"I need five minutes with Dan," she told his assistant. The young man nodded and took his seat behind a desk outside Honeycutt's office. Maggie watched him do her old job, only not as well. He should have asked why, put her off, sent her away until he could ask Honeycutt. The young man did none of those things. Instead he ate a piece of coffee cake and read the Detroit paper. Maggie might have her job because Georgia knew a judge, or because she had joined KCR, or even because she let Honeycutt "know" her, but she was also an asset to the office, to the state of Michigan. She worked hard. She was smart. She gave the taxpayers, the people, their money's worth. Her righteousness was close to a peak when Honeycutt arrived. He shot his assistant a look before smiling at her.

"Just a few minutes," Maggie said, rising from the sofa and walking into his office.

Honeycutt followed her, speaking as he did. He managed to say "Now is not a great time" before she cut him off.

"Bea is not coming to any more newcomer meetings or bible studies."

Honeycutt closed his office door behind him. "I'm surprised to hear that. She has been very enthusiastic, and she's a quick study."

"She's a *girl*. *My* little girl."

Honeycutt was silent for a second before he spoke. "She's a young woman."

The hair on the back of Maggie's neck stood up.

"Bea is not going to any more of your meetings, and our family isn't going to KCR services anymore. You won't be seeing her again. Or me, outside the office."

"I'm sorry your feel that way, but Bea is almost sixteen. The law says that's old enough to make some of her own decisions."

"Not this one. I don't know what you've been up to with my little girl, but whatever it was, it's over."

"I've been teaching Bea the truth about the lord, and what he wants for us. We spend a lot of time together, and we've become close. She needs a man in her life."

"She doesn't need a goddamned thing. Especially not from you."

Honeycutt's Bakelite telephone sat on his desk one stride away. Maggie considered snatching up the receiver and burying it in his head. He moved around behind his desk and sat.

"Really, Maggie. The lord's name in vain? In an office paid for with taxpayer money? To your boss? I know you haven't stopped smoking or drinking. I think that you aren't really interested in KCR. You joined because you thought that would help you keep your job. I'm not stupid."

Maggie thought she might be sick. Honeycutt was wrong. He *was* stupid. Too stupid to figure out her motives on his own. The smoking and drinking, lots of people could have told him that, but her scheming to keep her job, that could only have come from Bea. She had known she would lose Bea to the world, to her adulthood, maybe to a husband, but she couldn't bear losing her to this man.

"Have you touched her?"

"Maggie, you watch your tone. You wanted the benefits of the KCR, and you got them. I look out for you here. It was me who promoted you, me who found money in the budget for you. We made room for you in the KCR family. When you joined us, you agreed to follow the true teachings of our lord, including the teachings about men and women. If you didn't take your study seriously, that's your own fault. Bea has—"

"She's a child. You keep your hands off her. I'm not afraid to call the police."

Maggie turned on her heel and left, her threat in the air. She remembered to smile at Honeycutt's new assistant on her way past him. She was still a practical woman, and she knew she should hang on to this job. As Eld had often said, a smart man doesn't jump ship unless he has a lifeboat. She took the stairs up to her office as fast as was practical in the ridiculous fucking shoes she had bought to work in this office.

She was still breathing hard when she dialed Georgia's number.

TWENTY-EIGHT

Apparently, Bea had been eating fruit in the morning. Expensive fruit like oranges, bananas, and grapefruit. Bea did most of the shopping, and she always left the kitchen immaculate. Maggie hadn't noticed that before. Since she had started work for the state, in an office, Maggie didn't eat breakfast anymore. She drank coffee, and sometimes after Bea left for school she had a cigarette at the kitchen table.

Back when she had eaten breakfast, when she was still making food for Eld and Doc too, she fried eggs and sometimes bacon. Pancakes were an occasional Sunday treat. Maggie didn't like bananas and never bought them. She thought of bananas as the kind of fruit eaten by people who played tennis.

Bea peeled a banana and cut it into pieces. She cut up an apple and an orange as well, before mixing them together and adding a teaspoon of honey.

"When did you start doing that?"

Bea looked at her for a second before looking back to her bowl and speaking down into the table.

"I can't hear you when you mumble."

"I said I eat every day."

Maggie swallowed her anger. "I meant, when did you start eating fruit like that for breakfast?"

"It keeps you slim."

"You don't need to worry about that."

"I feel better."

"What do you mean, 'better'? Was there something wrong?"

"Nothing is wrong. Fran eats this for breakfast. She showed me."

"Fran isn't slim, though, is she?" It was a catty thing to say, and Maggie regretted the comment as soon as it left her mouth. Calling a woman fat, or ugly, though admittedly Fran was a little of both, was not an effective way of claiming the moral high ground.

"Cigarettes and whiskey will keep you thin too. But I don't think that's what god wants us to do with the bodies he gave us, do you?"

There was a cigarette burning in the ashtray. They both looked at it. Maggie had never stopped entirely, but she had cut down, and upon joining KCR had made an effort to smoke less in front of Bea. Since her conversation with Honeycutt, though, she had resumed smoking with the abandon that comes with falling from the wagon. She liked smoking.

"The president smokes. I don't think god would lead him to that office if smoking was so sinful."

"Maybe you should run for president."

They sat in silence while Bea finished her fruit, then rose to rinse the bowl in the sink. Her eyes swept the table, the ashtray, and Maggie, who was in her housecoat.

"Are you going to work this morning?"

"I have an appointment, but I'll be here when you get home from school."

"I have—"

"I don't want to hear it. Straight home. I'll be waiting."

Apparently one of the values Bea had absorbed from the KCR was politeness, so much so that even in the throes of adolescent rage she didn't quite slam the apartment door on her way out.

Maggie picked up a banana. Somebody had picked it. Somebody had put it on a boat or a train from wherever it was they grew bananas. Somebody had sold it. There were other lives she might have lived, maybe a life on the periphery of bananas, instead of the periphery of herring or whiskey, but that was not the life that found her. She peeled the fruit and took a bite. The pale flesh was sweet, but somehow pulpy and grainy at the same time. She spat it out and washed the taste from her mouth with a gulp of cold coffee. Warm weather and sweetness, fragrant blossoms and tropical oceans, that life had never been hers.

She poured herself more coffee and got dressed. Bea would come around. Or not. Either way, Maggie had to make decisions for the both of them, act for the both of them. She was lighting another cigarette when Georgia knocked and then let herself in.

"Jesus," said Georgia, waving her hand in front of her face. "The air is blue in here. A person might say you smoke too much."

She took the chair across from Maggie at the kitchen table.

"So," Georgia said, reaching for a cigarette herself, "you're settled on this life of crime, then?"

"I have reasons. I'll get to those in a minute. But you don't have to do this. I could do it on my own." Maggie said this because she thought she should give Georgia the chance to back out. But it wasn't true. Alone she wouldn't have the courage. Georgia's instinctual response to authority—that it was wielded by incompetents undeserving of it—was crucial for her plan.

Georgia lit her cigarette and shook out the match, the wave of her hand dismissing Maggie's comment. "Can you get me a badge? I've always wanted a badge. I'll flash my badge, tell them there's a new sheriff in town. Bust balls."

"I'll get you a badge. And a clipboard. We have those. What we don't have is time."

"What's the rush?"

Maggie told Georgia her fears about Bea and her argument with Honeycutt. At nine o'clock she paused to call in sick to her office. When she returned to the kitchen table Georgia was sitting quietly.

"What if we just killed him?" Georgia said.

"I think we go to California," Maggie said. "But we'll need more money than I have, for a stake. Enough for a down payment on a little bungalow someplace. Keep the wolf from the door for a few months until we get our feet under us. I figure we need about two thousand, maybe twenty-five hundred. I have three hundred saved."

"I'm down to about three hundred," said Georgia.

"We get as much as we can from the three refineries. As soon as we get the money, we leave."

"What if Bea doesn't want to go?"

"She won't. But I make the decisions. Sooner or later I'm bound to make a right one."

"You ever been to California?"

"No, but I was thinking Los Angeles."

"Well, California is the fashionable thing to do. I understand the Okies are all for it."

"There's deserts between us and the Pacific. Mountains too. Think the Ford can deliver us, one more time?"

"Sure. Why California?"

"They grow oranges out there, and grapefruits. Maybe bananas too. Eat that stuff for breakfast, keeps you slim."

"That sounds like bullshit."

"Probably. Anyway, I don't like bananas."

TWENTY-NINE

When she cracked the office door the box wasn't visible on Honeycutt's desk. Maggie tried to recall the details of when Honeycutt had given her her badge. She had been grinning like an imbecile and not paying attention. She remembered him taking it from a box of them in his office. The box was dark blue, the size of a bread box, with a hinged top and the name of the manufacturer embossed on the case above some sort of a seal. Even this tiny part of her plan would be hard. She took off her shoes so that she could walk quietly on the tile floor of the office. Her shoes in one hand, she pulled open the big lower drawers. It wasn't there either.

Georgia really didn't need one, but Maggie had promised, so she was in the Michigan Department of Agriculture an hour before anyone else, rifling Honeycutt's office for an extra badge. Georgia didn't like the plan, but she was willing, once again, to help what was left of Maggie's family. A badge was the least Maggie could do. She needed Georgia's easy confidence and her sly way of speaking to men. Georgia could ask for money like she was asking for a cup of sugar. If she said she needed a badge, Maggie would get it for her, but the truth was no one ever asked to see them.

She didn't want to turn the light on, but in the dark she couldn't find the case in Honeycutt's coat closet either. Would he have taken them home?

She froze at a noise from the hallway. A light went on in the outer office. She stepped around behind the desk and crouched down. There was no innocent explanation for standing in the dark of her boss's office, her shoes in her hand.

Maggie waited for the sound of an office door closing before she stood and opened the top drawer. A single badge slid into view. She dropped it into her coat pocket and crept from the office. She didn't put her shoes back on until she was in the stairwell.

The morning was spent on paperwork, but in between forms and reports she went through her own desk, looking for mementos of her time in the employ of the state. Georgia had given her a fancy pen with a stand. She put that in her bag, along with a desktop lighter. Briefly she held her brass ashtray, as large as a dinner plate and mysteriously stamped with the seal of the state of Ohio. It's provenance a mystery, she had found it in an empty office on the fifth floor. Whether it was a gift from a Buckeye state official to some long-gone employee or just stolen as a prank, it was too large to sneak out. The pocket bible that Honeycutt had given her she left in the drawer amid the office lint of staples and paper clips.

She was eating soda crackers from a wax paper sleeve at half past eleven, her hands in her lap, when she heard the slap of shoe leather on the marble floor of the hallway. As she turned her office chair to face the open doorway, Honeycutt appeared wearing the vest of his suit, though not the jacket. The brown tweed was nice, and it fit him closely, but he had inexplicably chosen a tie the sunny blue of cornflowers. He leaned against the door frame and crossed his arms. Maggie watched him and put another soda cracker in her mouth.

"I don't think we can work together right now," he said, "but it wouldn't be right to let you go. Even if you don't want to be a part of KCR, I know Bea still does. She's family, and you are too, when you come around."

Maggie chewed and swallowed. "So, you're quitting?"

"I put in to have you transferred over to the highway department. It hasn't gone through yet, but it will."

"What's the job?"

"I didn't ask. Mostly they mail checks. Money out to the counties to build roads."

"When?"

"A week from Friday will be your last day in this office."

"I see."

"I know you won't believe me, but everything I've done has been to help your family. Even now, when you have rejected KCR, the truth of the lord's teachings, I'm not casting you out."

"Real gracious of you."

"The truth is, it's Bea that's saving you. If it weren't for her, I'd wash my hands of you. But I know she's found a home in the KCR, and I won't let you sabotage that. As long as she's a part of KCR, and I have anything to say about it, you will have a state job."

Maggie understood that Honeycutt was proposing a bargain. The look on his face was confident, as if he were explaining himself to a child. How had this man wandered the earth for decades and no one had found the time to beat him to death?

"No," Maggie said. "You won't see her again. Ever."

Honeycutt rolled his eyes. "Don't be stubborn. You don't want to be out in those streets on your own."

He turned and left the way he came, with the same even footfalls. Maggie called Georgia, and after speaking for thirty seconds was out the door herself. She drove to the National Bank of Detroit in her Dodge. She kept her money there because Uncle Sam owned half of the bank, and the other half was owned by General Motors. With the runs on banks, sometimes they went bust, but GM and Uncle Sam had deep pockets. If they both went belly-up, she would have bigger problems than just being broke. There was snow in the bank's parking lot, but she had already slid into her galoshes. Inside, the ceiling was twenty feet above the floor, and they had a tree in a pot near the entrance.

"That's a lime tree," said a man in a gray suit. He was older, and his hair was white, but he was trim. He looked like the kind of man who would work for a bank owned by GM.

"I asked them to put that there," he said, stepping closer to Maggie. "See those tall windows? We move the tree around during the day so that it catches the light. If it ever grows limes, I'm going to take them home so my wife can make a pie."

Maggie thought about that, about being the woman who made pies out of limes for this man. A life like that seemed so small now, but that woman was probably happy, or at least not worried about going to jail. Men could be unpredictable, even dangerous, but undeniably useful.

"You can make a pie out of limes?"

"They do down in Florida," said the man, smiling. "A kind of cream pie."

"That sounds delicious."

"But you didn't come here today for limes, did you? At least I hope you didn't."

Maggie smiled at this man. He was friendly. Handsome. Married. Perfect for Georgia, but she wouldn't have time before they left the state.

"No limes for me today. I came to close my account."

"Well, I'm sure sorry to hear that. Can I ask why?"

"Moving out of state."

"I see. Tired of our winters?"

"Time for a change."

She followed the man to the counter, where he delivered her to a young teller. Maggie asked for a hundred dollars in cash, and the balance of her account in a cashier's check. She drove home with her bag on the seat beside her. The papers now in the bag were the sum total of her life since the day Eld left for the last time. It was hard not to take stock.

Too late for lunch, and too early for dinner, the diner was mostly empty. Georgia wasn't there yet. Maggie took a booth by the window and ordered coffee. She put her cigarettes on the table and poached an ashtray from another booth. Ten minutes passed and Georgia still wasn't there. Maggie worried that she had been caught, but then remembered they hadn't done anything yet. The big Ford rumbled up outside and parked on the street. The car had been their deliverance and she had affection for it, like she might love a dog or an old horse, but there was no denying it was showing its age. That was the way of the world now, the things you loved wore out and were replaced, to hell with how you felt about them.

Georgia came in with a shopping bag and took a seat, smiling. She motioned at the waitress and pointed at Maggie's coffee cup.

"I brought you something," she said. "A good-luck present."

This was why Maggie needed Georgia for this. This wasn't failure; this would be an adventure. Maggie felt the knot in her stomach loosen. She unwrapped a box. It was a hat. A blue beret. Georgia leaned in.

"I got three. One for each of us. Different colors, of course. They're just like Bonnie Parker's."

"I don't want to seem ungrateful, but you know Bonnie Parker is famous. Half the police in the country are after her."

"Looks good in that hat, though. And anyway, she's following that Clyde around. He might not be the brightest."

Maggie put the beret on.

"Honeycutt is transferring me to the highway department," she said. "Week from Friday. Whatever it is we are going to do, we need to do it by then."

THIRTY

When Maggie pulled up in the government Dodge, Georgia was already waiting at the door of her building. They rode in silence out of the city, the Michigan winter landscape at the edge of the car headlights. The black bark of leafless sugar maples stood out against week-old snow now frozen crisp on the top. Maggie knew the trunks would be like stone to the touch in the bitter cold, the bark smooth on the younger trees. Old trees would have deep furrows. Eld called them shaggy, said he tapped them because they produced the most sap. There would be no snow, no tapping maple trees, in California. Maggie was ready to give that up, ready to move, ready to take Bea back from the world. There was just this one thing that had to be done first.

They drove for forty minutes on empty roads, but it was still dark when they arrived at Midwest Sugar. Steam rolled across the parking lot under overhead lights on utility poles. The lot was nearly full.

"Aw hell," said Georgia. "Forgot that smell. It's like shit, only like someone is cooking it. Like you put shit in a hot oven and roasted it."

Maggie tried to smile. "Smells like money."

She picked a spot as close to the refinery entrance as she could find. The other cars were beat up, some missing fenders or windows. There were more than a few Model T trucks, a decade old now, slow on the highway but hard to kill. The men who owned these trucks would be small farmers or hired hands, working the sugar campaign in the winter and leaving wives and children at home to care for stock. A bushel basket in a truck bed was filled with conibear traps on muddy chains. Traps set for mink that probably caught only muskrat. Skinning muskrat, cold and stiff, was a good way to slice open your hand. These men and their families were scraping by on any trickle of income they could manage, tired from hard labor, worried about their future. You didn't get rich being honest.

Maggie reached for Georgia's hand and gave it a squeeze. She took her clipboard from her bag. Georgia was holding a badge in her hand. They arrived at the doors, which had a material that looked like carpet attached to the edges. The carpet dragged on the muddy concrete floor. Maggie put a shoulder to the door and shoved. A puff of steamy air came out that smelled worse than anything yet. Saliva pooled in the back of her throat, but she didn't stop. California sunshine. Bananas. She resisted a gag impulse and walked inside.

"Oh, for the love of Christ," said Georgia. "You didn't say I would need to throw out these clothes."

The noise inside was a deep mechanical throb with a regular chirp from something that needed to be oiled. There were no men present inside the door, but an empty stool sat under a punch clock. Maggie pointed at mud tracked in from the lot as they walked toward the source of the noise.

"That's maybe a violation," she said.

"Dirt on the floor? Pretty chickenshit. I'm going to say we saw a rat. Everybody hates rats."

"I don't hate rats."

"What?"

"Poison, traps, guns, a thousand years of all-out effort, and still they are right here, always close. I respect them. I learned that on this job."

"Okay, *regular people* hate rats. They don't like them shitting in the sugar, so I'm going to say I saw a rat."

The first employee they ran into was a chubby watchman in a rumpled blue uniform. He was hustling along the wall toward the empty stool. He put a hand up.

"I told you people, you can't be in here," he said. His uniform could have been that of a city cop, but the front of his shirt was untucked. A baton and a revolver were visible on his belt. The sight of authority, even this bedraggled variety, and Maggie's courage fled.

"What people is that?" Georgia said. The reason that Maggie needed Georgia, it was right there in that voice.

"Reds. Organizers. Whatever the hell you think you are. You can't come inside the factory. Workers only in here."

The man spread his arms out as if to corral them toward the door.

"Now you turn around and get your asses out, right back the way you came, and that will be the end of it. Now move, or I'll lay hands on you and you'll wish I hadn't. Broads or not."

Before Maggie could utter a word, Georgia had her badge in the man's face.

"These asses are with the Michigan Department of Agriculture. You so much as touch one of us and you will spend tonight in jail. This is an official inspection on order of the commissioner."

The watchman took a step back. Maggie thought Georgia's voice sounded different. A little Southern. It occurred to her that Georgia thought this was fun.

"In our report we could note that you weren't at your post when we came in. Not your ass, nor any other part of you. Any asshole could've waltzed in here."

The man took her measure for a moment. He was a thick-lipped man with heavy features. A series of emotions rose and fell on a face that needed a shave. Maggie thought she recognized annoyance, then resignation, then possibly fear. But not skepticism. He believed.

"I get a break to use the can," he said. "Once every other hour. Nobody told me you were coming. Besides, nobody comes in here, unless they have to. On account of the odor."

Georgia snorted. "That's what you call it, an odor? Stink could take paint off Satan's shit house. We'll be looking around either way, but you should let your boss know we're here."

"If I go tell him, there will be nobody on the door."

Georgia told him they would watch it for him. He seemed pleased with that and trotted off the way he had come.

"He was almost too stupid to be useful," Georgia said. She was smiling.

"Stick to our plan. Don't get too comfortable."

"Just leave it to me, sister. Here they come. Now you wander off and make notes and I'll negotiate."

Maggie looked up to see the watchman returning with another man.

The second man was smiling and nodding. He was wearing a duck-cloth shop jacket and a necktie. Maggie was a half-dozen steps away when she felt an urge to run. She could still stop this plan. Nobody here had her name. She could run and grab Georgia on the way and leave these yokels wondering what the hell that was all about. She looked over her shoulder. Georgia had her badge out again and the man with the necktie was beckoning her to come with him. He was smiling. It was too late.

Maggie pretended to examine machinery and found herself at a machine slicing sugar beets into thin strips. A bubble had formed around that particular machine where the smell was less intense, the air diluted by the comparatively pleasant woody smell of the cut beets. Two men attended the rattling equipment, pulling a lever every so often to allow another batch of beets to drop down from an overhead hopper into the slicing mechanism. They looked at her and nodded, but it was too loud to have a conversation. A stream of white strips poured out onto the belt below the machine that then raced them off to some other destination. Maggie thought that the smell got more intense in that direction, and anyway she was too scared to be interested in the next process. More minutes crawled by. She circled the machine, ready to leave, or be caught, or drop dead.

Georgia appeared and they were walking toward the door. The watchman was there on his stool, his shirt now tucked in. Outside it was still bitter cold, but the sun had come up. Maggie felt hairs in her nose freeze. They didn't speak until they were in the car. Maggie revved the engine and dropped the clutch. The tires chirped on the cold pavement and the engine threatened to stall.

"Just drive," said Georgia. "Just like every other day."

Maggie turned out onto the road.

"What happened?" Maggie's hands were tight on the wheel, right at two and ten.

Georgia lit a cigarette. "I told him that I would look the other way on the rats for fifteen hundred."

"Shit," Maggie said through her teeth. "That's too much, Georgia. More than we planned."

"I raised the price on account of the stink. Like I fell into a cesspool. I'll need to replace my clothes. Anyway, he took it from a stack in the safe. Nice as pie. Thanked me and said see you next year. Tell the truth, I don't feel like we even committed a crime there."

Maggie took her eyes from the road to look at Georgia. "Where's the money?"

Georgia put her cigarette in the corner of her mouth and went through her bag. Maggie realized she was speeding. She took her foot off the gas and looked out to the road. When she looked back Georgia was holding up a large, very tidy manila envelope.

THIRTY-ONE

Maggie had the second refinery on the phone before she had her coat off. She dialed with a pencil and stood by her desk. She was curt and said to expect an inspection first thing in the morning. She took her coat off and sat. This was the way men did it. The way Honeycutt did it. Even Max. If you saw something you wanted, you didn't feel sorry or pretend you didn't want it. You went and took it. She called the third refinery.

At noon she took lunch at the German place and drank two beers. The beer made her sleepy, and late in the afternoon she woke at her desk with her chin on her chest. She stood and left without looking at a clock. Bea was at the kitchen table doing homework when she got to the apartment. She looked up when Maggie came in the door but went back to work without speaking. Maggie saw columns of figures in Bea's neat handwriting as she took the chair opposite her daughter.

This next couple years, this would be the tricky part. Bea was so angry all the time, so open to every bad idea, so keen to follow the advice of anyone save her mother. But Bea was whip smart, nobody's fool, and she worked like a demon. Maggie felt sure that if she could see Bea through this time to the other side, to being a young woman, just a few years from now, well, then there was no telling what she might become. In the meantime, she would try understanding and gentle persuasion, even love. If that didn't work, brute force would do.

"I don't think this is the right place for us," Maggie said.

Bea looked around the room. "I don't mind."

"I don't mean the apartment. I mean Lansing. What if we went somewhere warm?"

"What would you do for a job?"

"There's lots of jobs out in California. Schools out there, the hallways are outside. 'Cause it never gets cold. We could swim in the ocean."

Maggie had never seen the ocean. The idea of it frightened her a little, but she liked the idea that her Bea would swim in it on warm days and lie on the sand after.

"I like it here," Bea said. "My friends are here."

"I think you are going to love it."

"Wait, is this going to happen? Are we moving again?"

"I'm doing this for you. Just think of what your life could be like out there."

Bea put her pencil down on the table and fixed her eyes on her mother. "You and I only have to live together until I'm eighteen. Three years. Then you can go wherever you want, have whatever plans you want. Leave me out of it."

"What if I told you Georgia was coming? The three of us will drive across the country together."

"What if I told you I won't go?"

"I'm your mother. You're going."

Bea picked up her books and stood. "Why do you have to ruin my life?"

Maggie laughed in spite of herself. Bea stared at her for a few ugly seconds and then fled to her room. Waiting for the sound of the slamming door, Maggie thought that Bea might have a point. In all her trying, Maggie might have ruined her daughter's life, and she had just now laughed in her face. She had looked for things that might help. She had joined her husband in a scheme to be more than what they were and lost him, and her son, in the process. She had run and hid. She had lain with a fleshy boss with some odd ideas about god. She had even sought bananas. None of that was working, but she was going to keep doing it, because it was all she knew how to do. She would try one more time. She would separate a few sugar barons from their filthy lucre.

The Seagram's and an ashtray were in the cabinet where she had left them.

At dawn the temperature hovered near freezing, a full fifteen degrees warmer than the day before. Maggie was less nervous this morning, but a little hungover, and she had poured three cups of hot coffee on her sour stomach. She was over giving a damn. She was going to save her daughter, the last survivor of her little clan, from Honeycutt and the KCR, even if that daughter would never forgive her for it. Everything after that was just gravy. Other than Georgia, and maybe Max, Maggie couldn't think of a soul who would say they liked her, but they were almost to California now, the chief task left to her in this life to complete.

"The last one I booked for Thursday," she said to Georgia. "After that, I'm ready to go anytime. The sooner the better."

"I'm ready too. What'll we do out there, the three of us in a bungalow by the sea?"

"I'm gonna go native," Maggie said. "Sit on my porch and drink whiskey. Look at the ocean. Boil cod bones like a sea hag."

The Huron Sugar Company had three refineries in the state, the largest of them an hour's drive from Lansing. When Maggie turned the Dodge into the gravel lot that morning, only one of the two stacks was in use. Pillows of white steam chugged into the morning air and dissolved in the wind. A handful of cars dotted the lot.

"They're wrapping up here," Georgia said.

"You collect one bribe and now you're a sugar expert?"

"Yesterday the plant superintendent and I had a nice chat in his office while he was giving me his money. He said the companies have mostly worked though their stockpiles. The campaign is almost over for the year."

"Maybe when we get to California you can open a beet refinery." Maggie pulled into a spot and turned off the ignition. "They say you get used to the smell."

They were laughing as they walked across the lot. Maggie was unafraid, wearing old clothes she counted on throwing out in the next few days. She had on a long camel coat that Eld had given her on a Christmas years ago. She had been pregnant with Bea at the time, and the coat had been too big ever since. She had a new coat now, a better one, that she'd bought with money from her own job. She had kept the camel coat in a box. When she put it on that morning it smelled to her of babies and Eld and her old house in Minden. Today she would stink it up with fumes and throw it out, and then she would be on her way to California.

They entered the plant through a broad hanging door that slid on a track. There was no guard, and the only workers in sight were far from the door. Maggie strode toward them, eager to get someone's attention and be done with this appointment.

"Place is spotless," Georgia said.

Maggie hadn't noticed, but when she looked she saw Georgia was right. The floor was a slab of concrete, sealed with a yellowing varnish. It had been swept and mopped recently. The idle machinery they passed was shrouded in canvas tarpaulins and smelled faintly of bleach.

"I'll say there were signs of rats," Georgia said. "Getting so I'm counting on the rats. Says a lot about my career choices."

"Say whatever you need to."

They reached the still-active line and found two men wearing blue coveralls. Georgia spoke to one of them and he pointed to a windowed enclosure above the factory floor. Maggie resisted the urge to have a cigarette when Georgia left. She ignored the two workers and followed the line back to the point where the beets came into the building through a hole in the wall high above the floor. They dropped into a rotating tumbler cage that shook free clumps of black Michigan farmland. Beneath the tumbler a man with a spade pushed the mud into a trough in the concrete. He stopped periodically to retrieve a hose and spray clean the muddy floor.

Maggie had her clipboard in front of her, but instead of an inspection form it held a Rand McNally Road Atlas. The thought of days in Georgia's car made her smile. She would work on Bea. Buy her slices of pie and ice cream at small-town diners in Illinois. They could stay in nice hotels in the bigger towns, splurge in the hotel restaurants.

She turned with a smile on her face to follow the line to the next stop. Georgia was between two men in suits. They each held an arm. A chubby woman in wool trousers and work boots was following two steps behind. Four people, walking fast and looking only at Maggie.

They were fifteen feet away when Georgia started shouting: *"Keep your mouth shut!"*

One of the men grabbed Georgia's chin with his hand and squeezed her mouth open, the way Maggie had done in a panic when one of her children put a button or a thimble in their mouth and she needed to fish it out. Georgia's voice changed as the man pushed her head back. She was shouting something at the ceiling, but all Maggie heard was vowel sounds. Georgia shook her head free.

"Shut. Not a word. They were hiding in the goddamned coat closet."

Maggie didn't move. She realized she was still smiling when the four of them pulled up a step away. The woman in boots spoke first.

"Never seen this one before either."

"Let's see your badge," said one of the men.

He was shorter than the other and wearing a fedora. Maggie knew a man shouldn't wear his hat inside, but she wasn't sure if a factory floor was really inside. The other man, the bigger one, had Georgia's chin in his hand. Georgia's eyes were darting back and forth.

"Georgia? Why do you—"

"You are under arrest. So's she." The man held out his own badge. "Attorney general's office. Public Integrity squad."

Maggie had her own badge in her hand. "What is this about?"

"Where's Max?" demanded the woman in work boots. "I know he put you up to this. Last year that son of a bitch came in here and—"

"Stop talking," the official said.

"—driving around Lansing in a Packard, like fucking Rockefeller. He took that money from us, from my father. I said this year was going to be different. My father built this—"

"Enough," the shorter one shouted. He turned his head and looked at her. "You'll get your chance. Some assistant lucky enough to land this case, he'll ask lots of questions. You can tell him all your hopes and dreams."

He turned back to Maggie, reached out, and took her badge. "What's your name?"

Before Maggie could answer Georgia made a noise, but the bigger one squeezed her chin so that the sound she made wasn't a word.

"Take her out, put her in the wagon. I got this one," the shorter one said before turning to the chubby woman again. "And you, the show's over. Go back to your office. Somebody will call you."

In a few moments Maggie was alone with the man in a fedora. Physically, her world looked the same, but Maggie knew it was spinning off its axis.

"Is there anyone here with you, besides your friend out there on her way to jail?"

"No."

"Nobody waiting in a car somewhere?"

"No."

"Max. Is he waiting? He gets a piece of this?"

"No."

"Look, your friend there, I heard her ask for a bribe. So did my partner. But you, I didn't hear you say anything. You can save yourself here. You don't owe anybody. You roll over on her, your other friends that were in on this, maybe you don't go to jail."

THIRTY-TWO

Georgia knew lawyers. When hers came to the jail, Maggie didn't understand who he was. A guard led her from her cell without explanation to a small room with a single table in it. Already seated there was a man younger than she was. His blond hair that needed a comb and red cheeks atop a gray suit made Maggie think of a farm boy at a wedding. He didn't stand when she entered the room.

The guard left and the lawyer said his name was Cyrus. He spoke for a minute while Maggie wondered what he wanted. He said he knew Georgia, and that he understood her family had worked for Mickey. She should plead not guilty, he said, for now, and he was arranging to have her released on bail. A friend of Georgia's had agreed to put up the money. Maggie guessed then that he was her lawyer, and when she asked him if he was he smiled.

"Of course." He laughed.

"Why didn't you tell me that?"

"I thought you knew."

She wondered if he had done this before, but she didn't ask. She would figure that out later. He was working to get her out. He would be the only one.

He asked about the terrible smell.

She had to walk to the store to get sugar for the cake. A month had passed since her arrest and Maggie still had a set of keys, but she never saw her little black Dodge again. The recipe called for three-quarters of a cup of sugar. She poured out the measure and sniffed at it. The scent was clean, almost soapy. Nothing of the stench of the process remained.

She made the frosting while the cake baked, so there was nothing to do as the cake cooled on the counter. She smoked cigarettes with the radio off and waited for Cyrus to call. Two hours until noon. Lunch in prison would be at noon, breakfast at seven. Five hours' wait. Then another five hours until dinner. No radio. Lights out at ten. She would need to get good at waiting.

Bea had said nothing on her way out the door. Maggie was sure that no one knew it was her daughter's birthday. There had been birthdays in Minden when Doc bought her a candy and Eld came home early. A little holiday only they observed. Maggie had made a vanilla cake back then, and every year since. She hoped the cake would do for Bea what it did for her. Just a moment of what they had, before it all mysteriously disappeared. If she was going to prison, she would need that. She would need an hour from her daughter that wasn't angry, a word that wasn't snarled at her. She could hang on to that. She didn't need much, but she needed that.

The phone rang. Before she picked it up Maggie knew it was Cyrus. Cyrus or a wrong number. He told her again that he was working on a deal.

"Nobody wants to go to trial," he said. "This is a government town. Nobody wants a week of press about a corruption trial, but they aren't going to let you walk either. Not if you don't give them what they want."

"I don't have anything to give," she said. Maybe that wasn't true. She had a nice cake to give.

"Answer their questions, tell them what you know about anyone, I could get them down to a fine, no jail time."

"I'm not looking for a bargain, Cyrus. I did it. It was my plan. Nobody talked me into anything. If anybody has to take responsibility, it should be me."

"This isn't Sunday school. You don't get what you deserve, you get what you bargain for. If you can't bring yourself to testify against Georgia, what about Max? If you tell them about Max, how he showed you how it was done, led you astray, they might let you walk."

"Max agreed to take Bea when I go to prison. He can't go to jail."

"Find somebody else to take Bea. Give up Max, and maybe you won't have to go to prison at all."

"*Maybe?* That's not good enough. If I go to prison, and Max does too, then what happens to Bea? I keep telling you, I am going to prison. I know that. What I want you to bargain for is Georgia."

"I don't represent Georgia, I represent you."

"Talk to her lawyer. I will confess, give the AG the whole story, if they cut her a break. They get two for one."

"Two detectives on detail from the Michigan State Police heard her demand a bribe. She had the money on her when they grabbed her. Clarence Darrow couldn't save her from doing some time."

Maggie refused to give them Max or Georgia because there was a difference between being broken and being broken utterly. Keeping her mouth shut was her only available act of defiance. No more of her people would pay a price for her decisions. She would go to prison denying the world what it wanted. She would hang on to that defiance. That and, maybe, a memory of kindness from the only surviving member of her family. With those two things, she could endure. She told Cyrus to offer her full confession in return for leniency for Georgia. Cyrus complained, but said he would do as she asked.

Maggie opened a window. Late-spring air came in, warm and heavy with the smell of turned earth from the empty park across the street. Workers in green coveralls were spading over the dirt in the flower beds. Their work left black scars through the matted remnants of last year's flowers. There was nothing to miss about this place. Not this apartment or this block, not Lansing. Since Minden she hadn't really liked any place she had been, and she was sure to have no affection for the women's prison in Jackson. If you can have only one home in this life, she had lost hers.

When Bea returned Maggie was in the bathroom. The cake was frosted and perched on a cake stand in the middle of the kitchen table. Maggie heard the front door close, then footsteps, then the thump of a bookbag dropped to the pine floor. She stood and washed her hands at the sink, getting a good look at herself in the mirror. Raising children is a decades-long project, the outcome uncertain. She had known this, and done it anyway. Maybe because the bible "tells us so." Maybe because she lacked the imagination for another kind of life.

Bea was seated at the kitchen table. She had two plates and forks.

"Happy birthday, daughter," Maggie said.

"I thought maybe you forgot." Bea's voice cracked. She sniffed. "You know, with everything going on."

"Not a chance," Maggie said. She was grinning now, which seemed to make Bea cry.

Bea held out a knife. "You cut it."

They ate cake and didn't talk about the future. Bea asked questions about her father and Maggie told her a story about a time when he fed a pan of hardened bacon grease to the neighbor's dog. The grease disagreed with the animal and it lost control of its bowels in the neighbor's house. Maggie laughed telling the story. Cake fell from Bea's mouth as she laughed too. Maggie tried to continue, recounting the chorus of shouts that had come from the neighbor's house and how the dog had shot out into the yard, assuming the position. She couldn't finish the story, which Bea had heard before anyway, but whatever came next, in the future that neither of them wanted to talk about, Maggie hoped this moment would be enough.

Georgia was in the hallway in front of the courtroom when Maggie arrived with her apple-cheeked lawyer. Maggie had been there before, when she was arraigned, so this time she wasn't surprised at the dim lighting from the high ceiling. More than a dozen men stood in clumps around the hallway, their tan trench coats dripping from the rain that fell outside. Some of them were probably reporters. The few women present sat on benches against the walls. They had the put-upon look of wives and daughters. Except Georgia. She was smoking, and wearing bright red lipstick.

Maggie took in the men standing around. She knew two or three of them by name, but they were more or less interchangeable. They had worked out the deal. For two days she had told her story to the prosecuting attorney. She didn't reveal her dalliances with Honeycutt until the second day, after some hard questioning, so that the prosecutors would think they got everything. She made no mention of the envelopes she split with Max. Georgia would do two years. Maggie one. Honeycutt was fired when the story made the papers. Even the Detroit papers covered the story, mostly on the gleeful angle that Georgia's dead brother had been a rumrunner. A day or two later the stories focused on Maggie. There were a lot of sugar puns made at her expense, how she was both taking it and giving it away. A grateful Max kept his job and fulfilled his pledge to take Bea for the year. Bea would finish high school in Lansing. All that was left to do was put the deal before the judge for his approval. Cyrus said that was a sure thing.

"Hey, cousin," Georgia said when Maggie was within a few steps. "Ready for our close-up?"

"Got my bag with me," said Maggie. She held up a canvas Gladstone bag that contained one dress, a set of underclothes, tooth powder, and a dozen bars of her favorite soap. Cyrus hadn't been able to find out where she was headed after this appearance before the judge, but she knew it wasn't home.

"There's only one outfit allowed," said Georgia. "They give it to you. On the house."

"These clothes are for the day I get out. Didn't you bring any?"

"They'll be two years out of style," Georgia said. "You can bring me some new ones when you come to pick me up."

The lawyers had drifted away. Georgia's lawyer was leaning toward Cyrus. Cyrus was getting out a pad.

Maggie spoke quietly to her friend. "I know I said we wouldn't talk about it, but I'd—"

"Stop." Georgia was loud enough to turn a few of the lawyers' heads. She went into her purse for a cigarette and they went back to their murmuring. "I made a decision. I knew the risks. We are going to be in there together for a whole year, and I can't imagine the other guests will be all that scintillating. I can't be ducking you for a year because you feel guilty and want to tell me about it."

The tall oaken doors to the courtroom opened. A uniformed bailiff stuck his head out.

"Everybody here on the sugar cases, come in and take a seat."

Georgia's case was first on the handwritten docket sheet thumbtacked to the wall just inside the door. She and her lawyer took chairs at the defense table. Maggie followed Cyrus into a pew. Lawyers and detectives slid into the other pews, as well as a clump of ragged-looking men Maggie took to be beat reporters.

When the judge entered the courtroom, Maggie stood, both hands on the handle of her Gladstone. The sooner she got started the sooner she would be out the other side. Cyrus leaned over and spoke in her ear. She lost what he said to the noise of the bailiff calling the court to order.

PART III

THIRTY-THREE

It was a healthy work sweat. The smell that rose from his shirt was not pleasant, but different from the smell of his sheets after fever sweats, or the chemical odor of sweat that came the day after drinking homemade liquor strained through a loaf of bread and shared beneath a railroad trestle. He took the smell of his sweat as one more sign that he was as healthy as he would ever be, but he wasn't leaving the hospital because he was cured. He was leaving because his last friend was gone.

Ivan was big, six feet six, over 250. A hard man to miss. One morning Ivan didn't appear at breakfast. When he didn't make lunch either, Eld asked after him. An orderly Eld didn't recognize said sometimes patients were just gone in the morning, their bed made and belongings gone. Eld described Ivan, said he was an Indian.

The orderly shrugged. "Are you sure he was an Indian? Ivan sounds like a Russian name."

Eld said he didn't know for sure. He realized he hadn't asked.

"Well, maybe he left during the night. Indians around here do that, come and go, no explanation."

Ivan had laughed at Eld's jokes, and he never asked why Eld didn't just go home. As Maggie would say, the man was good company. Ivan was the last of his ragged platoon of ghost friends, men Eld remembered through fog banks of fever and alcohol as crippled by poverty, disease, and industrial mishap, but somehow still funny. They laughed around campfires, laughed on empty freight cars, laughed at hands with missing digits wrapped around bottles. He'd met them on the road, in logging camps, and the jails of small Canadian towns. They came and went, but now that Eld was awake, or anyway more awake than he had been in over a year, he wondered if his troop had ever existed at all.

Real or not, Ivan the giant Indian was nowhere to be found, and Eld was alone. Worse, Eld was expected to do the work he and Ivan had done together, clearing rocks from the pasture. He'd been at it for three days and the flesh from the back of his head to a spot midway between his shoulder blades had ossified. Crossing the road from the pasture back to the hospital, he had to turn his body at the waist to look both ways.

The cots were set out on the big porch in rows, so the scarred lungs of patients would steep in the balm of fresh mountain air. Each cot was made with crisp sheets and a thick wool blanket. The faint aroma of bleach rose from the sheets and mixed with the breeze-borne scent of fir trees. The porch was made from foot-wide planks of the same fir trees, soft wood that made no creak when he walked across the floor to the bathroom in stocking feet. Eld had slept here better than anywhere since he was a boy. He would miss sleeping here.

Perched on the end of his cot, he wrote his wife that he was coming home. The last time he had written to Maggie he was in the army. He had been waking up then too. Waking up and going home.

He took his last breakfast at the hospital mess. As he ate he thought Ivan was foolish to have skipped it. Eld wasn't hungry, but he ate oatmeal with butter and a fried egg on top anyway. The food was good, but the pleasure wasn't the same as satisfying a hunger, and he didn't eat with the same hurry. When he first bused up the road from Vancouver to Tranquille Hospital in Kamloops he had weighed 125 pounds. The nurse had asked at registration, but he couldn't remember when he'd last eaten, or what that meal might have been. He said he wasn't hungry. He wasn't hungry now either, but he was back up to 160, the same kid-skinny weight he was the day he joined the army in '17. He was closer to 180 the winter day a year and a half ago when he went looking for Doc. The doctors had told him that tuberculosis takes your appetite and sometimes never gives it back.

The nurses said he needed to eat every day, and so he had. At their request he stopped drinking too. Quit tobacco. Bathed every day. When the weather permitted, he slept outside in cold air, swaddled in sheets the orderlies stewed in bleach every other night. Since the day he gave up on finding Doc, he'd done everything anyone asked because it was the easiest thing to do. He did what people asked until they asked too much and he found some easier way to live, and then he did that instead.

That policy served him well at Tranquille, where his life meandered back and forth over the line between guest and inmate. He was agreeable, spoke English, and—after a few months of treatment—was healthy enough to perform light work. The doctors and staff liked pliable patients who showed progress, so they liked him. Some of the other patients fought. They cursed and threw things and refused to allow surgical collapse of an infected lung. Not Eld. Most of the fight had leaked out of Eld the first three months he looked for Doc. Tuberculosis took what was left. When the doctor said he needed to collapse his lung, Eld had said, "Sure."

The same short, round doctor that had collapsed Eld's lung signed his release papers. He wore glasses and smelled like cigar smoke.

"You're not contagious anymore, Eldridge," he said, "and you are as healthy as I can make you."

"You have my thanks for that, Doctor." Eld couldn't say "Doc," the way the other patients did.

"You're American, aren't you? You have family down there?"

"I'm going to find out."

"Where you headed?"

"Michigan."

The doctor held out an envelope and Eld took it. When he saw it wasn't sealed, he held open the flap with his thumb. Pictures of King George decorated the notes. He had never held Canadian money in quantities greater than coins. Embarrassed, he looked up to find the doctor looking around in his desk.

"Here," he said, handing Eld a book. It was a bible, bound in green leather with a red ribbon bookmark.

"A little money and a bible. With those two things, a man can go far."

"Well, it's a fact I haven't had either in a long time."

One of the orderlies gave him a new pair of boots and a chambray work shirt from the supply closet. The trousers he had arrived in were railroad-issue conductor stripe. They were still in good shape, though he had no recollection of where they came from. They had been laundered and pressed, and the too-large waist brought in, by a woman in the laundry who did not speak any languages that Eld could recognize. She smiled when he came to claim them and motioned that he should try them on. He did so in front of her, dropping his hospital-issue pajamas without thinking, revealing his lack of underwear. He had stripped so many times in the hospital, and before that in jails, barns, or jungles under bridges, without regard for who might be present, that the concept of modesty was a half-remembered childhood rhyme. Sex more distant even than that. His seamstress held out a short stack of men's underwear. She waved her hands and stepped back to admire her work as Eld slid the pants up his thighs. His nakedness had elicited no reaction. She too, apparently, had been relieved of that part of her humanity by disease and circumstance.

Eld got a lift to the train station with a nurse whose shift ended at noon. She was picked up by her husband. The husband drove a truck with a single bench seat. Eld sat against the door, the nurse perched between him and her husband. She spoke happily of Eld's recovery, her voice full of affection. Eld could not remember her name. The man drove carefully but shot skeptical looks across his wife to Eld. Sexless with his seamstress, Eld was now a potential seducer. He got out of the truck at the train station and started to walk away when the nurse reminded him to retrieve his bag from the bed.

He picked up a paper from a bench in the station. It seemed the world, or Canada anyway, was still in a state of economic emergency. With a handful of exceptions, the names of Canadian politicians, sports teams, and cities were unknown to him, so the stories read like fiction. Little plots unfolded, with heroes and villains and conflicts that hung unresolved at the conclusion of the article. Several stories were good enough to make him want to buy tomorrow's installment, but then he discovered the paper he was reading was a week old. He noticed then that he was alone in the waiting area, his bag between his shoes. Dazed by his new freedom, he had forgotten to buy a ticket or even ask when the next train was due.

The agent behind the ticket window was sitting at a desk, his feet up on a drawer handle. He was reading that day's edition of the same Vancouver paper Eld had been reading. Eld asked him when the next train was due. The man looked at Eld, and then at his watch. Eld checked the clock over the ticket window. It was two o'clock. He had read through lunch. The ticket agent stood and brushed his hands on his pants.

"You going down to the coast, or back east?"

Eld didn't say anything for a moment. "Which one comes first?"

"Westbound, down to Vancouver. Ten minutes to four."

"And the eastbound?"

"Tomorrow morning. Eight fifteen."

Eld knew he had been down to Vancouver. He must have seen the Pacific Ocean, but he didn't trust his memory. He was plenty sick by the time he got to Vancouver, and he believed at the time that the whiskey was the only thing keeping him alive. His blood a scalding river of fever and alcohol that whirled up visions, he might have spent a week there or an hour. There was no way to tell. He thought he might have eaten a salmon pie and slept in a church hall.

"You been up at Tranquille? Trying to get home? Where's home?"

The agent spoke the words like Eld was a child.

"I'm American," said Eld, "from Detroit." He figured the agent would have heard of Detroit.

"You can stay this side of the border, take one train from here all the way to Toronto. From there you can get another train to Detroit. Or you can go down to Vancouver tonight, catch a train south over the border to Seattle. There's a ferry too. From there you can go anywhere you like."

"Maybe that would be best. Get back to my own country."

Eld had nothing against the Canadians. Even when he'd slept in their streets the police who rousted him were polite. They called him "buddy" or "friend" and told him to move along. They heard the bark of his American vowels and laughed, asking him why he didn't go back south, where it was warmer and FDR would give him a job. Hell, they even cured him of the white plague. Still, he was ready to go home. The differences were subtle, but their ways, especially that business with putting the King of England on the money and the postage and half the public buildings, reminded him he wasn't home. That was one reason he wanted to leave. The other was that he had lost Doc here. Somewhere. Coming west he had told more than one man that he would find Doc. That he would find his son in this empty, frozen country, or anyway he would die trying. But he wasn't dead, and he hadn't found Doc, and he was going home anyway.

The next morning in Vancouver he bought a ticket on the two o'clock ferry to Seattle. He would cross over water to his own country, the same way he had left. He thought he remembered a fish pie that tasted of butter and pepper, with rose-colored flakes of fish. Even absent the rich sauce of hunger he could appreciate the artistry, and he wanted it. With the general direction of water in mind, Eld had wandered into a narrow street of redbrick warehouses and scant pedestrians. With no one to ask for directions, he took three steps down from the street into a dark saloon. There was a woodstove and a dog asleep on the floor. A homely woman stood behind the bar. She had one black eye and two customers. The pair of them watched Eld from the end of the bar. The barmaid looked from them to Eld, and he remembered hearing, maybe in the army, that ugly women made better cooks.

It was the dog that got Eld to stay. A deep-chested Labrador bitch with cocoa fur that was coarse as a broom on the ridge of her back. Eld crouched and rubbed the back of her head. The bill of fare was written in chalk on a sign behind the bar. No pies. The dog picked her head up from the floor and made a grateful yawning noise.

"She likes you," said the barmaid, "but she likes all men."

"Like you," said one of her two customers. The words were spoken in a way more familiar than cruel.

She ignored the comment. "What can I pour you?"

"Oh. Right. Beer. I guess," Eld said.

"That's a good guess," she said, already turning away from him to retrieve a pint glass.

The dog got up and followed him to the bar. Eld climbed up on a stool and the dog resettled herself on the floor by his feet.

"Her company ain't entirely free," said one of the men at the end of the bar. "She'll be expecting a piece of your lunch."

"She wouldn't be the first female I've disappointed."

Eld was surprised that he had ready such a clever thing to say. He was a little proud of it, but the storm of cackles from the men at the end of the bar was suspicious. He had learned how some men looked for weakness. The two of them moved closer and introduced themselves. Eld forgot the names as soon as they were uttered. Both men were bigger than Eld, and younger. One had a mustache that didn't quite cover a harelip. That one did the talking. He asked Eld if he was American. Eld knew his own accent was as plain as theirs and that there was no point in lying. He said he was from Michigan. When the barmaid brought his beer he remembered that he had stopped drinking, but that could be remedied. He could start again.

Eld listened more than he spoke as the three of them drank beer together. They had a plan for him that they thought he couldn't see coming.

"Hey, friend, you like Pacific oysters?" The man with the mustache was speaking to him.

"Can't say as I've ever had one." Eld hadn't been a fisherman in a long time, but out of solidarity he was inclined to support the men who chose that life. He ate anything that came from water.

"We've got the best in the world, right out there." The man waved his arm in a direction Eld would not have guessed for the ocean. "You got to try 'em." He called to the barmaid. "Virginia, set us up with a dozen oysters."

The woman was on a stool reading a paper. She paused for a moment before getting up, and she didn't put the paper down.

"You running a tab? I need to see your money."

"I got it," said the second man. He had blond hair down to his ears and wore a buffalo plaid shirt. He put a wad of money on the bar and Virginia put down her paper.

Eld ate the oysters. They were cold and briny. He would eat them again if the opportunity arose. He knew there would be an ask, some request for a return of the goodwill, but he ate half a dozen anyway, putting himself in their debt. He was relieved when the blond one produced dice. The dice would be shaved, or there was some other trick. Eld had learned to roll in the army, and he had also learned that games of chance seldom were. He didn't mind. The money was given to him, and who was to say he deserved it any more than anybody else. He would have shared if they asked, but losing a little in a barroom game of craps was probably easier for everyone.

They rolled on the bar with a hunk of two-by-four as a backstop. Eld bet a dollar on the outcome and rolled a seven. The bets increased and he won three more times in a row. It was over in a few minutes.

"You cleaned me out, mister," said the man with the mustache. He was on his left, the blond man on his right. "I don't have money even for the lunch we just ate."

"Let's say we call it a friendly game," said Eld. "I'll cover the tab. You can keep your money."

"We will." It was the blond man speaking now.

Eld looked him over again as the man maneuvered between Eld and the door. The barmaid had disappeared. She was in on it. There would be nothing so elegant as cheating at dice. The play was simple robbery. Eld considered his position. He didn't mind so much parting with the money, but they would beat him, and he was tired of hospital living. They might take his clean clothes. His ferry left in an hour.

He turned back toward the bar and picked up a fork from the oyster tray. The utensil was more spear than fork, straight with two tines and a handle carved from antler that fit well in his palm. When he turned back again the blond man was a step away, reaching for him. Eld put the fork in the soft spot above his collarbone, then grabbed the man's hair and gave the fork a shove so that it sank to the handle. The man crumpled to the floor, grunting, hands to his chest and legs kicking like he was running for his life. The man with the mustache made a short vowel sound and stepped back. The dog sprang from the floor, considered the scene, and bit one of the churning legs of the man on the floor. Eld left their money on the bar and walked out.

He fell asleep in the warm air of the ferry cabin. He woke up thinking about what had happened in the saloon, if it had happened at all, and if it had, why he was so calm. He wasn't sure that the men there had really intended to rob him. They hadn't, after all, demanded anything. But he had sensed violence coming and brought it to them first, a step that he now understood to be the key to survival. He would give no more ground.

He was comfortable with the possibility that he had just stabbed an unarmed Canadian, likely killing him. He was an instrument of fate, his visit random and lethal, like a tuberculosis bacterium, a German artillery shell, or a button man hired by Detroit rumrunners. One of these things, or something similar, was coming for everyone. For every swinging dick, as his sergeant in France had said, until that particular swinging dick got his eternal reward and they gave Eld his job.

THIRTY-FOUR

In Grand Bend they had told him Doc had picked up a load and left. Business as usual. They described him. Eld had run to the bakery where Doc must have bought his sandwiches. The girl behind the counter smiled a little and agreed Doc had been there. She described his sweater. From the description Eld knew the sweater. Maggie had knit it. Doc wore it when he didn't want to wear a coat. Sometimes he wore just the sweater with gloves and a hat. He said he could move better without the bulk of a coat. Eld could see the boy, smiling as Eld told him he was foolish not to wear a jacket. The girl smiled and said she hoped he liked the sandwiches.

Within twenty minutes Eld had run out of people in Grand Bend to ask. When he didn't find Doc in Grand Bend, he went back up the trail the whiskey came down. First to Sarnia, then Windsor. He wouldn't go home without his son. He asked men who stared at him and answered only that they didn't know what happened over the border. In a week he was at the gates of the Waterloo distillery. There were no gangsters there. Instead, men in coveralls with lunch pails came and went at the shift change, walking together in groups of four or five. Eld stopped them and asked if they had seen his son. They called him "Mac" or "buddy," shook their heads, and told him they didn't know what he was talking about. They were working men, and when they spoke Eld knew they were telling the truth.

He stayed in a rooming house run by a French Canadian widow. The rent included dinner, served at six sharp to a long table of men like himself, alone on various tragic errands. During the day he looked for Doc and at night he drank. He interrogated teamsters, longshoremen, and distillers, anybody he could find who would admit they were connected to the liquor trade. When Eld said he was looking for his missing boy they were unfailingly polite. He saw their pity. The Canadians had been in the war too. Disappearing boys were not new to them, nor the people left in their wake to ask questions. None of them knew anything of Doc or where he might be found.

After a week of looking and drinking, two of his housemates took him to a saloon to meet a friend of theirs they thought could help. Eld hadn't been to a legal saloon since Michigan went dry. The noise and smoke cocooned him. A series of hand signals and an exchange of cash from his dwindling supply brought a drink. The friend was produced and Eld could see immediately that he too was American, and a gangster at that. He had American cigarettes and wore a double-breasted suit with half-dollar coins for buttons. The man tugged his sleeve and Eld followed him out into the quiet of the street. Nickel-sized snowflakes drifted down through motionless air.

When the gangster spoke his breath was visible. "This is just a favor I'm doing for our Canadian friends. They asked me if I could help, because of the organization I work for. I wasn't involved, you see, but I asked around, back in Detroit."

"Can you tell me where my son is?"

The man glanced at the ground before looking back to Eld. "I can tell you he's not here. Not this side of the border. Nobody up here would try to keep him from you."

"He didn't come home. I found his boat, with a full load. Nobody on it."

"He's not hiding. Nobody kidnapped him. I don't like telling you this, but nobody else wants to." The man drew on his cigarette. "Mister, your boy, you're not going to find him up here, or back home either. He's dead." The man's hand was on Eld's shoulder, pressing him down into the earth.

"How do you know this?" Eld said this with the last of the air he could expel from his lungs. His voice was tiny.

"The organization I work for, they soaked up Mickey's operations. All in one go. Your boy was in the wrong place. For what it's worth. Somebody shot up the guys who got sent after him. Your boy, he wasn't just a pigeon. Went out fighting."

"What if that's wrong? What if I don't believe you?"

"Like I said, this is a favor to the Canadians. It's them looking out for you, not me. I've done what they asked. What you believe, that's up to you."

Eld drank more and looked less. A week passed and there was nowhere left to look, so he drank full-time. At the end of the two weeks the widow told him at dinner that it was time for him to go on home. The other men looked into their plates and said nothing, but she kept speaking, in a voice that was clear, saying that he was loud at night, that when he drank his sobbing kept everyone awake.

"Everybody here, we all have something to cry about," she said. "You, you still got a home, right? Family? Go home. Take care of them."

The next morning he came down too late for breakfast, but the widow made him pancakes anyway. On the empty chair next to him he put down his canvas bag containing a single change of clothes and a Dopp kit. He could not remember buying the bag, or its contents, but he was sure he didn't bring them from Michigan. Cream-colored and still clean, with brown leather handles, the bag was something people put tennis clothing in for weekends away. Eld pulled the chair out. Maybe one of the other boarders of questionable character would pass and steal the bag so that he wouldn't have to return to Maggie with it, to tell her of her dead son with the handle of a jaunty valise in his fist.

The widow wanted to settle his bill. She charged him extra for the pancakes and took his American money at par. They were outside on the porch when he counted out the amount she asked. He was almost a dollar short. They looked at each other in silence for a moment until he offered her his bag. She shook her head and said he could mail her the money. Then she was closing the door behind her and he was alone.

He started down the sidewalk, employing the slow shuffle familiar to anyone accustomed to walking on ice. Snow was shoveled from the sidewalks and driveways of the tidy houses he passed. Women worked behind windows, busy taking care of somethings or someones. He wished he was about to turn up one of the walks to take his place at a table, but he was a trespasser here. He hadn't built anything like this for his own family and had no right to linger in the domestic security built by other men. He quickened his step. What he had wrought, what he would return to, was in panicked disarray. He had failed in his only mission, to provide and protect.

The pancakes burned off in the half-hour walk and he was hungry when the first westbound train rolled into the station. He climbed aboard with a vague plan to say he'd lost his ticket.

A conductor stepped in his path and gave him a tiny nod. "Ticket, please." The look on the man's face said he knew Eld didn't have one.

Eld didn't bother pretending. He didn't reach in his pockets or change the look on his face. All at once he knew he was unshaven, his clothes rumpled. His fingernails ended in dark crescents. Other passengers were taking their seats unmolested, averting their eyes from the small spectacle. Misfortune leaves its mark on a man, and the conductor apparently knew what to look for. He stepped close to Eld.

"The freight yard is less than a mile south of here," he said. "Get off the road. Walk in on the track." His voice was not quite a whisper, but he was trying to be quiet. There was a trace of sympathy there. "Lots of trains. Not a lot of guards. But you'll need a blanket."

Eld found the jungle first. He'd read about them, and soon he'd spend time in much larger encampments, but this was his first. Tucked into the woods alongside the track were crude shelters fashioned from discarded wooden pallets and cardboard. Too small to be houses, like a race of dogs had learned to use tools and built a village for themselves. Farther down the track a waxed canvas tarpaulin hung between trees, sheltering three men and a smoky barrel fire. The men were watching him from their perch on a log. Eld nodded but kept walking.

"Hey," one of them called. Eld looked up to see a man standing. "Much past here and they'll run you back out."

Eld stopped walking. The man turned around to look at the spot where he had been sitting on his log. Like a cat, he took short steps, inspected his space, and turned around again before sitting down.

"There's nothing coming through till tonight anyway," he said. "You may as well join us. We been talking about lunch."

Eld found a spot on their log. They had a small collection of canned goods but no whiskey. One of the men had a glass jug of cough suppressant they shared as a freezing rain drummed on the tarpaulin. Eld recognized the bitter taste of laudanum but gagged down a mouthful anyway. After several doses the beverage offered a different brand of comfort than whiskey. Whiskey helped him believe there might still be a way he could set everything right, by force of will or struggle or reckless courage. The cough suppressant showed him there was no use, but as a compensating and fatal anesthetic, revealed that nothing mattered anyway. Months later he understood that camp was probably where he first encountered the tuberculosis germ, probably why the man had a jug of cough syrup in the first place.

Two of the men volunteered that they were veterans of France, though they didn't have to. Eld recognized them for what they were. The man who had first called to him seemed to be, if not quite their leader, a spokesman. The other two struggled with conversation, an art that the spokesman evidently missed, as he engaged Eld immediately. He asked if Eld was American, then held forth on the bank failures and the new American president. He spoke for some time but never asked Eld how he came to be standing by the side of the tracks in Waterloo. Maybe there was some sort of vagrant code that called for respect of a man's privacy.

The spokesman wore mismatched boots, one of which flapped where it was separating from the sole. When he said they would share their food with him, Eld offered his bag in payment. The spokesman looked Eld's bag over and held it up with one hand.

"I thank you, but I fear it's not my style," he said.

"It's not at that," said one of his companions.

The spokesman explained they were waiting on a freight to Toronto, and from there they would go west by the same method, north around the Great Lakes, across the prairie, over the mountains, and down to the Pacific.

"I'm headed back the other way," Eld said, "to Michigan."

"There's one goes down to Windsor every day," the spokesman said. "Then through the tunnel to Detroit. That where you're going?"

"Close enough."

"That train's been through already. You can catch tomorrow's."

"Never done this," Eld said, "hopped a freight." He had read that expression in the newspaper.

"Price is right, but you know, they don't heat the cars."

The spokesman explained that the encampment where they sat was not theirs, or anyone's. They had only been there for a day and had no idea who built the small shelters.

"There's one in every town, or anyway just outside town. Most are bigger than this. Better than this. A dry spot might be tough to find, but nobody will bother you."

It was dusk when they finished the cough suppressant. Whether from the cold or the laudanum he didn't know, but Eld couldn't feel his fingertips. When his new companions began gathering their belongings, he left the shelter of the tarpaulin and surveyed the nearest small shelter. Coffin-sized, it had a pallet floor and stacked carpet trimmings for bedding. When he pressed on the carpet a rivulet of water trickled out.

"You could come with us." The man raised his arm to the west. "We're going all the way. All the way to the Pacific."

"I'm going home."

"Up to you." The man shrugged. "Me, I think I am home. For now anyway. Maybe not forever, but now."

His three companions shambled down the track toward the yard, raggedy men in whose company Eld felt he belonged. Bearing their own shames and tragedies, they wouldn't ask questions or tell him he had failed. Also, they were on their way to a city. Long afternoons on the lake, when they were picking herring from the net, Doc excitedly spoke of leaving Minden for the city as soon as he could. He had been talking about Detroit, but Toronto surely beckoned just as much. Probably any city would do. Maybe Doc had come this way. Maybe Eld could still be looking for him. Some part of him knew that he was chasing a poisonous deceit, but his love for the boy would take a long time to die. He picked up his bag and set off to kill it.

The four men waited behind an equipment shed for their train. Pressed against the weathered wood, the eaves kept the rain off, but only just. With the back of his head against the wall, raindrops passed the end of his nose. Eld started for the train as soon as it came even with their hiding spot. A hand grabbed his coat.

"We're looking for an open door," said the spokesman. "Somebody already on, to help us up. Don't want to fall under the train. You look like you might be able to manage on your own, but I need a lift."

"What if there's nobody to help us?"

"That would be a first. By now there's somebody on every freight going everywhere."

The train moved slow, at barely more than a walk, a deep metallic thud sounding out the rhythm of its progress. Minutes passed and the line of cars accelerated, but still no open doors were in evidence. Eld watched his new companions for a sign of what to do next, but they did not appear anxious.

"There."

Eld was already moving and didn't see who spoke. The side of a boxcar was opening and he ran for it. The door slid on a track. Men were revealed. Some appeared to be talking to each other, as if standing around a backyard on a sunny afternoon, but two were kneeling with their hands out. Eld jogged on the track bed, his speed limited by the poor footing. The track was atop a snaking barrow of crushed stone, the pieces the size of squared-off apples. He was there, the door open, the floor of the car at his shoulder, but he had to look each time he stepped to find a place to land. He swung his bag and threw it over the heads of the kneeling men. One of the talkers moved too late and the bag struck the side of his face. Eld trotted along for a dozen yards before he accepted that the footing would never get better. He held out his arms and jumped. His chest struck the bottom of the car and his legs folded underneath. His palms slapped the floor. He hung there for a moment, cantilevered over the tracks, but with nothing for him to get a purchase on, he slid backward.

A man on his knees took fistfuls of Eld's coat at the shoulders. He breathed curses in Eld's face through clenched two-tone teeth, but on his breath was the sugar smell of canned fruit. The other man crabbed over and grabbed Eld's belt below the small of his back. There was grunting and cursing and then they were in a pile on the floor of the boxcar. The two men who had pulled him inside scrambled back to their positions, now shouting to the men jogging alongside.

Eld remained where he was, flat on his back, palms on the floor, glad to be aboard and moving. A resonant thrum rose from the wheels and passed through his body. His fingertips rested on gritty dust. He had learned a trick in France: he was made of the earth, and so he could lie flat and *be* the earth, impervious to the Kaiser's artillery. The train was the earth too—ore dug by men from mountains and smelted into steel, trees cut down and planked—but all of it part of the earth that to the earth would return. His flesh, his mind too, was a part of the earth, like Doc, Maggie, Bea. They could all lie flat, be the earth, impervious. The freight car rocked. This was the best he had felt in many days, drunk or sober. Moving felt like doing something.

THIRTY-FIVE

"Eldridge Mackey, he's your husband, right?"

Maggie took a breath before answering. Cyrus had asked for this meeting, and Maggie thought Bea would be with him. The last meeting he had asked for was to tell her Bea had run off. Those were the words he had used, "run off."

Maggie had traded cigarettes for good soap and tooth powder so she would be ready for a reunion. In the shower this morning she had repeated to herself that she would not shout or lecture. Her prodigal daughter had returned, if not home, at least safe. She was prepared to be grateful, but Cyrus sat there alone, asking about Eld. She was tired of bad news.

"Yes," she said, without volunteering any more information, or asking for any. Her encounters with the justice system, and the people who worked in it, had taught her that avoidance was the best policy. Any information volunteered would be snatched up eagerly and pulled like a loose thread on a sweater. Things would unravel.

"He turned up in Canada," said Cyrus. "A hospital out west. A tuberculosis sanitarium."

"He's not dead...."

She wasn't asking Cyrus if her husband was dead, nor was she saying out loud something she had believed in secret. She spoke the words as a way of trying them out, testing what the world was like if the facts were something different. What if cats were dogs?

"Nope. Not dead," Cyrus said, sliding a postcard across the table. "At least not when he wrote this. Says he's headed home to find you."

Maggie read the message. She thought it looked like Eld's handwriting. Things she had believed moved around in her head.

"It's nicer here," said Cyrus.

Maggie looked up. It was late July, but Cyrus's cheeks were still apple red. She might have handed him a lollipop. She read the postcard a second time, concentrating on each word. When she finished she followed Cyrus's gaze to the walls. They were a dandelion yellow.

"This room," he said. "It's nicer than the visitor rooms in the men's prison. The paint, the smell, all of it. The men's prison smells like sewage. Not fresh shit, but sewage. Like the pipes don't work."

Maggie waved the postcard by a corner. "How did you come by this?"

"The postmaster in Minden. He's a dedicated civil servant. He tracked you down, sent it on to me."

"This is postmarked three weeks ago. It doesn't take three weeks to get here, even from Canada. Have you heard from Eld?"

"Just that postcard, but that leads me to why I'm here. If I do hear from him, what do you want me to do?"

"What the hell kind of question is that? He's my husband."

"Prison hasn't done anything for your manners."

"Believe me, you're getting only the sunshine."

Maggie tried to imagine Eld alive for the last two years, wandering the earth, without a care for his family.

"Was he in jail too?"

Cyrus laughed. "I don't know, but that would be something, wouldn't it, both of you in jail, and your daughter legging it from her foster parents."

The casual violence of prison life had taught Maggie that a slap could be useful. She could slap Cyrus's apple cheeks. A slap might get him to focus.

"Does this have anything to do with Bea?" she asked instead. "Is she with her dad? Have you heard from her?"

She could see on his face that he hadn't done anything.

"Max says he hasn't heard from her."

"Well, *of course* not. She ran away from Max after a month."

"The girl is fifteen, and from my brief dealings with her, she's going on thirty. She could be anywhere."

Maggie stopped the flicker of pride before it could become a smile. Before she disappeared, Bea had been in charge of paying Maggie's bills, including those from Cyrus. She had disputed several.

"You hear from Eld, you tell him where I am. Tell him I want to see him."

Georgia was in the Cunningham Wing. Three days passed before Maggie could get over there to talk to her. They were making sanitation uniforms that day, for the city of Saginaw. She sold a cigarette Cyrus had brought her for a penny and hid the penny in her shoe. When she put it under the needle of her Singer, the machine jumped. She showed the broken needle to the matron.

"Go get another one, but in the future, let's take it easy on state property, shall we?"

The Cunningham Wing was less than a decade old, but it was ugly. Uglier even than the original prison, which dated to just after the Civil War. Maggie was not by nature a woman given to pondering, but the free time afforded by incarceration had changed that. Walking through the old prison to the new wing made concrete a thought that had pained her lately. She grew up taking for granted that the world and everything in it slowly got better. Maybe her lot in life wouldn't improve, probably due to her own sloth and venality, but she never questioned that for the vast bulk of humanity, tomorrow was always better. Onward and upward was the default course of mankind. War, the Spanish flu, and even the Depression didn't change her mind about that, but walking to the Cunningham Wing did. The new prison wing wasn't quite witch burning or slavery, but by design cells were smaller, windows less frequently sprinkled across expanses of brick wall. Maggie understood, as did anyone who bothered to look, that the new wing was built to be more miserable than the original prison. The men who sketched out the plans, the legislature that approved the funding, the politicians who cut the ribbon, they all wanted women yanked from their families for some crime—almost always, Maggie had learned, committed at the behest of, or in response to the act of, a man—to suffer just a little more than they had six decades ago. Progress was not inevitable. Those men had turned the screws, proving that the world could be worse tomorrow. Christ only knew what darkness lurked around the corner. Her Bea was out there in that, on her own and cocksure, only a step ahead of the pursuing darkness.

Most of the women in the dayroom sat in twos and threes. Maggie slowed and took in the single large group that sat on the floor in a circle, around one who read to the others from a book. They would be some species of Christian in whose number Georgia would not be found. She didn't search their faces closely and gave them a wide berth. Striped prison-issue dresses obscured all but the most pronounced physical characteristics. She scanned a couple dozen faces. Many were familiar, and some smiled at her, but none were her old friend. Maybe Georgia wasn't there. She could be sick, or on some errand for the matron. Maggie would need to wait at least a week to invent another excuse. Eld could be coming tomorrow.

Georgia was at a table playing chess with an ugly lesbian. Maggie knew her name was Alice, though everyone called her Popeye. Alice was ugly because her plumber husband had used a pipe wrench to break the bones in her face. When it knit back together her face was lopsided with scars and one eye socket was tiny, like the sailor from the funny papers. Alice knew she was ugly, but when pressed she said she was homely before and that her husband's work might have improved her looks. She poisoned the man with lye. There were a number of husband killers in the facility, all held in high regard.

The steel benches were bolted to the concrete slab, as was the table. For all but the youngest and most athletic prisoners, the small gap between the bench and the table allowed entrance only from one or the other ends of the bench and required a person to slide in. No one wanted to be trapped in the middle of the bench when violence erupted, a not-infrequent occurrence, so the tables were occupied only at the ends, where quick escape was possible.

In prison the food was starchy and cold, and there was no privacy, but one encountered those things out in the world too. The thing Maggie most looked forward to upon her release was moving furniture around to suit her. Every day she moved from cell to yard, bunk to table, never making the least impression on her physical environment. Sometimes at night she stared at the underside of her cellmate's bunk and rearranged the living room furniture in her old house in Minden or dragged a chair to the window of her little apartment in Lansing so she could smoke and watch the snow fall.

"Alice," Maggie said, "do you think we might have the table for a minute? I'm sorry, but I'm on an errand and don't have time to be polite."

Alice didn't speak—as a rule, she didn't—but she nodded and slid off the bench. Maggie took her place, but Alice lingered to watch Georgia's move.

"She's losing," Georgia said. "We're playing two out of three and we each took one. I win this one and she owes me a pack of Chesterfields."

"What if she wins?"

It was hard to tell amid the lumps and scar tissue, but Alice might have raised an eyebrow. When she was out of earshot Maggie leaned across the table and spoke without stopping for several minutes.

Georgia tapped a finger on the table and looked over the chessboard. "I had her beat, you know. Maybe three moves, no more than six."

"I need to go. Bea, she needs me."

"What about money?"

"The lawyer said the other outfits who paid me wouldn't say anything, wouldn't come for their money back, because they wanted to keep it quiet. He was right about that. Of course, I paid him almost half of it, but there should be enough left."

"And Eld, you think you can count on him?"

THIRTY-SIX

Maybe he had never been here before. Maybe consumption and whiskey had put memories in his head that were some other man's stories. He was sure he remembered his children in that yard, remembered the town, the Pontiac Hotel, the harbor, even the individual trees. A big willow just off the road into town was right where it should be, welcoming him, but then a frightened woman told him through the door that she lived in his house now. He cried and she told him with fear in her voice that she would call the police if he didn't move on. He commenced kicking the door, but the scream of a child stopped him.

He started the walk he remembered to be four miles. Maggie's mother's house should be redbrick. There was a white porch and two barns. He saw things on the way that he didn't remember. When he got outside of town, a dog he didn't recognize bolted from a yard and stood before him growling. A man called the animal back and Eld kept on.

His mother-in-law's house was where it should be. Before he got to the door she had it open.

"I got no work for you. Keep on. My husband will be home soon and he's not as kindl—"

"Your husband's been dead for twenty years. Where's Maggie? Bea?"

His mother-in-law froze in the act of drying her hands on her apron. The woman had needlepoint stitched the word "welcome" across the front. He remembered that apron. This was the house where Maggie grew up. This was his memory. His family.

"Where are they?" Eld asked.

"Where have you been?"

"Are they here?" he said again. He shouted Maggie's name and looked up at the windows of the second floor. He started to jog around the back side of the house, calling for Maggie and Bea.

She turned her head to follow him. "I haven't seen them for almost two years."

Eld stopped. The woman spoke with an even voice. There was no lie in it. He sat on the grass, winded from his walk and the jog across this yard. He was not as cured as the doctors had said.

"You may as well come in and I'll tell you what I know. You're still family, far as I know."

When she asked him again where he had been, they were seated at her kitchen table, solid but pitted from decades of use, with a green runner. Over steaming cups of coffee she made fresh and poured into thick cups with a blue stripe around the rim, he said he had been looking for Doc, which was both true and a lie. He had looked for Doc, was right this instant looking for Doc, and would look for Doc every second he was in this world and the next, but the years he spent in Canada was time adjusting to the idea that looking for his boy wouldn't end with finding him.

She did most of the talking and Eld saw that she did not get many visitors. She talked about a woman dragging a child on the lam with another woman she called a prostitute. She described years without a word and then a scandal in Lansing and a jail term. She told him his house had been sold by the bank, and that all the whiskey money in town had disappeared with the end of Prohibition. She kept talking and said Roosevelt was a communist and he remembered that the last time he voted it had been for Roosevelt.

His mother-in-law offered to feed him, and after dinner she told him to stay in one of the empty bedrooms. She lent him an ancient pair of coveralls while she washed his clothes. He accepted each of her offers as they were made, each time doubting by degrees that this woman with her guilty kindness was his mother-in-law. He was up before six and she was already in the kitchen making coffee. He showered and put on his clean clothes though they were not quite dry.

Eld said he wasn't hungry when she offered breakfast. That was true. He hadn't lied since he left the hospital and he liked the lean way it made him feel, cutting like a blade through the fog of the world. He would keep it up as long as he could. Maybe for the rest of his life. He'd walk the earth telling the truth, an instrument of fate.

"You know where Maggie is? Which jail?"

"Prison. Not jail. Jail is for time less than a year. I learned that after I read—"

"Where?" he asked.

She startled and spilled some of her coffee. "I don't know. The court was in Lansing. I went to the post office here a month or so ago and the postmaster—you remember Bart—he told me he sent your postcard to a lawyer down there. He must know where she is."

"And Bea?"

"No worldly idea. Poor little thing."

He started to say it was a hell of a grandmother who leaves her granddaughter to fend for herself, but he only got the word "hell" out of his mouth. He was the first to abandon her, put her and Maggie in the spot they were in. Hell of a father. Hell of a husband. He amended his earlier commitment to walking the earth speaking truth. That was too much to ask of a person who had to accomplish things in a limited amount of time.

THIRTY-SEVEN

The matron came for Maggie before eight in the morning, then left her alone in the visitor room for more than an hour. Cyrus said the men's prison was worse, but Maggie thought she could smell the concrete of the walls. As a fisherman's wife and mother of two children she had encountered the many fierce stinks that came with that territory, but she knew that smells should fade with exposure. Not the prison. The walls had a moldering alkaline scent, subtle but always there. Always cold. Every breath, she took some of it in.

Breakfast time came and went. Eld might be late, but just as likely the prison machine had simply failed. Maggie had come to think of the prison that way, a giant unthinking machine that picked you up and spat you out at various times and places. The machine had no particular malice for anyone but equal malice for all. Sometimes, like a machine, the prison broke down. Food spoiled. Electricity went out. On two occasions in the time Maggie had been there a bewildered prisoner had been rousted early and bused to someone else's court hearing. A woman Maggie met on her first day swore she had been sentenced nine years ago to seven years. The woman was friendless. She could speak of nothing other than her tragedy, and the other inmates avoided her out of fear that her misfortune might attract more of the same. The machine rumbled on.

The door opened and a man stepped over the threshold. Drops of water were visible on his navy shirt. He smiled. Skinny. Sunken cheeks. A beard. Like the man she knew had been smoked and dried to a wiry jerky. He was not handsome anymore. Eld smiled and embraced her. Her arms around him, her fingers rested in the shallow divots between his ribs.

"We only have thirty minutes," she said, pulling away from him to sit down. They had ground to cover.

She tried to keep her mind on Bea and her feelings off her face. A small piece of food clung to Eld's beard. It was a pale color, a sort of beige. Maggie hoped it was food. It might be mucus, or a bit of lung. Cyrus had said tuberculosis. Cyrus had never seen Eld before, so the change would not have registered. He didn't know to warn her.

"I couldn't find him," Eld said. "God knows I looked, but I couldn't find our Doc. . . ." The words started a croak, ended as wind in dry cattails.

"Oh." There was nothing else to say to that, and no time anyway. A thought came, unsummoned. A gun to her head and forced to choose which of her men would return, it would not have been Eld.

His hands were on the table, palms up, and he looked at the ceiling. His head was shaking, his lips drawn back over his teeth. Was he crying? She had come prepared to persuade him, to overcome Eld's instinct for caution and careful plan. She had not expected this.

"We don't have time." She reached across the table and took her husband's hand. "That will all have to wait. You and me, we are here now, and Bea needs us. Your daughter needs you."

"Where is she?"

"I worked out a place for her to stay until I got out. A family. But she disappeared not long after I got here, and nobody is looking for her. I think I know where she is, or at least who's got her."

Maggie told Eld a streamlined version of the truth to make him understand that Honeycutt was a threat. She spoke for nearly ten minutes, explaining the fix they were in, and the few resources they had to do something about it. She watched Eld as she spoke, trying not to examine him. This presence was not quite the man she had known. Nor was he a total stranger. He was an Echo bounced back from the dark.

"You want your family back," she said, "it's going to take some doing."

The man that was her husband nodded. "Doing is why I'm here. I won't fail you again."

"That's good. We need you."

He smiled at that, a smile that frightened Maggie a little, an experience she did not associate with her husband. This man didn't look like her Eld, and he didn't talk like him either, but Maggie banished her doubts. Eld was all she had. She remembered from the gospel of John that the disciples did not recognize Jesus upon his resurrection. She leaned across the table and continued at just above a whisper. She spoke for another ten minutes and when she finished Eld took a deep breath.

"If that's what needs to be done."

"I get one visit per week. Can you be ready in a week?"

"I think so."

"If you'll need two weeks, say so now. Can't get word to me in here."

"I'll be ready."

"You don't have even one question?"

"No. You were always good at a plan."

She said she was glad to see him then. He started to cry again. She had never seen the man cry, and now it was twice in half an hour.

Maggie tried to smile. "My plan, it's risky, but not a suicide march."

"Might be at that," Eld said. Then he looked around the room. "The walls in here, color of dandelions."

―――

That night Maggie lay awake in the dark, hundreds of sleeping bodies stacked all around her. In their sleep the women made humiliating animal noises: gurgling coughs, bellowing snores, the occasional rumbling fart. Maggie paid no mind. Her months there had taught her she could pay no mind. She could wait out her sentence. She could, but Bea could not.

Her family had made some long-shot gambles, and so far every one of them had come up snake eyes. They were due.

THIRTY-EIGHT

The man at the table didn't look up from the papers in his hand. Maggie's panic rose and fell before she took a step into the room. Her breath came fast and shallow. By force of will she exhaled and paused before filling her lungs again. She rocked on her feet, gritted her teeth, and steadied herself. She would say nothing to this man. She would start again. A new plan. Bea needed her.

She sat down across from the man and got a good look at him. In a week he'd had a haircut and a shave. Eld. The gray suit he was wearing was finer than anything he'd ever worn to church. The knot in his navy necktie was straight. A white canvas valise was open on the floor, papers sticking out in a tangle. He was as unfamiliar as he had been on his first visit, but now in a different way.

Eld looked up and nodded at the matron. When she closed the door Maggie let out a long breath.

"Made the appointment as your new lawyer," Eld said. "Signed in as Clarence Darrow. They didn't read it. Barely checked the bag. They're not worried about women, I guess."

"Didn't anyone ask—"

"Smile. Act like you belong there. Nobody asks you anything. Learned that in Canada."

"What happened in Canada?"

Eld waved her question away. "When do we know?"

"Georgia is on breakfast shift. She's got a mop head with bacon grease on it. She's going to put it in the oven. Any minute now."

"They let that woman cook?"

Maggie had seen Eld face dangerous circumstances: drunks who wanted to fight, bad weather blowing in off the lake, a visit from the bank. Always he started spooked but slowly filled with a cold resolve. Today she didn't see any of that. His wiring, the lay of his bones, the man was unfamiliar. He seemed eager.

"Every fire drill has gone the same way," she said. "When the alarm goes, one matron is supposed to gather any visitors and walk them back out through the main gate. I think that's just you, but there might be someone else in one of the other rooms. Everybody else, matrons and inmates, they go out to the yard."

"Okay. You, me, one matron."

"God willing."

She told him about his daughter then, about how she had grown tall and pretty, but all business. When he smiled, the ghost of old Eld crossed his face. The instant Bea saw that grin she would forgive him his absence and his every foolish act. Of course, Maggie would never be forgiven. Not for her years of sacrifice, not for the risks she had taken, not for the time in jail, and god help her, not for the time spent with Honeycutt. But Bea and Eld, the survivors of her little family, would be reunited and happy. That was a pure mother's bargain, and one that Maggie was happy to strike.

A far-off alarm bell gave a short, weak ring, then stopped. They looked at each other without speaking. The bell started and stopped once more, and then other alarms sounded, one after another. Finally, a bell somewhere nearby joined the din with a mechanized peal that did not stop. Eld reached across the table and took her hand.

"This will be fine," he shouted over the alarm.

A few minutes passed, during which Maggie said nothing. When the door opened they were still holding hands. The matron standing in the door took in the scene.

"Not a drill," she shouted. "But it's fine. Just a kitchen fire."

Maggie recognized her. One of the decent ones. Older, heavyset, her long gray hair in a bun. Doing a job. She was loud and firm, but not cruel or perpetually angry. The matron pointed at Eld.

"You follow me. You, inmate, you sit tight. I'll be back for you."

Eld stood. Maggie hadn't been specific with him about how this part of her plan should work. Eld was a man, her man, and this was his part. She expected him to speak sharply, maybe use profanity, perhaps shake the matron.

Eld stepped forward and his elbow was in the air. He punched the woman in the face. The back of her head bounced off the steel door and she collapsed into the room. Eld grabbed the door to prevent it swinging closed.

"My bag," he said.

Maggie stood and handed him the white valise. He used it to prop open the door while he knelt next to the woman and fished a ring of keys from her pocket. He unfastened the buttons on her dress. The woman groaned.

She had asked for Eld's help, and here he was. This had to be done. She wouldn't question how he chose to do what she asked.

Eld looked over his shoulder at her. "Quickly now."

Maggie pulled her striped prison frock over her head and took the matron's uniform from Eld. Body odor and the perfumed scent of old women's soap rose from the cloth. The dress slipped over her easily. Her eyes covered by the fabric, she heard Eld speaking to the matron.

"Put this on," he said.

When the dress fell to Maggie's shoulders she saw the matron sit up, one hand on the floor and one hand across her chest. Her nose was bleeding. Eld took up the inmate dress with both hands and pushed it over the woman's head. He stood then, pulling the woman up by her arm. Maggie stepped forward and struggled to pull the hem down the older woman's large frame. Close to her now, Maggie saw mottled skin and gooseflesh. The matron was whispering. Maggie listened as she pulled the fabric down. The woman was praying.

"Put her in a chair," said Eld. He had the valise in his hand. Maggie did as he asked. Her hands in the woman's armpits, she lowered her with care.

Their faces inches apart, the woman whispered at her. "You won't get far. Whatever plan he has, it won't work. Let him go. Do your time."

The words surprised Maggie. She stood and slapped the old woman across the face.

"*My* plan," she said.

The hallway was full of the continuous sound of the alarm, but empty of bodies. Instructions for visitors were painted on the walls in red block letters. Maggie trotted after Eld without reading them. Eld shot looks over his shoulder as they turned the corner toward the main gate.

"Don't worry," Maggie said. "Visiting room door can't be unlocked from inside, and anyway you've got her key ring."

"When I came in there were two men in an office at the door."

"They'll be up on the wall by now. Watching the other direction, into the yard, but even if they're not, they're looking for inmates. In this dress, I'm not an inmate."

The hall ended at a steel door. A dozen feet inside the door a red line was painted across the floor, above the words WAIT HERE. A window, waist high on the wall at the red line, stood open. Maggie had passed it only once, on her way in for the first time, but she remembered the tiny office there, barely more than a closet, where a guard sat and monitored the door. The door to that space was shut. She approached quietly and tried the knob, but it was locked. Eld stopped before coming even to the window, then jerked his head at Maggie. She stepped forward with a smile for whoever might be there. A desk chair sat vacant.

"Empty," she said, and Eld was past her in a stride. She leaned through the window and looked around. A telephone and a notebook sat on the tiny desk. Papers were thumbtacked to a bulletin board. She saw the seal of the state of Michigan. A hat. A brown paper bag with the top rolled over and crumpled where it had been carried. Black galoshes in the corner. She'd told Eld there was a button in this office that would open the door. There must be.

The alarm stopped.

"Now would be a good time to open the door," Eld said.

Maggie turned around so her back was to the window, then hopped up so she was sitting on the sill. She tucked her knees to her chest and spun, then stood up inside the small room. It smelled like old paper and bad breath. There were no obvious buttons or switches. She moved the papers on the wall and felt around the door frame. Eld's torso was through the small window.

"I can't find it," she said.

"Look for wires," he said. "It's electric. Follow wires."

She flipped the light switch down and the overhead light went out.

"I can hear voices," said Eld.

She pulled out the chair and felt under the desk. Nothing. She cursed.

"The floor," said Eld. "Check the floor."

Maggie sat in the chair and pushed it back so she could see the floor. There. She mashed the steel pad with her foot. Now she heard the voices, but she heard the buzzer too. Eld ran to the wide steel door and pulled it open. She was most of the way back through the window when she saw two uniformed men down the corridor. They had stopped walking and were looking at her.

She smoothed her dress and waved. "Don't run," she said.

"Right," Eld said. "Not just yet anyway." He too smiled and waved.

She passed Eld and stepped outside onto the lawn. There were shouts from behind. The door closed and they were running. She hadn't run hard in years. The big red Ford, alone in the visitor's lot, was fifty yards off. She didn't look back until she was in the passenger seat, facing the gate. The steel door was opening and uniformed men came out, sending Maggie to a girlhood memory of hornets barreling out of a nest struck by a broom. The car was moving backward and Eld was shouting. They drove over something and she bounced from the seat onto the floor. She looked up to see the side of Eld's face. He was concentrating, looking over his shoulder and then back out the windshield. He pulled his head down into his shoulders and the windshield bloomed a spiderweb of cracks. Tires squealed and the car swung sideways. They were moving forward again. Maggie pulled herself up onto the seat. Within a minute Eld was driving the speed of traffic. They passed grocery stores and a hardware. People walked the sidewalks. There were two bullet holes in the windshield, but otherwise they could have been driving to church.

"This machine," said Eld. "It doesn't disappoint. Picked it up at the garage where you sent me. New battery and it started right up."

Eld was talking about the car. They had beaten a woman senseless and been shot at while she was escaping from prison and Eld was admiring Georgia's car.

"Indiana," he said. "Rented us a place in Indiana. You ever been to Indiana? I been over the border and back a couple times, but never spent the night."

"Yeah. I've been to Indiana."

He looked over at her, then back at the road. He was nodding. "Yeah. Okay. Well, we're going to Indiana."

Maggie was dizzy then, and as thirsty as she could ever remember.

"Do you have water? Anything to drink?"

"Well, shit. No. Sorry. I brought you some clothes. They're in the back seat, but I didn't think of water."

Maggie threw up on the floor between her shoes. It was the memory of the matron, the blood under her nose when Maggie slapped her.

"Open your window," Eld said. "We get some miles behind us, then we can stop. Get you cleaned up and maybe a couple of Coca-Colas. A cold one sounds good to me too."

He turned his head and smiled at her. They gave him a medal in

France, and she knew that medals were given for terrible things, but she had married him for his decency, and because he was handsome. She thought that the whisper of a monster in him, unsummoned and forgotten, had disappeared long ago. But now here he was, neither handsome nor decent, boiled down to that monster so that she could call on it.

THIRTY-NINE

Eld stopped the car at a hand pump on the shoulder. On the edge of a vast cornfield, he pumped the handle until water spilled out on muddy ground already slick and shiny. Maggie gulped water cold enough to make her teeth hurt, and then she washed her face. The prison water had reeked of chlorine, but this free water smelled of sulfur. She checked for traffic up and down the gravel farm road before taking off the matron's dress.

"I brought you underthings too," Eld said. "The kind you like."

And so he had. Her size, and a larger set as well. When she held up the larger set and looked at him, he shrugged.

"Wanted to be sure," he said. "You know, all that rich prison food."

She stood naked while Eld pumped water into her cupped hands. She felt him looking at her, but the idea didn't appeal. Maybe tomorrow. She poured water from her hands over her head and gasped as the cold water ran down her body.

"I looked for Honeycutt," Eld said. "Like you said, he's been gone for months. I checked with his church, but nobody there was talking. I think they were expecting somebody to come looking. This wasn't the first time they played dumb. Dead end there, but your lawyer, Cyrus, he got me your money from the bank, and he gave up Honeycutt's lawyer too."

"You had a busy week."

"I paid him a visit."

"Oh god."

"No. The man was in fine health when I left him, and he's twenty dollars richer for his trouble. He told me Honeycutt's family is from a place called Platte Landing, out in Nebraska. I got an address. He thinks Honeycutt went there. Bea left town later. When school got out for the summer. Nobody has heard from her, and she didn't tell anyone she was leaving."

"It's a good bet she's with Honeycutt," Maggie said. "Wherever he is."

"Your man Max seemed happy to be rid of our girl. He said she took a suitcase from his attic and most of her clothes. He tried to tell me she was old enough to make her own decisions."

"Max is not a young man, and Bea is a difficult child. I'm sure she encouraged him to think of her as an adult."

A half mile back a truck turned from a farm drive onto the road, headed their way.

"Let's go," Eld said.

Maggie wadded up the matron's dress and used it to clean her sick from the floor of the car, then threw it into the ditch below the water pump. This spot, right here, this would be the end of prison for her. She told herself she would not think of it, or the matron, again. In the car she pulled on the white shirt and denim overalls Eld had brought.

"You in your lawyer's suit, me in brand-new overalls—people will wonder what we're all about."

She put her feet on the dashboard to roll up the pant legs, but otherwise the clothes were a close fit, and she said so.

"It was easy," Eld said. "You look the same."

"Been two years," Maggie said. "Not easy ones. I don't look the same."

"The same as when I met you."

Maggie laughed. "I was nineteen."

"I was eighteen. I remember."

Eld was smiling. She could get used to this new version of him. She knew her talent was for getting used to things, for enduring, and anyway he was useful. Not handsome anymore, but useful in other ways. Thoughtful even. He had just broken her out of prison through a hail of gunfire and brought panties. Something to be said for that.

Eld drove like he wasn't worried about the police. Since he wasn't worried, she wasn't either. This new life they were headed into, whether it was California and a new name or something else, not worrying would be a full-time occupation. She rolled the window down to dry her hair.

"I'm sorry I left you and Bea alone," he said.

Maggie looked straight ahead. "I'm not going to forgive you, if that's what you're after."

"I don't need forgiveness. But we're starting again, and I want you to know I wasn't trying to get away from you. I was trying to find Doc. At least at first. I didn't want to come home without him. Long as I stayed out there looking, the question wasn't settled. If I came home to you, he was gone. I couldn't give up on him like that. I know that doesn't make sense."

"That took almost two years?"

"No, but even after I stopped looking, coming home felt like giving up. Then I got sick."

"We thought you were both gone. Was a lot to take."

Eld changed the subject to where they were headed, and Maggie was grateful to be done with that conversation. There was too much to talk about. Whatever he had done in Canada, whatever had happened to him, it didn't matter now. They were going to get Bea, then go to California. They would salvage what they could.

"We need gas," Eld said, "and those Cokes like I promised."

They were in flat country and the roads were laid out in a grid. The busier paved road was visible for most of a mile as the big Ford approached, pulling a plume of yellow dust. They passed a set of rhyming Burma-Shave billboards just after the turn, but Maggie only read the last one. Within a few miles they pulled into a Sunoco station. Eld jockeyed the car into line at the single pump. He reached into his pocket and handed Maggie a dollar.

"Cokes," he said, "and cigarettes."

The squat cinder-block station was on a small lot against a bean field. Maggie's skin felt clean in the breeze. There was no smell of prison. She stood for a second to let the clean air wash over her. Two uniformed attendants handled cars, and a cashier manned the snack shop. Three of them ran the place, and there was a line at the pump. This kind of business, attending to the machines, this was the future. One of the attendants pumped the gas while the other cleaned dusty windshields. They would start something similar in California. She asked the boy washing windows and was directed to the ladies' room around the back.

A raked gravel path led around the corner to a bathroom both empty and clean. The door had a functioning lock. After months of doing her business in close proximity to others, the privacy of Maggie's first visit to a free toilet was thrilling. She enjoyed it for longer than was biologically necessary. Minutes passed. She washed her hands, smiled at herself in the mirror, and felt in her pocket for the dollar Eld had given her.

She had the doorknob in her hand when she heard shots.

FORTY

When Maggie came around the corner of the building the door to the shop was swinging closed. Eld was in his shirtsleeves, leaning against the hood of the Ford, looking down at his shoes. He looked to be catching his breath. She ran to him, noticing as she went.

His suit coat was on the ground near the Ford, which was pulled up in front of the shop. There were half a dozen cars, but the customers and pump crew had disappeared. A police cruiser, black with a gold shield painted on the open door, was pulled in at the pump. The driver's door was open and the engine was running.

When she reached him the first sound Eld made was a gurgle. He coughed and a string of blood hung from his lip. She saw then that his right hand held a pistol. A uniformed policeman was sprawled on the concrete in a position no living person would assume. There was movement inside the station. The cashier had a phone in his hand.

She put Eld's arm over her shoulder. She had walked him home like this once or twice, years before, when he'd had too much to drink. He would wake up the next day sheepish and she would pretend to be annoyed. She walked him around to the passenger door, but that's as far as he got. Her fist was closed on the door handle when he collapsed on her. Blood saturated his white shirt and soaked through to her new overalls on contact. She got the door open with one hand, but Eld went limp and fell to the ground. His eyes were open and the look on his face was surprise. She tried to pick him up, but even the skinny version of Eld was too much for her to lift.

"It was a good plan," he said. "You know I'm sorry."

The fabric on the left side of his shirt lifted off the skin of his chest on a pulse of blood.

"Eld," Maggie said, "I'm going to leave you now."

He didn't answer, but he was looking up at her. All those years ago, when she'd told him he had a son, he'd put his shoulder to the wheel. She'd taken this man's life. Twice now.

She felt in his pockets.

"The keys?"

Eld lifted a hand and pointed at the car. He put that same hand on her arm and blinked slow.

"You can drive?"

FORTY-ONE

In Fort Wayne she stopped at a Sears Roebuck to buy a screwdriver, then used it to remove the license plate. The August air was much too warm for the jacket she'd found in the back seat, but it covered the blood smeared on her overalls. She worked up a heavy sweat just getting the plate off and left the car parked with the keys in the ignition. Maggie was sorry to leave it behind, but too many people had seen the big red Ford with the bullet hole in the windshield.

Eld had her money and Georgia's driver's license in a leather tool bag in the trunk, along with the Mexican road maps she had asked for and a note card with the address of the Honeycutt ranch in Nebraska. She left the Mexican maps on the floor, tucked the old plate in against the tight bundles of cash, and carried the bag to a used-car lot. Prices were written in soap on windshields. She asked a loitering salesman about a Dodge coupe. The man looked Maggie over and then saw something interesting on his fingernails.

"Is your husband going to join us?"

"I'm a widow," Maggie said, remembering that was finally true.

They had a black one. She overpaid and drove it off the lot, the temporary plate issued in Georgia's name good for thirty days. The salesman threw in a free tank of gas.

From Fort Wayne she drove west on the Lincoln Highway and didn't stop until she crossed into Illinois. Two states away and in a different car, she relaxed enough to buy Coke and cigarettes. She knew enough about small-town living to know a woman staying alone would be remembered, so she drove on to Joliet and booked into a busy motor inn right on the highway. The desk clerk was an old man listening to a baseball game on the radio. He said nothing other than the few words absolutely necessary to their transaction.

A bottle of Seagram's from the liquor store across the street put her the rest of the way at ease, but three drinks reminded her she hadn't eaten all day. She walked the side of the whirring highway to a fried chicken drive-in shack. The lot was full of families on summer trips, back seats full of pillows and squabbling children. She had no choice but to watch them while waiting for her order.

In the morning the drive became pleasant. Warm clear weather held through Illinois and into Iowa. The rolled-down window brought air that smelled of growing things and the occasional barnyard. She decided not to think of Eld and found that wasn't difficult. He had been gone for years, and the man she had seen die bore only a passing resemblance. She focused on Bea and drove like a woman without a house to take care of or a family to keep fed. The Dodge stayed in high gear, pointed straight down a high-crowned road through tall corn that stretched to the horizon. She bought her first pair of sunglasses at a five-and-dime.

She didn't know Ames was a college town, but when Maggie got there she couldn't miss Iowa State. The skeleton crew of students still there in the summer included handfuls of young women in skirts and saddle oxfords. She watched their faces switch from serious to easy laughter. That was just exactly what she wanted for Bea, and there was no reason her Beatrice couldn't join them. She parked to find a diner and stumbled over a plaque that said Iowa State had admitted women since its founding. From the diner she went straight to the Memorial Union and booked a room. She walked the campus in early evening, taking in the limestone and red brick with something close to wonder.

She left early and stopped for lunch just over the Nebraska line. She was in Platte Landing by late afternoon, but there wasn't much to indicate a town, and nowhere to ask for directions to the address written in Eld's scribble. She drove to Columbus, the closest town of any size, and bought the most detailed map she could find. She studied it in a motel room and left in the morning by six.

The X she had penciled on her map was only a guess, and it turned out to be a bachelor farm on a dirt road. The bachelor was in the yard throwing handfuls of feed to chickens while she parked the car. He watched her approach but didn't move.

"There's no lady of the house," he said by way of greeting.

"I'm sorry to hear that, but—"

"There's nobody here to buy Avon or brushes, or anything else you might be selling."

"I'm looking for the Honeycutt ranch. Think I got turned around."

"It's all around us. Every inch that isn't mine is Honeycutt land."

"Where would I find the lady of that house?"

"They got their own road." He pointed. "Half a mile, on the left."

"Many thanks," Maggie said, turning back to her Dodge.

"There's a lot of ladies of that house, you know which one you looking for?"

He had his hands on his hips. Living surrounded by Honeycutts. Maggie took another chance.

"My daughter. She's just a girl." The last words came out strangled.

"Right. Well, you aren't the first to come looking. They think they've cornered the market on god, can do whatever they want to the rest of us 'cause they're so special."

"I'm not sure she's there, but I've come a long way. I just want to find out if she's there, speak to her, tell her she can come home."

"They see you coming, they'll hide her. And they own the sheriff. He'll come and run you off."

"What do I do?"

"The boys, they've been right on my fence line last few days. Digging some drainage. Probably fixing to send it all down on me." He waved a fly away from his face. "The boys, they aren't too bad, and they're not the sharpest. We get them talking, maybe we find out if your girl is there. They'll be along directly if you can wait. I just put on a pot of coffee."

Maggie wiped her eyes. The people who helped her paid a heavy price. Georgia was in prison, Eld dead in a gas station.

"Thank you," she said. "Why would you help me?"

"Those people," he said. "They piss me off."

The boy rode in the passenger seat. He had turned down Maggie's money, saying he had nowhere to spend it, but said he would ride with her right to Bea's front door if she gave him a cigarette. He might have been thirteen. She handed him the pack.

The drive was less than a mile, all of it on gravel roads through rolling fields of wheat. They pulled up to a shotgun shack with a covered porch. The boy was out of the car before it stopped rolling. Maggie had drunk half a pot of the farmer's boiled coffee and her heart was racing as she opened her door.

She had lied to Eld, told him he was Doc's father. She had lied to him because she needed a provider, and a protector for her son. She had lied and now she was out both of them. She had tried, god knows she had tried, to make a go of it without them, but her daughter ran away to a cult just the same.

All the things we did to each other, maybe a moment like this, where her feelings were as pure as she could make them, maybe that would redeem her. If come Judgment Day the lord said this wasn't good enough, then to hell with him.

FORTY-TWO

They told her it was a wheat ranch. That sounded romantic, like a western movie. Bea had waited at the train station in Sioux City for most of a day before a boy she had never seen came to get her. He didn't apologize for being late. He said he had chores to do, every day, before he could be running errands like picking up girls at the train station. It was sixty miles in a pickup truck to the house they had for her. She was sick the whole drive.

The little house they put her in was a long way from where anything much might happen, and a five-minute walk from the big family house. The two young girls who were waiting for her when she arrived told her that Fran liked it that way. They had been scrubbing the house and the three rooms smelled of Murphy's Oil Soap, a scent Bea had always liked. Now the smell only added to the strangeness of the place and she fled outside to vomit in the unpainted privy.

The girls said they were cousins. That first day Bea saw more than a dozen kids within a few years of her age and they all said they were cousins. She was seated with them at the first dinner, instead of with Dan and the other adults. The kids laughed when she asked if there was a radio.

"City girl," one of them said.

Three months and the size of the sky still dazzled her. She watched clouds from her little porch and got by without a radio. She was probably better for it. Out here, she could focus on the important things: god, family, and her health. In the world, but not of it.

Like Fran said at the first dinner, her health was the thing she really needed to concentrate on. She needed to prepare, body and mind, for the first few months. Once the baby was sleeping through the night, she could move into the family house, but the first few months she and the baby would stay in their little house alone. She lived on a working ranch now, and they all needed their sleep. Everyone had a job, and in time Bea would get hers, but for now her job was to be healthy.

She didn't like oatmeal, but she ate it every morning with a tablespoon of molasses and some heavy cream. Fran said it would keep her regular. When she asked if they had any bananas, Fran frowned.

"You'll have to forget that life, those exotic things from far away," she said. "In the city, sure, we live like that. But here, here we are closer to god. Most of the girls here have never seen the like. We eat what grows here."

Bea started to cry then, though she couldn't say why. Fran said she was a silly girl to cry over something like bananas and that she needed to grow up. Life was about to get much harder.

"You are a woman in this family, by your own choice," Fran said. "That's not an easy job. Don't cry to me. I'm not your mother."

Fran was not her mother, and Dan was not her father. Dan came to visit her little house once a week, on Thursday nights, and he was surely not her father.

Staying healthy didn't require much labor, so she had lots of time to think. Occasionally a cousin would come by with a bushel of potatoes that needed peeling for dinner, or she made clothes for herself to replace those that didn't fit her anymore, but otherwise she watched clouds and wondered if she was in the right place.

On the train from Michigan she had been excited. She would start her own life in the wide open of Nebraska, be her own woman with her own child, and live closer to god. But she could see she wasn't starting her own life here. This life already belonged to someone else. Fran. The baby inside her. Maybe every life was like that, no matter what you did. Anyway, hers was.

When there was no work and no clouds, she eventually came around to thinking of her father and Doc. She loved them too, but her mother never acknowledged that. That was the rotting heart of everything. Doc, Dad—they were gone and right away she was in a car, a string of new houses, a new school. Her mother never home, then the scandal. The escape from that permanent chaos was god. God and family. She knew that. Like Fran said, this was her choice, and it would not be easy.

But Fran was not her mother. Bea threw up every morning and wished for her mother.

On a hot morning in August a cousin came to her door. She had just been sick and was still coughing.

"What is it?" she said through the screen door.

"There's a woman here says she knows you from Michigan." The boy turned and hopped over the steps on his way back to whatever task had been interrupted. Mud from his lug-soled boots sat in clumps on her porch. Bea stepped to the screen and saw that a woman stood in the open door of a small black car. She didn't cry out. She pushed open the screen door and saw her mother smile.

The thing that happened next was what always happened when she wanted to run to her mother. She got angry. She saw the conversation they would have in ten minutes in the car, her mother dismissing the "crackpot" religion of these people. The first big decision Bea had made for herself would be undone by her mother on a rescue mission, saving her from her own bad judgment. She slid the string of her apron down so that it pulled the fabric tight under her belly. Some of her decisions would not be unmade. She stepped out on the porch and felt warm sunshine. An ocean of wheat, green turning to gold, rippled in every direction. She turned to frame her profile in the doorway and placed her hands on her stomach.

She saw what that did to her mother and she was sorry, but it was too late.